VAMPIRE BEACH

BLOODLUST & INITIATION

ALEX DUVAL

Simon Pulse
New York • London • Toronto • Sydney

SIMON PULSE

An imprint of Simon & Schuster Children's Publishing Division

1230 Avenue of the Americas, New York, NY 10020

Series created by Working Partners Ltd.

Bloodlust copyright © 2006 by Working Partners Limited

Initiation copyright © 2006 by Working Partners Limited

All rights reserved, including the right of reproduction in whole or in part in any form.

SIMON PULSE and colophon are registered trademarks of Simon & Schuster, Inc.

Designed by Steve Kennedy

The text of this book was set in Adobe Caslon.

Manufactured in the United States of America

This Simon Pulse edition May 2007

10 9 8 7 6 5 4 3 2

Library of Congress Control Numbers:

Bloodlust: 2005938357

Initiation: 2006923501

This 2007 edition of Vampire Beach created exclusively for Barnes and Noble, Inc.

under ISBN-13: 978-0-7607-9496-8 • ISBN-10: 0-7607-9496-0

These titles were originally published individually by Simon Pulse.

CONTENTS

VAMPIRE BEACH

BLOODLUST

For Amber Caravéo—there would be no Vampire Beach without you.

Special thanks to Laura Burns and Melinda Metz

ONE

𝕸alibu.

Jason Freeman took a deep breath of the fresh California air. He *lived* in Malibu now. This was him, driving his VW Beetle down the Pacific Coast Highway. The thought was as blinding as the sun on the ocean, as dazzling as the white sand stretching out alongside the car—*right* alongside the car. He could pull over and be down there in—

"How insane is that house?"

Jason reluctantly dragged his gaze away from the . . . the *Malibu*, and glanced at the house his sister, Danielle, was pointing to. She'd pulled her sunglasses down for a better look, and her gray eyes were wide with curiosity.

"It has a tennis court!" she declared. "And I bet that glass dome is for an indoor pool. They don't let you see much, do they? All those trellises and flowers." Dani glanced over her shoulder as they drove by, trying to eye-TiVo every detail. "That new job of Dad's, the un-pass-by-able job, the one I had to leave all my friends for? It pays a gazillion dollars. Why aren't we living in a place like that?"

"Places like that cost multiple gazillions," Jason told her. "Besides, we have a pool at the new house."

"An *outdoor* pool," Dani complained. But Jason could hear a hint of amusement in her voice. The idea of complaining about anything in this city was ridiculous.

"Don't knock the pool. 'It's a lovely kidney shape, with colored tile detailing,'" Jason said, quoting the real estate agent with a wry smile.

Dani adjusted her Oliver Peoples sunglasses that had been a gift from their aunt Bianca: the aunt who—aside from having impeccable fashion sense—had also first mentioned the new job to their dad *and* helped find their new house.

"True. But the pool doesn't make up for being dragged halfway across the country two weeks before junior year," Dani said flatly.

Jason sighed. He knew the leaving-all-her-friends part of the situation had really upset Danielle. She'd had at least thirty "best friends" back in Michigan, and she hadn't wanted to part with any of them.

"Hey, so I heard about this guy called the Surf Rabbi," he said, trying to get Dani's mind off her homesickness. "He's an actual rabbi. He's, like, fifty years old, and he gives surfing lessons: spiritual surfing lessons. He's all about, I don't know, giving yourself over to the water, or something. He teaches in Malibu."

"Hmm," Dani managed.

Jason shot a look at the surfers already out in the ocean. Sweet. He couldn't wait to get out there himself. But he might need to pay a visit to the rabbi first, seeing as he'd never set foot on a board.

The lifeguard stations on their long wooden legs reminded him of another thing he needed to do. He had to find out where to apply for a job as a guard. That was seriously on the top ten list of things to do now that he was living in California, right after joining a gym. He figured he had a decent shot at getting a lifeguard job since he'd been on the swim team back home and he'd already taken a lifesaving course.

"Jeans!" Dani gasped as they neared the school gates.

"Huh?" Jason queried.

"I have to change," Dani said, as if that was actually an explanation. Jason raised his eyebrows. She rushed on. "Those girls we just passed were all wearing designer jeans!" She shook her head, her chin-length auburn hair flying around her face. "And I'm in a skirt. I'm not dressed right."

Jason sighed. "We don't have time for you to change. We just got here. Besides, what you're wearing is fine," he assured her.

Danielle pulled out a brush and whipped it through her hair. "It's different for you. You're a guy.

You have the vintage bug. You have the blond hair–blue eyes combo. You look like a combination of Chad Michael Murray and . . . somebody not so WB. Nobody's going to care what you're wearing."

"And you're the only one who cares what *you're* wearing!" Jason countered. "You look great. You always do. Chill out, Dani."

Jason swung the car into the parking lot of DeVere High. DeVere, as in DeVere Heights: the gated complex where they now lived. And DeVere University. And DeVere Museum of Modern Art. And DeVere Library. And DeVere Athletic Complex, et cetera, et cetera, and et cetera. He killed the engine and opened the car door.

Dani remained motionless. Her gray eyes were filled with apprehension behind her shades. She hated change. She always had. She'd actually insisted on moving every single Narnia book she'd ever owned across the country, even though she hadn't read them in years. She seemed to think that the world would end if she didn't have them stuffed in her closet in Malibu, just the way she'd had them stuffed in her closet in Michigan.

Jason had handed out his belongings left and right. He wanted to start clean here. No mooning over his past life, no calling his old friends every five minutes, no thinking about Michigan like it had been some kind of paradise. He wished he could give Dani a transfusion of some of his excitement. They were in Malibu now. Life was going to change. And Jason wanted it to. In Fraser, the suburb where he'd lived since birth, he had been able to see every day, every week, every month stretching out in front of him. Not bad. But boring. Here, he had no idea what was going to happen—and it was a total rush.

"Listen. You had more friends than anyone else at our old school," Jason reminded his sister. "It's not going to be any different here." He climbed out of the car. The bug looked like a toy among all the ginormous H2s and Range Rovers that filled the lot. Still, Jason spotted a number of Mercedes SLK convertibles and several other vintage cars like his own. Not everyone was an SUV freak.

He glanced at Dani. She was still in the car. A couple of girls around his sister's age—sixteen—walked by, laughing and gossiping to each other just like girls everywhere. "They don't seem so evil," Jason pointed out.

With a sigh, Dani climbed from the car and gave the girls a once-over. "They definitely wouldn't survive a winter in Michigan," she said at last.

"There's the old Dani attitude," Jason joked. He smiled as he led the way to the main building. It looked nothing like a school—an art gallery, maybe, a mansion, sure, but not a school. It had arches and parapets and red roof tiles. A bell tower rose up from one side, and a wide porch wrapped around the second floor.

They stepped through the largest archway and found themselves in a central courtyard with a manicured lawn in the middle, surrounded by palm trees. Jason still wasn't used to seeing palms all over the place. And flowers grew like weeds out here, not in neat little gardens, but everywhere: on the medians of the freeways, on the sides of buildings—he'd even seen some growing around the trunks of palm trees.

"I'm this way," he announced, stopping in a cool, dim walkway next to the courtyard. Stone steps led up to a side door, and his school map showed him that his first class should be right inside. He looked at the class schedule Dani was clutching so tightly that the blood had drained from her fingers, leaving them bone white. "You're over there . . . ," he added, nodding in the opposite direction, where another set of stairs led into the wing across the courtyard.

"Yep," Dani replied shortly. She looked terrified at the prospect of going it alone.

"Look, just make it through this first week. You can do that," Jason told her encouragingly.

"And then what?"

He tried to think of something that would keep her

going. "I'll take you to the movies on Saturday," he suggested. "Even if it means sitting through a chick flick."

Dani laughed a little shakily. "Okay." She took a deep breath. "See ya after."

Jason nodded. "I'll be at the car," he said, and headed away from her, into what he hoped would be . . . the unexpected.

Nothing unexpected in the first three periods, Jason thought as he joined the cafeteria food line. Well, nothing if you didn't count the fact that all the kids looked as if they had dermatologists and orthodontists and any other -ontists and -ologists that kept you perfect. And the fact that the cafeteria was mostly taken up by a terrace overlooking the Pacific—which was kind of a surprise. He couldn't wait to grab his food and get out there.

Somehow, when he'd moved here, Jason had thought his life would . . . well, *start*. And so far, school was still school. Beautiful. But still just school.

"Would you hand me the last green Borba?"

Jason turned toward the voice. And instantly felt as if his body had caught fire. He could feel the blood rushing through him—pulsing, throbbing. He suddenly felt alive in a way he never had before. And life was full of possibility.

The girl who stood there was the most beautiful thing he had ever seen, hair spilling down over her shoulders like a black waterfall, eyes almost as dark. Her lips were a little plump, as if they were full of something sweet, filling Jason with an almost overwhelming desire to kiss her. It struck him that he had never found a girl so instantly desirable before.

"Green Borba?" the girl repeated.

How long had it been since she'd asked the first time? A second? Five? Long enough to make him look like a complete moron? Jason dragged his eyes away from her and over to the lunch counter. There was an array of sushi in front of him. But he'd never heard of a sushi called Borba. Not that he'd heard of every type of sushi in the world, but he wasn't sushichallenged or anything.

"Okay, you said it was the last one. And that it was green. One more hint and I know I can get it," Jason told her.

The girl shook her head and smiled. "Oh, right. You're from a flyover."

A "flyover." That didn't sound especially good.

The girl reached across Jason and picked up a green bottle of water from a shelf above the sushi. She started toward the cashier, but Jason wasn't ready to let her go.

"So, what makes green Borba different from"—he

took a quick look at the other bottles of water—"from purple or pink Borba? And which one should I be drinking?"

She looked him up and down thoughtfully. "Some things you just have to find out for yourself," she said with a smile. Then she gave him a half wave and walked away.

Jason stared after her. He couldn't help himself. The tight T-shirt she wore with a short cargo skirt showed off the curve of her waist above a long stretch of tanned legs.

He realized he was holding up the line, so he grabbed one of the waters just to see what the deal was, slid his tray down to the burgers, acquired one with some seasoned curly fries, paid up, and headed toward that unbelievable terrace.

The sun hit him full force the second he stepped out the door. It was a little windy, but the sound of the surf pounding the beach below more than made up for it. He glanced around. Stone tables in a variety of shapes dotted the terrace, most of them already taken.

"Hey, Freeman. Over here."

Some sandy-haired guy—Alex? Adam?—from Jason's history class was waving him over with one hand and pointing a small, sleek camcorder at him with the other.

"European history," Jason answered, wanting to

show he remembered him, even though they hadn't actually met.

"Yep," the guy answered, still filming. "I'm Adam Turnball. Give me your impression of DeVere!"

"Are you making a documentary?" Jason asked.

"It's more of a Christopher Guest/Richard Linklater semi-scripted, lots-of-improv kind of thing," Adam replied cryptically.

Jason glanced at the other guy who had staked out the far end of the table. He was hoping for a translation, but the guy didn't look up from his book.

"Come on. Talk to me. Anything," Adam urged.

"Uhh—cool cars in the lot, great views." *The hottest girl I've ever seen.* Jason silently added, then continued. "A wide selection of chow. Speaking of which"—he sat down—"my food is getting cold."

"Oh, sorry." Adam shut off the camera and turned to his pizza.

Jason twisted the top off his purple Borba and took a slug. It tasted like water with a little berry thing happening. "Five bucks a bottle, you'd think they could throw in a little more kick!" he mumbled.

"Well, yeah, but it's not about the taste," Adam said, his hazel eyes twinkling. "It's about the protection."

"What?"

"It's a prophylactic," Adam said, nodding at the

Borba with a sly smile. "Against aging. Of course, you need to drink two a day for maximum effectiveness."

Jason read the side of the bottle. Crap, it *was* for aging skin. Why were they selling it in a high school cafeteria? He ran his hand over his cheek. "I heard the sun out here is very drying," he said to Adam. "Also, I didn't read the label."

Adam laughed. "So, should I pretend I don't already know where you're from, et cetera, and ask you all the normal questions?"

"I guess if you already know, it's a little pointless," Jason answered. "But *how* do you know?"

"You live in the Heights. Everyone in Malibu knows who lives there. Movie stars, moguls, music producers, and, to keep to my 'm' theme, magnificent, newly successful ad execs from Michigan, like your dad. We hate you. And we all want to be you at the same time," Adam said. "You're all we talk about. Real estate agents pass on the dirt, along with landscapers and interior decorators. There's a whole information infrastructure."

"And who exactly is this 'we'?" Jason asked, taking a bite of his burger.

"You know, the people from the wrong side of the tracks," Adam replied. "Not that there is a wrong side of the tracks in Malibu. Let's say the wrong side of the gate that leads into DeVere Heights."

"So I'm guessing you're not mogul or movie star spawn," Jason said with a grin.

"I am the child of the poor but hardworking chief of police," Adam answered, so cheerfully that Jason suspected he didn't give a crap about not living in the Heights.

"Can I ask you something?" Jason ventured.

"I live to serve," Adam quipped.

Jason shot a glance at the guy at the far end of the table. He was still reading. "What's a flyover?"

Adam half stood up and spoke in one of those whispers that are supposed to sound like shouts: "Hey, everybody, the new guy doesn't know what a flyover is!"

Nobody responded. Nobody even glanced at them. "It's one of the states you fly over to get between California and New York," he told Jason. "You know, those two being the only worthwhile states."

As I suspected, she basically called me a loser, Jason thought.

Adam polished off the rest of his pizza. "So what else? Ask me anything."

Jason wanted to ask about the girl who had turned him inside out. But he wasn't ready to be quite that pathetic—and obvious—yet. "How about a who's who?" he asked instead. "I need to put some names to faces."

"Well, there's me," Adam said. He struck a pose. "Adam. Turnball. Remember the name, and when I'm the next Scorsese you can say you knew me back in the day."

"I'll try to remember," Jason joked.

"And over to our left is Luke Archer, whose position as 'new boy' you are currently usurping. Hey, Luke, how long has it been?"

"A year," Luke said without looking up.

"Huh. Time flies," Adam replied. "Supply an interesting factoid about yourself for the new guy, please."

"Uh, I have a dachshund named Hans," Luke volunteered, finally glancing up and shoving his longish blond hair out of his green eyes.

"I never knew that about you," Adam said, but Luke had already returned to his book.

"Give me some social survival hints," Jason said. "Like, who's cool, who's psychotic. Basically, who should I hang with and who should I stay the hell away from?"

"Ah. That will take a while," Adam replied, and grabbed a curly fry off Jason's plate. "But I'll give you the Cliff's Notes version. You've got your two basic groups here: the normal people and the rock stars."

"Rock stars?" Jason said skeptically.

"I exaggerate," Adam said cheerfully. "What I mean is, there are normal people—like myself. And

then there are people who live in DeVere Heights—
like you. Although you don't quite fit the mold. No
offense."

"What mold?" Jason asked.

"Not to sound too much like I'm describing some
hideous teen soap, but DeVere kids are rich, they're
beautiful, and they're painfully cool," Adam explained.

"And I'm not?" Jason laughed, pretending to be
insulted.

"Don't get me wrong, you seem decent and all. You
just don't have that 'je ne sais quoi' that the DeVere
Heights natives possess."

"I can live with that," Jason replied. "So tell me
about these rock stars. Who are they?"

"The first name you need to know is Zach
Lafrenière," Adam began. "Mom's a writer—with an
Oscar. Dad's a music producer. So, he's got good blood.
And Zach cares about that crap, even though he likes to
pretend he doesn't. His own credits aren't bad. Basketball star—he led us to victory last year. He's also had a
little part in a movie—not one of his mom's. And he
went to the senior prom with Paige Devereux, when he
was still a *freshman*—which is impressive, to say the
least. Now that he's a senior, he's the big enchilada, as
we like to say around here. Actually, only I like to say it.
You probably shouldn't. You don't have enough of the
ironic vibe to pull it off. Not that I'm judging you."

"Which one is he?" Jason asked, glancing around the terrace.

"He's not here. Monsieur Lafrenière will not be joining us for a couple weeks, as he's in France with his parents," Adam answered. "Visiting the homelands."

Jason tried to steer the conversation without being obvious about what exactly it was he wanted to know. "So, who's the female equivalent of this Zach guy?" he prompted.

"Who's the woman?" Adam shook his head. "No contest. Paige passed the It Girl torch to her little sister, Sienna. She's a senior now. Paige is off in college."

"And where's Sienna? Hawaii?" A little too late, Jason realized that Hawaii probably wasn't a big deal when you lived in Malibu.

Adam grinned as if he could read Jason's thoughts. "Nothing so mundane," he joked. "She's right over there. A couple of tables behind us. Black hair, a body that's impossible to miss . . ."

Jason knew who he'd see before he turned around, but he took a fast look anyway.

She was looking back at him, and she raised an eyebrow when she spotted the purple Borba in his hand.

Kill me now, Jason thought. He raised the bottle in a toast, trying to cover his embarrassment.

Sienna smiled—a slow, painfully sexy smile—and

raised her Borba in return. Then she turned away, laughing at something one of her friends had said. And suddenly, Jason felt cold, as if the sun had gone in.

"Besides Sienna and Zach, we have Brad Moreau. . . ." Adam continued.

But Jason wasn't listening. All he could think about was how well her name matched up with her: Sienna. It was sexy. Exotic. Unusual. Unexpected . . .

TWO

Thank you, God, for the alphabet, Jason thought, *which led to alphabetical seating, which led to this Freeman sitting directly across the aisle from Sienna Devereux.* English was now officially his favorite class.

The teacher, Ms. Hoffman, started doing the what's-expected-of-you-this-year speech. She explained what percentage of your grade came from homework or from tests or from class participation; she went through the reading list; she told them the number of papers and when they were due; and so on and so on. Jason knew he should be paying attention; English wasn't exactly his best subject. But the thing was, Sienna was so close, he could smell her perfume—a mix of green apple and vanilla and the ocean. Tangy-sweet and yet somehow also mysterious.

"Jason Freeman."

The sound of his name jerked Jason out of his trance. The way that Ms. Hoffman was looking at him made it clear that she'd just asked him a question. Everyone in the room had turned to stare at him in his moment of embarrassment, an assortment of smirks and grins on their faces. He felt a flush creep up the back of his neck, and it only got worse when he saw Sienna watching him.

"Uh, can you repeat that?" he asked. "I'm a flyover, and everyone knows we're kind of backward."

"You're *from* a flyover," Sienna corrected him, but she was grinning.

He winced. "See? Backward."

A few other kids chuckled, and Ms. Hoffman smiled. "I asked if you've already studied *Macbeth*," she said. "That's what we'll be starting with."

Score—Jason had.

He managed to keep his focus on Ms. Hoffman for the rest of English. He noticed she had a pair of Peoples sunglasses hooked over her white T-shirt, just like Dani and half the other girls he'd seen today. Clearly, being tragically underpaid was not a problem for teachers at DeVere. Either that, or Ms. Hoffman skipped meals in order to keep herself in eyewear. He wondered if even the janitors here wore designer shades.

When the bell rang, Jason joined the throng of students in the hallway. Soon he realized that Sienna was also walking directly to the door of his next class. The day just kept getting better.

His physics teacher wasn't into the alphabetical thing, so Jason took a seat by the window. Physics was one of his strong subjects, so the distracting view of the surfers riding the curls wouldn't hurt his grade too badly.

After watching them for a few minutes, Jason couldn't wait to hit the water—even if it was just the pool. Thankfully physics was his last class of the day. He'd already put his name on the list for swim team tryouts right after school that evening. The second the bell rang to end class, Jason bolted from his seat and took off toward the pool. He found the locker room— the only one he'd ever been in that didn't smell of sneakers and feet—and suited up.

"I hope you've been practicing over break," Jason heard someone in the next row of lockers say with a laugh. "With the electronic plates installed, you're not going to be able to cheat your way into beating me."

"Bite me," came the muttered reply.

"There are electronic timing plates?" Jason asked in surprise. He knew that for Olympic competitions they had timing plates in the starting blocks and contact plates installed underwater. That's because in relays, it was all about tagging. The relay team member wasn't allowed to leave the starting block until he'd been tagged, and the contact plates left no room for error. If a swimmer left the block before his team mate hit the underwater plate, an alarm was sent to the meet official's headphones and the team would be disqualified. It was pretty hardcore.

This has to be the only high school in the country with an Olympic-level system, Jason thought with a grin.

A guy from Jason's calc class, Brad Moreau, appeared around the corner, carrying his goggles. "We've also got high-speed cameras now," he told Jason. "Absolutely nothing is left to human error." He sat down on one of the polished wooden benches and looped his towel around his neck.

Jason remembered that Adam had put Brad in the DeVere Heights "rock stars" category, and he could see why. He had brown hair and brown eyes—nothing remarkable there—but there was something compelling about him that Jason couldn't quite put his finger on.

"From what I hear, you're going to give us some much-needed aid in the relay," Brad continued.

Do they give out files on all the new kids, or what? Jason wondered.

"Small school," Brad said, reading Jason's expression. "And Coach Middleton has a big mouth." He stood up. "Come on, I'll take you out there."

"Cool." Jason grabbed his towel and followed Brad toward the pool door. He was struck by the fact that Brad seemed pretty friendly. He'd gotten the impression from Adam that the DeVere Heights kids didn't let outsiders in too easily.

But I'm from DeVere Heights too, he realized suddenly.

Jason was so used to thinking of himself as ordinary that he'd forgotten his new status as a semi-wealthy dude. Maybe that was why Brad was acting as if they were already friends. Was Adam right about DeVere Heights? Did living behind that gate—a gate, incidentally, that looked like it should be in a museum as a piece of sculpture—mean that much to everyone out here?

"There you have it," Brad said.

Jason's mouth actually dropped open when he saw the pool. He estimated it to be fifty meters by ten lanes, with two movable bulkheads so that courses could be set up for twenty-five yards, twenty-five meters, or thirty meters for water polo. It looked like it had a movable floor to change the depth, too. And the water was so blue, it left an afterimage when he blinked.

"Nice, huh?" Brad asked.

"Yeah, sure, but where are the inner tubes? A pool isn't a pool without inner tubes," Jason joked.

"And a few girls in bikinis," Brad agreed.

"Get in there and do some warm-up laps," Coach Middleton called from the bleachers.

Jason was underwater almost before the last word was out of the coach's mouth.

I could do this forever, he thought. It was like listening to music to the point where you're gone, not in your head anymore, not exactly anywhere—more like *everywhere.* Jason lost himself in the moment. He could feel nothing but his muscles working, the water pressing against him, the feel of it flowing over his skin. Perfection.

Too soon, the coach blew his whistle and waved everyone over to the side of the pool. "Okay, everybody who's trying out for the team, Assistant Coach Simkins will take you through your paces." He gestured to a twenty-something guy with a face tanned almost the same color as his freckles.

"Let's head to the other side," Simkins called, starting around the pool toward the far side. Jason began to swim over with the other newbies.

"Not you, Freeman. I want you with me," Coach Middleton said. "We lost a key man on our 200-meter medley team, and I need to get you in place ASAP. From what I hear, you're up to the challenge."

"You got it," Jason replied. He was up for anything that involved water. And he was starting to get used to the idea that everybody here seemed to know everything about him already.

"Let's try you with Moreau"—he pointed to Brad—"Van Dyke, and Harberts."

Jason recognized Van Dyke from English. He didn't think Harberts was in any of his classes.

"I'll take anchor—the freestyle leg," Van Dyke said.

"You sure you're up to it? You don't look like you're feeling so—," Brad began.

"Don't be trying to nab my spot!" Van Dyke joked. "You need me as anchor, even though it pains me to have to do the last leg because it means I have to watch you clowns burn up time on your laps that I have to make up." Van Dyke turned to Jason. "I hope you can hang."

Jason hoped so too. All three of the guys, but especially Brad and Van Dyke, looked like serious athletes, at least judging by how ripped they were. Although, Jason could see why Brad was concerned about Van Dyke. His face was pale, death pale, the kind of pale that often precedes a massive puke.

"I'll start us out with the backstroke," Brad said. "You can swim breaststroke, Freeman. Then Harberts with fly. Then we'll see if Van Dyke can stay afloat as anchor."

Jason and Harberts nodded. Somehow it felt natural for Brad to call the lineup. Jason walked over to his block and got into position with his feet at the back. He liked to do a single step to launch himself. He was glad he'd been assigned the breaststroke leg. His freestyle wasn't bad—he'd taken the anchor slot a few times back at his old school—and his butterfly was decent, but his backstroke could use improvement, to put it kindly.

Jason watched as Brad got into the pool at the other end.

"Swimmers, take your mark!" Coach Middleton yelled.

Brad compressed himself into a ball. The coach gave them the signal, and Brad exploded out of the blocks, using his legs to push free. Man, he was fast. Eyes narrowed, Jason watched Brad closely. He couldn't start before Brad touched the plate in the wall, but he didn't want to waste one tenth of a second of his leg of the relay by starting late. He only had fifty meters to show his stuff. Then it would be over to Harberts, who would swim butterfly back to this end, where Van Dyke would be waiting to dive in and take the final, freestyle leg.

Brad touched the plate. *Now!* Jason ordered himself. He took a step and flew into the air, then hit the water swimming the breaststroke. *Go through the smallest hole in the water,* Jason coached himself. *Don't pull your arms back. Just scull.*

And then he was done.

Harberts flew over Jason's head and plunged into the water as Jason climbed out of the pool and watched him swim down to Van Dyke. *These guys are good,* he thought as Van Dyke made a low, clean entry at the start of his leg.

But then Van Dyke sank. Like his body had turned

to lead, that's how fast he went down. Straight to the bottom of the pool.

Jason's lifesaving training kicked in and he plunged back into the pool without even thinking. In a second he had looped one arm around Van Dyke's chest, pulled him to the surface, and towed him to the side. Brad and the assistant coach, Simkins, helped hoist him out of the pool.

Van Dyke had been pale before, but Jason saw that even his lips were white now.

"Should I get the nurse?" Jason offered. He wasn't sure, but he thought he'd seen the nurse's office somewhere near the principal's.

"Nah. We just need to get him rehydrated," Brad said confidently. "And get him some air." He waved Jason away, then Brad and Simkins led Van Dyke into the locker room, clearly supporting most of his weight.

Harberts jogged over to Jason. "What the hell was that? Is Van Dyke all right?" he asked.

"I don't know. He looked completely out of it," Jason replied, amazed. He couldn't believe Van Dyke wasn't on a stretcher right now. It didn't look like a take-two-aspirin kind of thing.

"Guess he should have listened to Brad and taken it easy," Harberts said. "Although 'easy' is not Van Dyke's style."

"Competitive, huh?" Jason asked, trying to push the image of Van Dyke's limp body out of his mind.

"Extremely, in everything, and mostly with Brad—probably because they usually come in within a second of each other," Harberts answered. "And because Brad ended up with the girl Van Dyke had his eye—"

"Set me up, Harberts!"

Harberts broke off as Van Dyke's voice interrupted.

Jason couldn't believe his eyes. Van Dyke was powering over to his starting block as if nothing had happened.

"Are you sure you know what you're doing?" Simkins called, following Van Dyke out of the locker room. Jason noticed that the assistant coach's face was pale under his tan, each of his freckles now clearly visible. Obviously, he'd been as freaked by Van Dyke's collapse as Jason had. Except that, other than being pale, he seemed fine. In fact, Jason thought, he looked more like he'd just scored a buzz.

"Sure, I'm sure," Van Dyke replied cheerfully.

"Well, *I'm* sure you're hitting the showers," Coach Middleton yelled. "I want you in top form for the first meet."

At least somebody around here is sane, Jason thought. His old coach definitely would have sent Van Dyke to the nurse—and maybe even would have ordered him to go to the doctor and get blood work done.

"I'm in top form already!" Van Dyke protested, with a grin. And he looked fine. His cheeks were flushed too, like he'd been running a marathon.

"I got juiced up," Van Dyke announced. "Simkins supplied the sweet, sweet Gatorade."

Gatorade? Jason shook his head. Clearly they made it differently out here.

After practice Jason meandered toward his car, enjoying the warmth in his body from the exercise and a hot shower—not to mention that omnipresent Malibu sunshine. How disturbing would it be to have a seventy-five-degree Christmas this winter? Somehow, decorating a palm tree on the beach wouldn't be quite the same as stringing lights on a pine tree—but Jason thought he could handle it.

"Hey, Michigan! Can I borrow your cell? Mine died."

Jason already knew that voice. Sienna. He felt his pulse quicken as he walked over to her and the imported Alfa Romeo Spider—hood up—that she was leaning on. "What did you do to your car, Malibu?" he teased.

Sienna shrugged. "It's temperamental."

"Oh, well, temperamental, that's beyond me. I could fill up the wiper fluid thing. You out of wiper fluid?" Jason asked.

"Nope," she answered. "So I guess you're no help to me."

"And that's where you're wrong. I know exactly where to get you a cell phone," Jason said. But he didn't make a move to retrieve it.

"So are you going to? I'll say thank you and everything," Sienna promised.

"Yeah. But instead of saying thank you, just tell me something about yourself." *Not bad,* Jason thought. "It's not right that this whole school seems to have the 411 on me when I don't know anything about anyone."

Sienna laughed. "'The 411'? I haven't heard that since elementary school."

Oh. "What? You have no appreciation for retro?" Jason asked, attempting to recover.

"I'm all about the new," Sienna breathed, taking a step closer. "So what do you want to know? I answered your retro question. I'll give you two more."

Two questions. Jason's mind started to spin. *What did you think of English class? What kind of movies do you like? What are the chances you'd go out with me?* All moronic. "I'll think about it while I go get the cell from my car. My sister has it."

"You drive your sister home?" Sienna asked.

"Yeah."

"Most guys wouldn't do that."

"I guess I'm not most guys."

Sienna smiled that slow smile of hers. "Good. We need someone different around here. New blood."

Is she flirting with me? Jason wondered. He felt a huge grin struggling to break across his face and quickly turned away from her. "Be right back."

Dani was waiting for him in the passenger seat, flipping through a magazine. "Finally," she said when she spotted him. "I need to get home and have a nice, private panic attack."

"It can't have been that bad," Jason said.

"First day at a new school? First day ever in my life as the new girl?" Dani gave him her patented sarcastic head shake. "Are you kidding? I've definitely had better days!"

"I need two more minutes," he told her. "And I need the cell."

Dani handed the phone over, sighed, and returned to her magazine.

Jason hesitated. He wanted to come up with something memorable to ask Sienna. Something that would intrigue her, not something unimaginably lame, like, "If you could be any kind of animal, what animal would you be?"

Maybe something with girl appeal, like, "When were you the happiest ever?" Jason thought as he walked back to Sienna. *Or maybe... "Do you have a boyfriend?"* If he could bring himself to ask what he really wanted to know.

As it turned out, he didn't have to waste a question on the boyfriend thing. Because Sienna wasn't leaning against the Alfa Romeo anymore, she was leaning against Brad Moreau. Her arms were wrapped around his neck, his hands were plunged into that amazing black hair of hers. And they were kissing as if they never planned to stop.

THREE

The next day after lunch period, Jason headed straight to the locker room. A bunch of younger guys hung around near the bulletin board just inside the doorway.

"Don't even think about it, bro," Brad said, clapping Jason on the back.

Jason jumped. He hadn't noticed Brad in the throng of guys. *But what was Brad talking about?* Had he seen Jason flirting with Sienna by her car yesterday? Was he pissed?

"No need to check the list. You definitely made the team," Brad continued, steering Jason away from the group.

Oh, that. Right. Jason's heart rate returned to something around its usual beats per minute. "Great," he said.

"So listen, I'm having a party this weekend," Brad told him as they joined the crowd of students making their way across the sunny courtyard to the next period. "I stuck an invite in your swim locker with the info. The whole team will be there."

"Sounds good," Jason replied. "Is it just a guys' night? Team bonding?"

Brad laughed. "No way. It's a house party—my parents' place on the beach. Bonfire, barbecue, bikini-clad chiquitas, absent mother and father, the whole deal." He slapped hands with Van Dyke, who was waiting outside a classroom. "Van Dyke will be there. But he shouldn't bring us too low."

"I tolerate that only because . . . actually, I don't tolerate it," Van Dyke said, disappearing into the room.

"Best friends since preschool," Brad explained. "See you at practice."

"Yeah, later." Jason made his way toward English. English and Sienna. Would it be awkward to see her? *Screw it*, he told himself. He'd managed to cover his awkwardness yesterday when he had found her and Brad making out. It would be no big deal to see her today, especially now he that he knew he didn't have a chance with her. The pressure was off.

And at Brad's party, he'd make sure he made the acquaintance of a few other DeVere "chiquitas," as Brad called them. Sienna couldn't be the only female around who would make his pulse race.

But the moment he stepped into the classroom, his gaze fell on Sienna. She wasn't even looking at him. She was deep in conversation on her cell. But Jason suddenly felt intensely alive and aware of her—she was the only thing in the room that mattered.

She's Brad's girlfriend, Jason thought. *And Brad's a*

good guy. Like today with the team list and the party invite. Besides, Jason just wasn't the kind of guy who hit on somebody else's girlfriend.

But none of that seemed to matter when she was so close.

"Hey, Michigan." Sienna's voice jerked Jason out of his thoughts. He turned toward her, steeling himself to meet her eyes as if she were just a normal girl who got a normal reaction out of him.

"Hey," he said, happy to hear that his voice came out steady.

"Did Brad tell you about the party?" she asked.

"Yeah. Sounds cool."

"And . . . ?" Sienna prompted. When he didn't answer, she turned in her seat to look at him more closely. Jason got an extra jolt when she brought her long, honey-tan legs into sight. "Are you coming?"

"I don't know," he said. "I have to cart my sister to the movies first. Sacred promise. But maybe after."

Sienna laughed. "Hold it." She pointed her cell at him. "I need a picture of a guy who would rather spend time with his sister than go to one of Brad's parties." She hit a button, capturing his image with her phone.

Jason felt a blush creep up his neck—caused by both embarrassment and pornographic thoughts about those legs of hers. At least the blush had started post-photo. "She's having a hard time here," he explained. "Adjusting, I mean. She was, like, the queen of the school back home."

"Dani, right?" Sienna asked.

Jason raised his eyebrows. So everyone really did know everything about him and his family. "Right."

"Well, bring her to the party," Sienna said. *"Pourquoi pas?"*

Jason thought, from the one year of French he'd taken, that that meant "Why not?"

She turned away from him, using both thumbs to click in a text message before class started. He hoped it wasn't about him and what a family-centric, boring little mama's boy he was.

Jason stared at her back. Her silky hair shone in the soft light from the wall sconces. What did it mean that Sienna wanted him to go to the party? It was Brad's party, which meant it was basically her party too. So maybe she just wanted to be sure they would have a good turnout. *Don't be an idiot,* he told himself. *They're two of the most popular people in school. Everyone will be at their party.*

Sienna threw back her head and laughed at something—probably the return message. She'd completely forgotten Jason was there.

He busied himself pulling *Macbeth* out of his backpack. What did it mean that she wanted him to come to the party? It meant nothing.

• • •

"Do you have any idea what this means?" Dani cried. "Brad Moreau is the hottest guy at DeVere! This party will be *killer*."

Jason couldn't help smiling.

"Nobody said you were allowed to go, missy," their mother pointed out from across the new cherry wood dining room table.

"*Allowed* to go?" Dani repeated. "Since when do I have to ask permission to go to a party?"

Jason shot his father a look. His dad shrugged. They'd both learned to keep out of arguments between the women in the Freeman family. Mostly because neither Dani nor Mrs. Freeman ever paid attention to anyone else when they were arguing with each other.

"We're not in Fraser anymore," Mrs. Freeman said. "Things are different out here."

"What are you talking about, Mom?" Dani exploded. "Aunt Bianca knows all these people, remember? She found us the house here because it's a safe place to live! I'm probably safer here than I was in Fraser."

"Bianca doesn't live in California full-time," Mrs. Freeman argued. "And she doesn't have children of her own. She doesn't know the kinds of things that go on."

Dani rolled her eyes. "Like what? What 'things'?"

"You know what I mean," Mrs. Freeman responded.

"These kids grow up too fast. Who knows what kind of parties they have?"

Dani sighed, exasperated. "You've been stealth-watching *The OC*, haven't you? Just because 'these kids' live in Malibu doesn't mean they're not normal."

"So this Brad Moreau's parents will be there?" Mrs. Freeman asked. "And there won't be any drinking?"

Jason took a bite of his mashed potatoes, hiding what he was sure was a guilty expression. He agreed with his mom that the kids out here seemed a little more experienced than his friends back in Michigan. But if his mother thought that Michigan parties were supervised and alcohol-free, she was dreaming. "Mom." Dani put on her "reasonable" voice. "Even if there is alcohol there, I won't drink it. I'm not stupid. And besides, you have to let me go. This party is vital."

"Vital to what?" Mr. Freeman asked.

"Vital to making friends. To achieving some kind of happiness at the new school you're *forcing* me to go to. Isn't that what you want me to do?"

Their parents exchanged a look. Dani's constant misery over the move had been worrying them, Jason knew. Dani was totally using it to her advantage.

"Look. I ate lunch with Kristy Blane today and yesterday," Dani said. "She's really cool. And if I can get her an invitation to a party like this, it will solidify our friendship. Jason, help me out here."

Jason sighed. The last thing he wanted to do was chaperone Dani and this Kristy person. But this was the first time he'd seen his sister excited about anything since they'd arrived in California. "Mom, Dani's been going to parties for years. You can't change the rules just because we moved."

His mom sighed, still unsure.

"And besides," Jason added. "I'll be there to keep an eye on her."

"Okay. But be careful," Mrs. Freeman reluctantly agreed. "I hope I don't regret this."

I hope I *don't regret it*, Jason thought.

"Dani, we're going to be late," Jason called up the stairs on Saturday night. He was talking *late* late, not just don't-want-to-look-desperate late. He'd been sitting on the couch for half an hour, waiting for Dani and Kristy to finish getting ready.

"What do you think?" Dani asked as she came down the stairs. She did a turn in front of him. "Too slutty?"

"Oh, that is so not a question you ask an older brother. An older brother does not even want to *hear* the word 'slutty' come out of his sister's mouth," Jason replied, covering his ears in mock horror. Then he looked at her outfit. It was a tight, short T-shirt and some kind of ruffled miniskirt.

"It's a Stella McCartney. How can it not be perfection?" Kristy demanded from the stairs. She was wearing almost the same outfit in different colors and had her shoulder-length blond hair styled just like Dani's. "Besides, it's a beach party."

"Fine, then. It's great. Wear it." Jason stood up. "Let's go."

"No, now you've ruined it for me. I have to change," Dani said.

"How did I ruin it for you? I didn't even say anything!" Jason protested.

But Dani had disappeared up the stairs, taking Kristy with her.

Jason sank back down with a sigh. Maybe it didn't matter how late they were. He had a feeling that this party would run all night. The way kids at school had been talking about it for the whole week, you'd think Brad's parties were the wildest bashes ever thrown, with people hooking up on the beach until sunrise. He was curious to see if the reality lived up to the hype.

He grabbed the remote and clicked on the TV. There was never anything good on, on Saturday nights, but he had to distract himself somehow. He couldn't just keep staring at the wall until Dani was finally ready. Why did girls work so hard at their clothes, anyway? Were they all like that? Was Sienna? He wondered if she'd be wearing some little Stella

McCartney skirt to the party. He wouldn't mind seeing her in that. Then again, maybe she'd just wear a bathing suit—it *was* a beach party, after all. Would she wear a bikini?

"Dani!" Jason yelled. "We're leaving. Now!"

"Valet parking?" Jason murmured as a guy in a white jacket waved him to a stop in Brad's car-studded driveway.

"Of course," Kristy said. She shoved open her door and tumbled out of the convertible, followed by Dani. The two of them took off toward the house without a backward glance. Jason gave the valet his keys and looked around. The house was a Spanish-style mansion with a red tile roof. And glass. Lots of glass. Floor to ceiling, in some places.

It didn't look much like a beach house. He'd always pictured them as sort of small and rustic. Places you could track sand into, where you could let your bathing suit dry on the porch rail and leave giant towels lying around. But this place oozed elegance.

Remember your mission, Jason told himself as he walked up the granite path. *You are here to meet girls who go to your school. Unattached girls. Converse with them. Share a beverage. That sort of thing.*

"The newbie gets his first look at a hot Malibu party," a voice said from behind him. Jason glanced over his shoulder to see Adam with his camera. "Stay right there." He circled Jason, filming him from all sides.

"I'm beginning to suspect that your movie's about me," Jason cracked.

"It would be classic," Adam replied. He turned off the camera and walked with Jason toward the house. "A stranger arrives in town and shakes up the small, tight-knit community. Very *Footloose*."

"I don't think I'll be shaking anything up," Jason said. "Or dancing like Kevin Bacon."

"You never know. Maybe you'll end up being the hero of DeVere Heights," Adam joked.

Jason stepped through the open door into Brad's house and surveyed the scene. "I don't know, it looks like a typical party to me. No one in need of heroics."

Adam sighed. "Then I'll go to Plan B: find a girl to film. Point a camera at a girl and she's your new best friend. " He clapped Jason on the back and waded into the crowd of kids at the large bar in the living room. Jason headed for the back door instead. He wanted to see the beach part of the beach house.

The wide French doors led out to a perfectly mani-cured lawn surrounding an enormous, lagoon-shaped pool with a hot tub at one end. The hot tub over-flowed in a waterfall into the main pool, and a couple was making out under the spray. Eight other people crowded into the steaming hot tub, giggling and kissing. Two girls floated on lounge chairs in the pool while a few guys splashed around in the water beside them.

Jason followed a stone path lit with five-foot-high tiki torches. The path wound around the pool and through a thicket of fruit trees heavy with flowers. Voices floated on the warm summer air—from people hiding in the darkness under the trees. Probably making out where they could get some privacy, Jason figured. So far, he wasn't too impressed. Sure, the house was nice, but the party seemed like any other party he'd ever been to.

Then he stepped out of the little orchard—and gasped. He stood on the edge of a tall bluff. The Pacific Ocean spread out in front of him. The moon hung low in the sky, casting a silver path across the water and right up to Jason's feet.

"You don't get that in Michigan," he murmured.

A tangy, vanilla scent drifted by on the warm breeze. Jason's heartbeat sped up. *Sienna.* He didn't even have to turn around to know she'd come up the path behind him—he recognized her perfume.

"Welcome to California," she said. "Nice view, huh?"

"Yeah." He kept his eyes on the ocean. He knew *she'd* be a pretty nice view as well. But he wasn't the kind of guy who went after someone else's girlfriend. And not looking at her sure helped him stay that way.

"Have you seen the beach yet?" Sienna asked.

"Uh . . . no. I thought maybe this *was* the beach."

"Do you see any sand?"

"No," Jason acknowledged. "But the water's at least fifty feet below us. I thought maybe the whole 'beach house' thing was a euphemism."

Sienna snorted. "We don't do euphemisms. Coming up with clever wordplay would take valuable time away from the grooming and shopping that is essential to SoCal life. You've heard how vain and materialistic we are out here, right?" she joked. "When we say 'beach house,' we mean it. Come on."

She led the way over to a jumble of rocks on the edge of the cliff. In the middle of a boulder a deep step had been cut. Jason peered over Sienna's shoulder to see a steep stairway plunging down the side of the cliff. In the moonlight he could make out a stretch of pale sand below. "Looks dangerous," he said.

Sienna shot him an amused look. "Sometimes dangerous is worth it," she said.

They don't do euphemisms. But do they do double entendres? Jason wondered. Was Sienna trying to tell him something? He shoved the thought out of his head and followed her.

She skipped down the steps as if she'd done it a

million times. She probably had, Jason knew. Adam had told him that Sienna and Brad had been together since they were freshmen. She must've spent a lot of time at his place.

When they reached the beach, Sienna slipped out of her sandals and took off across the sand barefoot. Jason pulled off his Tevas and left them in a pile of other shoes at the foot of the steps. He looked around at the soft white sand and the ocean—black in the darkness, except for where silver moonlight rippled across the surface. It took his breath away.

He turned his attention to a giant bonfire that had been built about twenty feet out from the base of the cliff. He hadn't seen it from the top. He got it now: This was where the real party was. A bunch of kids from school ranged along the beach, some swimming, a few playing Frisbee. But most of them were just sitting in groups and couples around the fire, drinking beer.

"Think fast!" Sienna tossed him a bottle from the row of huge coolers set up away from the heat of the fire. He caught it easily but didn't open it. For one thing, it might explode from being shaken up by her throw. For another, he didn't plan to drink tonight; he had to drive Dani and Kristy home.

"Come meet my best friend, Belle." Sienna tugged him over to a tall girl with short blond hair. Jason's skin tingled where Sienna's fingers touched him. "Belle, this is the new guy," Sienna said.

Jason nodded at her. He vaguely recalled Adam saying something about Belle in his rundown of the DeVere High hierarchy. But he'd been too distracted by Sienna to pay much attention.

"You didn't tell me he was an 'Absolut' cutie," Belle purred. She smiled at Jason and a dimple appeared in each cheek.

Now here's a girl who seems friendly, Jason thought. *And she herself is a cutie.* She had blond hair tousled around her heart-shaped face, and pearly skin that gleamed in the moonlight. Her green eyes were bright with intelligence and playfulness. Jason felt that this was a girl he should want to get to know better. But that electricity—that snap he got from Sienna—it just wasn't there with Belle.

"'Absolut' is a word that you can only use once in a while," Sienna answered. She flicked her eyes from the top of Jason's head to his bare toes. "But I guess he's worth it."

With Sienna, the electricity was never far away. As she gave him her seal of approval, Jason immediately got a rush. *Okay, not everything happens instantaneously,* he told himself firmly. *Give Belle, like, five minutes.*

He turned to Belle and looked her up and down, in what he hoped was a not-obvious way. She didn't have

Sienna's curves, but her body was thin and athletic, and she moved with the grace of a dancer. He noticed a diamond sparkling from a ring in her belly button, and smiled. It was sexy. "Did that hurt?" he asked, with a nod at Belle's navel.

"God, yes." Belle ran one finger over her piercing. "I wish someone had told me that before I got it! Do you like it?"

"Yeah," he said honestly.

"Good," Belle murmured. Somehow she'd gotten so close, he could practically kiss her.

"Hey! Back off, loser," a harsh voice interrupted.

Jason turned in surprise. A lean guy with shoulder-length brown hair was glaring at him, his blue eyes boring into Jason's.

"Excuse me?" Jason said.

"You heard me. Back off." The dude stepped closer—close enough for Jason to smell his extreme beer breath. Then, weirdly, he began to giggle. "Check it out! I totally freaked the new guy!" He slapped Jason on the back in what was supposed to be a friendly way, but the blow was just a little too hard. "Relax, man."

"Who are you?" Jason asked.

"Dominic. Belle's boyfriend," the guy said, his words slurring a tiny bit. "Didn't she tell you about me?" He dropped his arm across Belle's shoulders and gave her a drunken kiss.

"Her boyfriend?" Jason couldn't hide the astonishment in his voice. This guy looked way too moody to be with the beautiful, bubbly Belle.

"Yeah." Dominic looked Jason up and down, his eyes hard even though the smile stayed on his face. "What's so weird about that?"

"Nothing," Jason said quickly, trying to cover his surprise. "I just didn't know."

"Dom, let's go sit by the fire," Belle suggested. "You're wasted."

"So what?" he demanded. "It's a party."

Belle pulled him by the hand. "Let's just go sit." She gave Jason a lingering smile as they slowly walked off.

Jason shook his head. "Let me guess. It's a prerequisite for every girl in the Heights to have a boyfriend?" he asked Sienna.

"Well, DeVere's a small school. And we *are* all seniors," Sienna pointed out. "We've had plenty of time to hook up with one another. But you never know what might happen."

Jason gazed at her thoughtfully. "I'll keep that in mind."

"Stay away from Belle, though. Dominic's the jealous type. And you're already on his bad side."

Jason gaped at her. "I met him, like, thirty seconds ago. How am I on his bad side?"

"Because you were standing within a hundred yards of his woman," Sienna said, rolling her eyes. "Just ignore him."

"The new boy has clearly hit his stride early. Look at him hanging with the most flammable girl at the party." Adam appeared in front of them, filming and narrating as usual. "Unfortunately he's in for a disappointment. The lovely Sienna is as untouchable as she is irresistible," Adam continued.

"You're going to give me a copy of that tape, right?" Brad asked, coming up from behind Adam. He plucked the camcorder from Adam's grasp in one easy movement and turned it on the film junkie. "Let's take a look behind the camera," he said, imitating Adam's narrator voice. "Who is the mysterious voyeur who sneaks into our parties and films our every move?"

"I didn't sneak in," Adam said. "I came with Jason. Right?"

Jason blinked in surprise. He hadn't realized that Adam was crashing. But Adam was his first California friend—he had to back him up. "Of course."

Brad turned off the camera and handed it back to Adam. "I'm just kidding," he said. "The police chief's son is always welcome. It'll keep us from getting busted for underage drinking."

"I'm flattered," Adam said dryly.

"What the hell are you *thinking*?" a guy shouted. "I could kill you, loser!"

They all spun toward the bonfire. A bunch of kids were rushing to get away from the commotion, and for a moment, Jason couldn't see what was happening. Then the way cleared, leaving Dominic and another guy alone in front of the fire. The guy towered over Dominic. He looked like a football player. This was not going to be pretty.

"I'll kill you," Dominic shouted drunkenly. "That's my girlfriend you're enjoying."

Jason shot a look at Belle, who stood off to one side. She didn't seem particularly bothered by the scene. But Dominic was almost apoplectic. He shoved the bigger guy in the chest.

"Hey, man, she asked me if I wanted to do a body shot," the guy snapped. "Why don't you yell at *her*?"

Dominic didn't answer. He just charged at the bigger guy, ramming his head into the guy's stomach. Jason expected him to bounce right off the shelf of muscle, but instead, the other guy went down, crumpling to the sand as if he'd been stabbed in the gut.

Dominic fell on top of him and began punching him with both fists, moving faster than Jason would've thought possible. The mountain of flesh groaned and tried to push him off, but Dominic didn't budge.

Jason shook his head. The guy was twice as big as

Dominic, but Dominic was going to beat him unconscious. Or worse. Jason was running across the sand
before he'd even made a conscious decision. He hit
Dominic from the side, using his own momentum to
bear him to the ground. They both fell hard, but
Dominic didn't seem to feel it. He had squirmed out
from beneath Jason in a second.

He turned and straddled Jason's chest, eyes burning
with rage. Lightning-fast, his hand shot out and
grabbed Jason's neck, squeezing with unbelievable
strength.

Get him off you! a voice screamed in Jason's head.
He remembered the jujitsu classes he'd had as a kid—
just because an opponent was stronger didn't mean
you couldn't beat him. Jason knew he simply had to
out-think Dominic. He concentrated on his own
movements, forcing himself to ignore the crushing
pain in his windpipe. Then he reached up and stabbed
his thumbs into pressure points on either side of
Dominic's neck, just above his collarbone.

Dominic's body went slack. Only for an instant,
but it was enough. Jason scrambled away and got to
his feet, turning back to face his opponent.
Amazingly, Dominic was on his feet already. He
glared at Jason, his blue eyes crazed. *He's going to charge
me,* Jason realized, and dropped into a fighting stance,
ready for Dominic's attack.

But just then, Brad grabbed Dominic in a head-lock. He gave Jason a grim smile. "I'll take it from here."

Jason nodded and stumbled away from the fight. But he could feel Dominic's eyes on him. Filled with hate.

FOUR

"Are you all right?" Sienna asked as she and Belle rushed over to Jason.

"Yeah," Jason answered. The word clawed its way out of his damaged throat. He felt as if he'd swallowed a mouthful of sand.

"Well, you shouldn't be!" Sienna snapped. "Are you crazy, going after Dominic? You're lucky you're not dead."

"He's not *that* strong," Jason muttered. But, in truth, Dominic was a lot stronger than he looked. Jason could usually size up his opponent pretty accurately, but Dominic's strength had caught him completely off guard.

Jason's eyes moved back to the fight. Brad had Dominic pinned, and Dominic had stopped struggling. Their faces were only about an inch apart as Brad talked Dominic down. The situation had clearly shifted from red alert to yellow.

"Give the boy a break," Belle told Sienna. She turned to Jason. "I think you were seriously brave."

Jason didn't answer. He wasn't really in the mood to be praised by the girl whose boyfriend had just tried to strangle him.

"He wouldn't have had to be brave at all if you didn't love seeing Dominic pull his jealousy act," Sienna said, and sighed. "You knew what would happen when you asked Matt to do a body shot."

"Oh, please," Belle said, waving off the criticism.

Matt was the huge football player, Jason surmised. His thoughts came slowly, as if his brain had been scrambled with a fork. He'd been in fights before, but Dominic had really done some damage. He sucked in a deep breath of the chilly night air. It still surprised him how fast the temperature in Malibu dropped at night. Part of being so close to the ocean. He glanced over at the water. It was utterly dark now. Some clouds had drifted across the moon, blotting out the sparkles of silver light on the waves.

Suddenly, the ocean didn't seem beautiful anymore. The inky water looked . . . ominous. Like it was hiding secrets. Jason had the urge to go check on Dani, make sure she was okay. "I'm going to head up to the house. See if I can find any fights to get into up there," he told Sienna and Belle. Belle laughed, but Sienna didn't look amused.

"You've had your share of fighting for one night," she answered, her dark eyes stormy.

She was scared for me, Jason realized. He didn't know how to respond to that, especially because her boyfriend had just saved his ass. So he didn't say anything at all, just turned and headed over to the stairs in the cliffside.

The trip back up to the house felt like it took forever. He was really feeling the effects of the fight. He wanted a beer—or three—to take the edge off the pain radiating through several key body parts, and there was a cooler full of them right inside the door. But being the designated driver for the night, he decided he'd have to stick to something nonalcoholic.

Jason managed to find a can of Mountain Dew stuck in among the Hansen's kiwi and strawberry diet soda in the fridge.

The sound of girls shrieking, guys bellowing, and then all laughing led him to the living room. Harberts and a couple of other guys were playing Madden NFL on the Xbox. Dani's friend Kristy was cheering them on, along with a couple of other girls who looked like freshmen. No Danielle in the mix. Jason wasn't crazy about the fact that she'd split from her friend. He figured it would have been harder for her to get into trouble if she'd stayed with the group.

On the sofa—a shiny-slick, half-moon-shaped burgundy sofa—two couples were half undressed and making out. Neither of the girls was Dani, which was good. Jason wasn't up for a second fight tonight.

Behind the sofa, a bikini-wrapped girl was stretched out on the floor, ingesting some vile-looking blue liquid through a funnel held by a guy who had the words "papi chulo" written on his naked chest in Magic Marker. Jason didn't think bonging a drink that looked like it should be served with a little umbrella and some plastic seahorses was particularly advisable. Gladly, no Dani present.

He popped the top of the Mountain Dew and took a swig as he headed into the kitchen. The carbonation bubbles felt like bombs against the inside of his throat. It was as if Dominic's fingernails had actually broken the skin and gouged out a layer of flesh.

Just like it would be back in Michigan, the kitchen was another party hot spot. A guy who looked as if he played actual—as opposed to virtual—football was doing push-ups with two girls sitting on his back. Another girl was counting the push-ups. A couple of guys had co-opted the granite top of the kitchen island and were mixing up a batch of brownies, with much controversy over exactly what went into them. And in the far corner of the kitchen, Jason's friend Adam was talking to a girl from their history class, Carrie Smith.

Nice, Jason thought. Carrie was a surfer girl. He'd spotted her with her board driving home one day. She kept her dark brown hair short, and she had pointy Jack Nicholson eyebrows—the girl version—which made her look kind of devilish, in a cute way. Jason thought Danielle would give the two of them her potential couple stamp of approval—if she was anywhere in sight. But she wasn't.

From the way Adam was leaning in and the way Carrie was smiling, Jason figured he might be interrupting something, so he didn't head over. Besides, he wanted to find his sister. He told himself he was worrying about nothing. Danielle had been to lots of parties without Jason playing chaperone. In fact, she was more of a party animal than he was. But that feeling of darkness that he'd gotten down on the beach hadn't let up. It was probably just a side effect of getting half asphyxiated by crazy Dominic, but still. . . .

Where was she? Jason exited the kitchen and passed by a spiral staircase. He didn't even want to think about Dani being up in the bedroom territory. Instead, he veered through the first open door he came to—and there she was, playing pool with Van Dyke. Well, at that precise moment, she was actually perched on the edge of the table, flirting for all she was worth, but it came to the same thing.

Jason smiled. Dani had always been a hustler when it came to pool. She looked like a giggly girl who didn't know how to hold a cue. But she played like a pro—she'd been learning from their dad since she was five.

Dani hadn't noticed Jason's arrival. Van Dyke,

however, had. "Freeman!" he bellowed in greeting. "Your little sister is kicking my ass!"

"Well, you shouldn't have told me girls can't play," Dani retorted. "You deserve what you get."

"Harsh," Van Dyke said, shaking his head and grinning.

Dani bumped him out of the way with her hip, then leaned over to line up her next shot. As she did, she glanced up at Jason.

He raised his eyebrows questioningly.

Dani laughed and answered his unspoken question. "I'm fine. I'm not drunk, and I can handle your friend here."

"Yeah, no kidding," Van Dyke mumbled.

Jason grinned. "Okay, then. Later." He kind of wished Dani were hanging out with a guy her own age. But Van Dyke had been friends with Brad for years, and that made Jason think he was probably a decent guy. Besides, Danielle was clearly having fun, getting evidence that her life in DeVere Heights didn't have to suck, and that was all good.

Back downstairs, Jason grabbed another Mountain Dew and headed out to the pool. Couples were making out at the edge, but he could still find space in the middle. He'd worn board shorts just in case. It *was* a beach party, after all, and they didn't do euphemisms. Sienna's teasing voice came back into his mind, and

Jason smiled at the thought of her. He peeled off his T-shirt and got ready to dive into the pool.

"Oh, come on, that part's no fun," a girl called.

"Yeah, come over here," another added.

Jason glanced over his shoulder and saw two girls in bikinis, one blond, the other Asian with glossy black hair, leaning on the little wall that separated the hot tub from the pool. Water from the hot tub flowed over the wall into the pool like a waterfall, making the girls' long hair swirl about them mermaid-style. Hot.

"What?" Jason asked.

"The pool. It's boring. The Jacuzzi is much more interesting," the blond girl called.

Jason walked over to her. "Why is that?" he asked.

"Because there are bubbles," the Asian mermaid replied. "And steam. And all sorts of things a regular pool doesn't have."

"Like me," the blonde added.

"Hey, no trying to hog the new guy!" her friend protested.

Jason grinned. They were both cute, they were both flirting with him, and it was about time the party offered him something to think about besides Sienna. "Okay, you've convinced me," he said, and eased himself into the hot tub to sit between the two girls. "I'm Jason."

"We know," the blond one told him. "I'm Cindy, and this is Jin."

The other girl smiled.

"How is it possible that every single person in school knows my name?" Jason asked.

"You're a celebrity," Jin replied. "We don't get new boys around here very often."

"Plus, you're a cute new boy," Cindy added. "We *really* don't get those! You were seen moving in and the texts and calls started immediately."

Jason laughed. "On behalf of Luke Archer, former new kid, I'm offended."

Jin wrinkled her nose. "Oh, Luke. He's such the loner. He's no fun. At least you hold a conversation. I'm not even sure Luke knows how to talk."

"Well, talking is just one of my many talents," Jason answered with a laugh. "So, are you two seniors? Wait, you can't be. All the senior girls are off the market," he said, thinking of Sienna, even though hanging with Cindy and Jin was supposed to be blocking the Sienna thoughts.

"We're lowly juniors," Cindy told him.

After hanging out a while with Cindy and Jin, including some dancing, caught on film by a grinning Adam, Jason was pretty much done. He also knew their mom probably would stay up worrying until he and Dani appeared at home. He pushed himself to his feet and headed for the pool room to see if Dani was still there.

"Are you the one who's been hogging all the Dew?" a familiar voice called as he passed the coolers near the front door.

"Does four qualify me?" he asked Sienna.

"That makes you an 'Absolut' piggy," she answered with a smile, but her voice lacked its usual animation, and Jason noticed that her face was pale.

Jason gave the soda can in his hand a test shake. "I'd say there's a good third left. With maybe only five percent of that being backwash. Want it?"

"Ewww! But even if it was fifteen percent saliva, I'd have to say yes," Sienna answered. She took the can and drained it in one long swallow. "Ahhhh. That should keep me going a little longer. True, Pepsi One has more caffeine, but what's caffeine without sugar?"

"Uh, I'm trying to come up with something clever here, but failing," Jason told her. "Milk without the chocolate? Tonic without the vodka?"

"Better stop now before you hurt yourself." Sienna's smile took the sting out of her words. "Did Dani have fun tonight?"

"Looked like good times were being had last time I saw her," Jason answered. "She was—"

He broke off as Brad rushed through the open back door. "Somebody puked in the hot tub. I've gotta see if the pool guy will come out tonight to drain and refill. My mom will have a convulsion if she doesn't get her morning soak. Something about pores and heat and toxins. Honestly, I don't listen."

"So I guess this means you won't be able to take me home anytime soon," Sienna said. "I'm wiped."

"Are you sure you're not just dehydrated?" Brad asked. "Want me to find you something to drink?"

Sienna shook her head. "I just want to crash."

"I can take you home," Jason offered. "I was about to head out anyway."

Sienna nodded gratefully.

"Great, thanks," Brad said, rushing off again.

"I'll go get Dani and her friend and we're out of here," Jason told Sienna. For a second he allowed himself to think about what it would be like if his sister and Kristy weren't at the party. If he'd been handed this chance when he could have been alone with Sienna. There was something about being with a girl in a car—it was like the two of you were in your own private world.

Which is why you should be glad to have Dani and Kristy along, Jason told himself. *You definitely need chaperones. And what about that whole meeting-other-girls thing? What happened to that plan?* He had to admit he hadn't been all that aggressive about his other-fish-in-the-sea fishing. He hadn't even asked for phone numbers from Jin or Cindy. Neither mermaid had been nearly as intriguing as Sienna. Which is why chaperones equaled good and safe. He might attempt something brainless, disloyal, and all things bad without someone to watch him.

Jason headed for the pool room, but a familiar giggle stopped him in his tracks. Dani was in the living room, on the big burgundy sofa. He could hear her laughing, but the back of the sofa came up too high for him to see her. A brief stab of worry went through him; was she drunk? Was she with a guy? Van Dyke? He stepped around the couch and stopped in surprise. His sister was practically convulsed with laughter, all trace of the pouty, self-pitying Dani gone. Kristy sat next to her, also laughing her butt off.

"What's so funny?" he asked, going over to them.

Danielle took one look at his face and laughed even harder. She looked a little pale, and her gray eyes were kind of spacey. "I don't know," she answered, her giggles finally subsiding slightly. "I'm just happy."

"Oh." Jason wasn't sure what to say to that. He settled for, "So you had a good time?"

Kristy snorted, which got Dani laughing again. Kristy joined in.

"O-kay," Jason said. "You two have obviously had enough to drink."

"I'm not drunk," Dani protested, slurring her words. "I only had one beer."

"Yeah, I'm not drunk. I mean, she's not drunk,"

Kristy agreed. She sat back on the couch and gazed at Jason with a huge grin on her face.

"Need some help?" Sienna asked, coming up from behind him.

"I've got two drunk girls who say they're not drunk," Jason told her. "Any help at all would be appreciated."

She smiled at him, then reached out her hands toward Dani. "Up," she ordered cheerfully. Dani giggled and grabbed her hands. Sienna hauled her to her feet and steered her over to Jason. Then she pulled Kristy up and led her toward the front door, holding on to her arm.

Jason kept hold of Dani, too. Not that she seemed likely to fall over—he just got the feeling she might wander off toward something funny or pretty or shiny if she got the chance. If he didn't know her better, he'd think she was stoned.

He and Sienna got both girls outside and into the tiny backseat of the VW. Sienna took the passenger seat, and Jason climbed in beside her. *Eyes on the road,* he told himself as he pulled out of the driveway. The last thing he should be doing was looking at Sienna's long legs stretched out next to him. *Remember, there are other people in the car.*

Except, after he dropped off one of his chaperones —Kristy—the other one fell into a nothing-will-wake-me sleep in the backseat. Dani, usually a night owl, was snoring before Kristy even reached her front door—which left Jason and Sienna unsupervised in the front.

Just keep your hands on the wheel and your mind on the road, Jason instructed himself firmly.

"What are you thinking about?" Sienna asked, ruining the plan.

He couldn't exactly tell her the truth. But what was he supposed to say? "Dominic," he said, surprising himself.

"Dominic?" Sienna repeated. "Why?"

"He was really strong," Jason replied thoughtfully. "Like, freakishly strong."

Sienna leaned her head back against the headrest and gazed at him with a tired smile. "Dominic was just drunk," she assured him. "Some people have anger issues that come out when they drink."

Yeah, but they don't usually get stronger, Jason thought.

Sienna sighed and turned to look out the window.

"You okay?" he asked.

"Mmm," she murmured. "Just tired."

He took the hint. She didn't feel like talking. Which made it a tiny bit easier to concentrate on the road—until he pulled into Sienna's driveway.

Her house wasn't in the Spanish mission style, like

a lot of the places in Malibu. It was spare and clean, with no ornamentation, almost like something carved out of one piece of stone. It managed to distract him from Sienna's presence for, precisely, no time at all.

"Thanks for the ride," she said, putting her hand on the door handle.

"Sure," Jason replied. Better to say too little than too much.

"And sorry if I was sort of a bitch to you before— down on the beach, after the fight. It's just that seeing you getting mauled by Dominic . . ." Sienna's voice trailed off.

"I know," Jason said thoughtfully. "You were scared for me."

She didn't answer. Instead, she leaned toward Jason and kissed him on the mouth.

Then she pulled away and jumped out of the car before he could respond. Jason was left staring after her as she ran up to the house, his whole body tingling from that one electric moment of contact.

Why the hell did she do that? he asked himself. And why the hell did she stop?

FIVE

"Get up, Dani," Jason called the next morning. He winced as he lifted his hand to knock on her door. Somehow Dominic had managed to bruise his arm as well as his throat during the fight the night before.

No response.

Jason opened the door and stepped into Dani's room, taking in the totally still form huddled beneath the duvet. "Dani!" he said, more loudly.

He still didn't get a response, so he reverted to his eight-year-old sibling warfare tactics. He leaned over his sister and flicked her ear. "Danielle! Now!"

She ignored him, pulling the covers all the way over her head. "Go away," she muttered. "Do not come back until . . . ever!"

"Mom is making pancakes," he told her. "You love them. You have to get up and eat them."

"I'm not hungry," his sister said. "I just need to sleep."

"Fine. But don't come crying to me if Mom and Dad don't let you go to any more parties anytime soon," Jason declared, and turned toward the door, waiting for the reaction.

"What do you mean?" Danielle demanded, sitting up slowly, worried.

"I mean that not coming downstairs for your favorite breakfast is like wearing a sign that says, 'Hello, my name is Dani. I have a hangover and can't be trusted to behave responsibly until I'm at least eighteen,'" he explained.

"But I hardly even drank last night," Danielle protested. She looked down at herself and frowned. "Why am I still wearing these clothes?"

"That is not the question of someone who barely drank," Jason told her. "And you're still wearing those clothes because I had to haul you up here and throw you into bed last night. You passed out in the car."

"Not possible," Danielle said, yawning.

"And yet true," Jason answered. "I hope Van Dyke didn't have anything to do with your beverage intake or I'm going to have to kick his ass."

"Van Dyke?" Danielle crawled out of bed and gave a catlike stretch.

"Michael. You know, the guy you were playing pool with. We're on the swim team together."

"Oh." Dani frowned, clearly searching her memory without success. "Yeah. Him. He was, uh, cute."

Absurd. She obviously had no idea who he was talking about. "Do you remember *anything* about the party?" Jason asked.

"Damn straight." A big smile broke across his sister's face. "I remember it was the best night of my young life!"

"Dani actually said it was the best night of her life!" Jason told Adam as they slid their trays down the cafeteria food line at lunch on Monday. "I've been hearing stuff like that from people all morning."

"People at DeVere do love the parties," Adam answered. "And that one was especially wild. Not that I've gone to many of them before. I mean, I go to lots of parties—and not just ones with paper hats and Pin the Tail on the Donkey, either, thank you—but I don't get asked to many soirées taking place behind The Gates." He added a salad to his growing collection of food. "By the way, thanks for, uh, inviting me."

Jason laughed. "Thanks for, *uh*, letting me know that I did before you showed up and all." He grabbed a pomegranate-blueberry juice. He felt the need for some antioxidants before swim practice. The fight at the party had been seriously debilitating. His neck still hurt every time he turned his head. He'd actually had to find a turtleneck to wear yesterday to hide the bruises from his mom so she wouldn't freak.

"I can see why you, a near decent-party virgin, thought it a ten on the grand scale," Jason said, grabbing a turkey sandwich. "But I still don't know why everyone else is acting like it was Mardi Gras and the Super Bowl all rolled into one."

"Hey, I got to hang with Carrie Smith. A girl who is hot and actually attainable. Unlike you, who was busy being friends with Sienna and Belle." Adam led the way over to the cashier. "Not to mention your lame showing with the two babes you actually managed to dance with. No wonder you didn't think the party rocked the Casbah. You were basically there as a eunuch."

"Rocked the Casbah?" Jason repeated.

"You have a problem with The Clash? They're on the *Royal Tenenbaums* soundtrack, and nobody knows music like Wes Anderson." Jason's face must have shown he had no idea what Adam was talking about, because Adam shook his head sadly. "Wes Anderson, pretty passable director of *The Royal Tenenbaums*," he explained.

"Never heard of him," Jason said. "However, I believe that The Clash—and I only know this because of the younger sister factor—was also on the sound-track for *What a Girl Wants*."

Adam stumbled backward, a hand on his heart. "I'm not sure that our budding friendship is going to survive this conversation," he said, mock-hurt. "At the very least, I'm taking you to the Blockbuster in the mall right after school. It's no Mondo Video A-Go-

Go—the best video store in L.A., by the way, and a true videophile's paradise—but with your level of ignorance, it'll do. We'll start with a few Wes creations, then move on to David Fincher."

"Sounds cool," Jason said. He was always up for watching new movies, not that he had the slightest idea who their directors were—and not that he cared. Adam headed over to the usual table. Luke Archer had already staked out his regular seat and was barricaded behind a book.

"So let's talk about Carrie. She looked somewhat into you, my friend," Jason said. "Clearly you were managing to keep your true self hidden."

"She was grooving on the unadulterated Adam," his friend protested. "She even helped me pro and con the soundtrack picks for my movie. Unlike you, she has an appreciation for the art that is film."

"Again, I can see why you're giving the party the big two thumbs up—that's the movie geek term, right? And I can even see why Dani was blown away by it." Jason took a bite of his sandwich. "But I was expecting something more. And I'd definitely have thought that your average DeVere High senior would need more than what I saw to label a night 'wild.'"

"Wait. You didn't find the true party, did you?" Adam leaned in and lowered his voice. "Dude, you gotta go through the passage behind the bookcase and take the staircase down to the dungeon. That's where the real depravity takes place. The absinthe fountain, the orgy—"

"You're an ass," Jason muttered.

"But I had you going for a second. Admit it," Adam said.

"Ass," Jason repeated, smiling. But he couldn't help feeling that he had missed something at the party. Not a secret room, but something . . .

Jason winced as he passed a long mirror on his way out of the locker room for swim practice after school. His neck was covered with splotches of blue-black. And his arm, where Dominic had grabbed him, had an impressive dark brown bruise over the bicep.

"Christ!" Van Dyke mumbled when Jason headed out to the pool.

"I second that," Harberts said from his seat in the bleachers. He took a pull on his POWERade.

Jason suspected it would take Harberts more than a little carb boost to handle swimming—he looked awful. He had dark circles under his eyes, and his skin was waxy and pale.

Harberts must have found something more entertaining than the Xbox at the party, Jason thought. He'd had at least a day and a half to recover. That should have been plenty of time to recoup from most forms of fun.

But the guy still looked exhausted, just like Dani had this morning.

Kyle Priesmeyer, one of the divers, dropped down next to Harberts. He was clearly in a similar state. His skin looked ashy instead of its usual warm brown and he kept yawning. Jason thought he'd been half of one of the couples he had seen rolling around on the Moreaus' sofa. "Can I have a drink?" Kyle asked, nodding toward Harberts' POWERade.

"Sorry, man. I need it more," Harberts replied, and drained the bottle.

Kyle rubbed his shaved head with his fingers. "I can't wake up today. And I slept half of yesterday!"

"I think I'm going to have to start kicking off my parties on Friday afternoons," Brad called as he headed over to the group. "You ladies clearly need a little more convalescence time."

"Ha-ha," Harberts muttered. Kyle yawned again.

"You probably need some convalescing yourself after that. . . ." Jason let his words trail off. He'd expected to see at least a few bruises on Brad from the fight. Dominic had gotten in some solid hits before Brad subdued him. But Brad looked more like a swimmer on one of Dani's beloved WB shows. There wasn't a bruise or a scratch on him. He stood in front of the bleachers, bouncing up and down on the balls of his feet. Clearly he didn't need a POWERade.

"What are you guys waiting for, an e-vite?" the coach yelled as he strode out of the locker room. "Pool. Laps. You don't need me to be telling you this."

Jason was in the pool three seconds later. The coolness and buoyancy of the water soothed his body aches. Thankfully Monday practice consisted mostly of laps of all the different strokes—he didn't feel up to much hardcore relay action today. And, judging from Harberts' slow-ass laps, neither did he.

But with each different stroke, Jason loosened up different muscles, and by the time Coach Middleton brought them over to do a couple of relays, he felt at least marginally human again. He got himself in position opposite Brad. The coach had kept him in the Moreau, Harberts, Van Dyke lineup.

Brad hurled himself off the block with his usual blast of speed. If he was feeling any pain, Jason couldn't see it in the smooth motions of his arms and legs. Jason, on the other hand, still felt his muscles protest with every movement. But he refused to let it slow him down. *One fight should* not *make me this sore.* He punched the sensor in the wall hard when he reached it and saw that he'd managed a fairly decent time.

He could tell from the splash he heard as he swung himself out of the pool that Harberts had made a sloppy start. He turned to watch Van Dyke and saw every muscle in his body tense as he waited for Harberts to reach him. "Come on!" he shouted, agitated.

But it was as if Harberts' limbs were weighted with lead. He was trying, but the guy was just too tired to swim as fast as usual. Jason's eyes moved to the huge clock mounted on the far wall and watched the seconds click away. Their time was going to be crap.

When Harberts punched the sensor, Van Dyke threw up his hands in annoyance. "What's the point of me even getting in the pool?" he yelled at Harberts. "We're past our slowest time!"

"Sorry, man, I'm just beat," Harberts replied.

"Dude, he's got after-party. Cut him some slack," Brad put in, keeping his voice low. Jason figured Brad didn't want the coach to hear.

"Well, maybe we should think about exactly who gets invited to our parties," Van Dyke shot back. He glared at Brad as if it were all his fault.

"Look, I'll get to sleep early tonight and—," Harberts began.

"I don't want to hear it." Van Dyke grabbed a towel, wrapped it around his shoulders, and stalked back to the locker room.

"Come on. Let's call it a day," Brad said. "We're out of here."

Jason glanced up at the coach. They still had a few

minutes of practice left. But Coach Middleton gave them a nod.

"You had a fish taco from Eddie's yet?" Brad asked Jason as they headed for the locker room.

"I don't even know where Eddie's is," Jason answered. He also knew that Adam was hanging around so he and Jason could hit Blockbuster after practice. "Besides, I've got plans today."

"The sister? Bring her," Brad said as he dialed the combination into his lock.

"No, Adam Turnball's decided I'm too film-challenged to be allowed to live this close to Hollywood. We're hitting the video store," Jason explained as he toweled off. "He might be up for the taco thing instead, though."

Brad shook his head. "Nah. I should probably just head home," he said. "My mom did not have on a happy face all weekend—and it wasn't just the BOTOX. She heard about the puke in the hot tub. It wouldn't hurt to put in some face-time."

Jason nodded. But he had the feeling that if he hadn't mentioned Adam, Mrs. Moreau's good son time would have waited. Clearly Adam wasn't in the same social circle as the DeVere Heights crowd. Although, for some reason, Jason himself seemed to be perfectly acceptable. *Guess that's the beauty of living behind the gates of DeVere Heights,* he thought.

"Let's hit Eddie's after the next practice. It'll be better after we've had an actual workout. We'll need the fuel more for muscle repair," Brad said as he tied his sneakers.

"Sounds like a plan," Jason answered. They headed out of the locker room and into the bright blue and yellow of a Malibu afternoon. Jason still thought it felt unnatural for the weather to be so predictable. But when it was predictable in a perfect-beach-day-every-day way, he figured he could definitely get used to it.

"What's he doing?" Brad asked, coming to an abrupt stop.

Jason followed his gaze across the quad. Adam had his video camera pointed at the giant football player, Matt, from the party. Even at this distance, Jason could see that Matt's lip was puffy, and his black eye could probably be seen from space—more of Dominic's handiwork. "Adam's shooting something for his work of genius, I guess," he said.

"But why that guy?" Brad asked, sounding annoyed.

Jason shrugged. "I haven't quite figured out exactly what Adam's movie is about. I'm not sure even *he* knows."

Brad's eyes narrowed as he continued to study Adam and Matt. "You know what? My mom might still be too pissed to stand the sight of me. I think I'll hang with you guys after all." He raised his voice. "Hey, Adam! Mind if I join you?"

Adam shut off the camera and slapped hands with Matt. He grabbed his bag and headed over to them. "Sure. You can help me educate Freeman."

"You take care of the film stuff. I'm working on his knowledge of fish tacos," Brad replied. Adam laughed.

Brad flashed him a big grin. "Besides, I don't know what you're talking about half the time with the movie lingo. You'll have to educate me along with Michigan boy."

"Always a pleasure to help the film-challenged," Adam told him happily.

"Let's take my car." Brad clapped Adam on the back and led him toward a Mercedes convertible. "You want to drive?"

"Are you kidding me?" Adam asked. "My vehicle is a used Vespa. Of course I want to drive the Merc."

Jason followed them, confused. Brad hadn't seemed eager to hang with Adam at all, but now he was acting like they were old friends. What was the deal?

SIX

"Sorry, Danielle. I'm with your mom on this one," Jason's father said at dinner the next night. "A yacht, alcohol, and no way to get someone to come pick you up if there's trouble . . ."

"It's a bad idea," Mrs. Freeman finished for him. "I'm surprised this girl's parents are even allowing her to have a party on their boat."

"Yacht," Jason corrected automatically. Nobody in Malibu said "boat" unless they were talking about a really old, huge car. And Belle's party was definitely taking place on a yacht. He'd heard enough about it at school today to be absolutely sure of that, along with the exact length of the yacht and how many separate cabins it had.

"But Jason will be there," Dani pleaded, eyes darting hopefully from one parent to the other. "And Belle is completely responsible."

Jason couldn't agree with his sister on that one. Belle was sweet and very cute. But, responsible? Hell, no. Inviting a guy to body-shot her in front of her insanely jealous boyfriend—that was pretty much the anti of responsible.

"When we've gotten to know some of these kids personally—," Jason's mom began.

"Fine. Pick a night. I'll invite them all over for charades and square dancing and Hi-C fruit punch. Or is that still too racy for you?" Dani demanded sarcastically. She stood up, grabbed her plate, dropped the silverware on top with a clatter, and headed into the kitchen.

Jason glanced at his watch. The Dani–Mom-with-a-minor-assist-from-Dad conversation about the party had lasted under three minutes. It wasn't like Dani to give up so easily. But it was only Tuesday night. The party was on Saturday. Jason figured his sister was plotting round two even now.

By the time Saturday rolled around, Danielle still hadn't made another play to get herself on the yacht. She didn't even shoot their mom a my-life-is-hell-thanks-to-you look when Jason took off in the VW, leaving her behind. Obviously she had something up her sleeve; Danielle was not the type to allow a parental party ban to ruin her night. Jason just hoped that he wouldn't have to deal with the fallout.

Not that he regretted finding himself on the aft deck of the *Moulin Rouge* with no little sister to watch over. He leaned on the rail and took in the sight of Surfrider Beach turning golden in the sunset, the sand and the high bluffs behind it practically glowing in the evening light. Surfers riding the waves seemed to skim over swells of molten gold, and when Jason looked up at the sky, his breath caught in his throat; the sun looked huge, a pulsing orange orb that appeared to be sinking directly into the ocean a few miles away. Jason almost expected steam to rise when the fiery circle hit the water.

Orangey-pink light glinted off the dark wood decks of the yacht, a sixty-foot-long vintage Chris-Craft Commander in pristine condition. Between the sunset, the cool ocean breeze, and the gleaming chrome and wood of the yacht, he felt as if he'd stepped into some kind of fantasy world.

"Kissabull?" a laughing voice demanded behind him. Jason turned and saw Belle balancing a tray of drinks in one hand. She was barefoot and wore a bikini top with one of those skirts that is basically a piece of cloth and a knot. Plus, the little diamond glittered next to her belly button, and silver rings shone on a couple of her toes.

"Aren't I, though?" Jason asked, not sure what she meant.

"Wait. No. For you, a Malibull. Cause you're new to Malibu. Ever had one?" Belle asked as she selected a pale green drink from the tray and handed it to him.

"This will be my first," Jason admitted, suspecting he hadn't been missing much.

"It's MIDORI, pineapple juice, and Red Bull," Belle told him. "If you don't like it, the Kissabull has Grape Pucker and the Bullionaire has gin, o.j. and cranberry juice."

"Practically a sports drink, then!" Jason said with a grin. He took a sip of the drink, a weak, sweet concoction, with only the tiniest bit of a kick. It tasted exactly like something he'd expect Belle to serve. He smiled at her. "Thanks."

"I live to serve. But only the first round. Then the crew takes over." Belle moved on with her tray.

A moment later, Harberts took her place in front of Jason. He shook his head when he saw the drink in Jason's hand. "If you're trying to get a buzz, I should inform you that that thing is only a few steps above nonalcoholic beer." He shook his glass. "Vodka tonic. Now *this* is a drink."

Jason grabbed Harberts' beverage and took a pull.

"Hey!" Harberts protested.

Jason grinned. "I'm doing you a favor." He handed Harberts the Malibull. "You'll thank me at practice on Monday. Don't want a repeat of last week."

"Aaron, I've been looking for you." A tall girl in a shortie wet suit sauntered over to them. "You said you'd snorkel with me."

"I thought you meant the kind of snorkeling we did at Brad's party," Harberts joked.

The girl gave him a playful slap on the arm. "I'm Maggie, by the way," she told Jason as she twisted her long, golden-brown hair into a bun at the back of her head. "Since Aaron's too rude to introduce us."

Harberts rolled his eyes. "Maggie's on the girls' relay team. A medley swimmer like us," he said. He ran his hand down the form-fitting neoprene that fit Maggie like a snake's skin.

"I should have known you're a swimmer," Maggie said. Her hazel eyes meandered over Jason's body. "You've got the build for it. You want to be my snorkeling buddy if Aaron isn't—"

"Aaron is," Harberts interrupted. "And Jason has plans of his own."

Jason took the hint and wandered to the other side of the deck. This yacht left plenty of room for wandering. He spotted Luke Archer standing by himself, as usual, and staring into the foamy white wake. "Hey," Jason greeted him. "I didn't expect to see the mysterious school loner at a party. I don't think I've ever seen you away from our lunch table."

Luke's lips twisted into a wry smile. "Sometimes I like to do the lonely-in-a-crowd variation. Just to mix things up."

"First time I've seen you without a book in your hands, too," Jason commented, leaning on the rail next to him.

Luke pulled a novel out of his back pocket. Jason took that as another hint.

"All right, then. I'll let you get to it," he said, and headed down the stairs and into a lounge with a wide-screen TV and a killer sound system. Guster bongoed away out of multiple speakers, and he noticed Adam standing in the entrance to the hallway across the room, filming as always.

Jason finished off his vodka and tonic as he wove through the crowd and over to his friend. He followed the angle of Adam's camera and found himself look-ing into one of the cabins. More specifically, at the bed. Even more specifically, at Carrie Smith sprawled on top of some guy, on the bed. Her hands were wrapped in said guy's longish blond hair, and her mouth was suctioned onto his.

Uh-oh, Jason thought.

"This is not the movie you want to make," he told Adam, grabbing him by the back of the shirt and pulling him out of the hall. "What would Wes Anderson think? Or were there some pornos on his credit list that you forgot to tell me about?"

Adam lowered the camera. "Scott Challon. *Happy Gilmore* is probably his favorite movie, and she's in there. . . ." His voice trailed off and he just stood there, looking crushed.

Jason decided a change of subject—and locale—

was necessary. "I heard there's a hot tub on the fore-deck. Let's go check it out." He nudged Adam back into the lounge. "And by *it*, I mean the girls in it. Carrie's hot and film-literate, granted, but don't tell me she's the only one for you. There's no such thing," he said, immediately thinking of Sienna.

"Scott Challon," Adam said again, shaking his head as if he couldn't believe it.

Jason gently pulled the camera out of Adam's hand and stowed it behind a chair. He snagged a couple of drinks from a passing waiter in some faux naval uniform, handed one to Adam, and held his own up in a toast. "To moving on and meeting new girls," he said firmly. "Drink up."

Adam reluctantly clinked glasses with him, then drained his drink in one long swallow. "That's disgusting," he commented, wiping his mouth.

"I'll say," Jason agreed, finishing his own drink. "But hopefully effective. Let's go." He led the way back to the stairs.

Two girls were coming down as they started up. Two girls who looked very much like his sister and Kristy.

"Hi!" Danielle said brightly.

Jason groaned. He'd been hoping he was wrong about Dani's secret plans for the night. "I knew you were going to pull something like this," Jason said, and sighed. "How dumb are Mom and Dad not to guess where you are tonight?"

Dani's eyes sparkled. "What they don't know won't hurt them."

"They think she's sleeping over at my place," Kristy explained.

"*Shhh,*" Dani told Jason, putting a finger to her lips.

"You'd better watch yourself if you expect me to '*shhh,*'" Jason said, nodding toward the two drinks in her hands.

"Don't worry. The rum is for my new friend Caleb. Mine's just plain o.j." Dani crossed her heart, without sloshing either drink, as she and Kristy slipped past Jason and Adam.

Jason shook his head. "You know this Caleb?" he asked Adam, sliding into big brother mode.

"Senior. Basketball player. Hangs with Zach Lafrenière, when Zach deigns to attend school. Hasn't spent time with my father, the chief of police, if that's what you're asking," Adam replied with a grin.

"No record. I guess that's something," Jason said, and laughed. He stepped out onto the deck and followed the sounds of laughing and splashing to the hot tub.

He stopped in surprise when he reached it: a huge hot tub filled with people drinking, laughing, making out. Well, really only one couple was making out, but that was the only one that mattered. Brad Moreau was facing Jason. And he had in his arms a girl with long black hair and honey-tanned skin, kissing Brad like she was drowning and he was oxygen.

Jason's face flushed and his muscles tensed. He couldn't get in the tub. He couldn't sit two feet away from Brad and Sienna making out. He'd done his best to forget Sienna's kiss after he'd driven her home from the last party, and to remember that she and Brad were together. But that didn't mean he wanted a front-row seat for their groping.

Brad moved his lips from Sienna's mouth to her shoulder, turning her head a little in the bubbling water, and revealing not Sienna's face, but the face of Lauren Gissinger, a girl in Jason's physics class.

Not Sienna. Relief spun through Jason's body. It wasn't Sienna making out with Brad.

Then he realized exactly what he was seeing. *Not Sienna.* Jason's relief quickly turned to shock, then bewilderment. Brad was cheating on Sienna.

SEVEN

Jason's mind was a jumble of emotions. Confusion—Brad didn't seem like the kind of guy to cheat so openly. Anger—on Sienna's behalf. And frustration on his own—here he was trying so hard to keep away from Sienna because she was Brad's girlfriend, and Brad didn't even care enough to be faithful. What kind of an idiot cheated on a girl like Sienna?

Then Jason told himself that maybe Brad had had a bit too much to drink, and maybe, since he was supposed to be a friend, he should go and attempt to save Brad from himself—before Sienna happened upon the spectacle in the hot tub.

Reluctantly he strode over to the hot tub and tapped Brad on the shoulder. "Hey, Brad. Are you sure you know what you're doing, man? Sienna's definitely at this party somewhere," he warned.

Brad looked up, startled. "Er, yeah, it's okay. I know what I'm doing," he said in a slightly bemused kind of way.

Jason shrugged. "Well, it's your funeral," he said. He figured there wasn't anything more he could do.

Lauren stood up, droplets of water sliding down her body. "Maybe I should, um, go somewhere else," she offered. But she looked kind of spaced out, as if she wasn't really sure what was going on.

Brad gently pulled her down onto his lap. "You're fine, right where you are," he told her. His eyes met Jason's. "But *you* might want to go someplace else," he said pointedly.

Jason abruptly got up to go.

"And, hey—don't worry, dude!" Brad called after him. A grin broke across his face. "Sienna's just as bad. It's all cool." He twisted Lauren's long, dark hair around his hand and used it to pull her face closer to his. Then he turned away from Jason and kissed her.

"Let's go," Adam said as Jason came back to join him.

Jason nodded briefly, and they turned and walked away. "Bet you wish you'd had your camera on for that special moment," he muttered to Adam as they circled round to the aft deck.

"No. Not dramatic enough," Adam joked as they approached the bar. "Wait!" he exclaimed suddenly. "They've got better stuff downstairs. Let's go there instead!" He veered in front of Jason, but it was too late: Jason had already seen.

Sienna and Kyle, the diver from the swim team, were sitting on one of the leather couches near the bar, performing a little show of their own. And it was definitely Sienna, this time—Jason had a great view of her as she lifted her body to move onto Kyle's lap, pulling him closer. Jason couldn't look away as Kyle slid his hands down over her ass while she traced the shape of his top lip with her finger.

"Jason!" The sound of Adam's voice broke the spell. Jason blinked, then headed directly to the bar. The confusion and frustration he'd felt with Brad had turned to ice in his veins. He didn't know whether to be mad at himself for trying to defend Sienna, or mad at *her* for totally not deserving it.

"I think there's a poker game going on in the master stateroom. We should check it out," Adam said, talking at warp speed. "These rich boys need to be relieved of some cash." He mock winced. "Oops, sorry, I keep forgetting you're a rich boy too. You haven't acquired the vibe. You should work on that. You can start by observing the others of your kind during the game."

Jason could tell Adam was trying to distract him. He felt bad—after all, the girl Adam was crushing on had been all over some other guy too. And Jason wasn't even officially crushing on Sienna, so why was he taking it all so badly?

He took a shaky breath, trying to get a hold of his whirling thoughts. "You go. I'm going to be too busy getting seriously drunk."

Adam hesitated.

"It's okay. I'll catch up with you later," Jason told him.

Adam nodded and disappeared down the stairs. "Vodka and tonic," Jason told the bartender. With the amount of consumption he intended, he didn't think it would be smart to start mixing his drinks. He'd been such an ass. Brad was clearly right about Sienna. And why wouldn't he be right? He was her *boyfriend.* He should know her.

The bartender handed him the drink, and Jason drained it in one long swallow. "One more," he said.

The bartender raised an eyebrow, but didn't comment. He was probably well paid to keep quiet about what kids were drinking at parties like this. Jason took the second drink downstairs. He figured he might as well find out if the stuff was truly better down there.

But he didn't have the chance. Erin Henry met him at the bottom of the stairs. "New boy. You are going to dance with me," she said, sounding emphatic and slightly drunk. Those were the first words she'd ever said to him. Or wait, maybe she'd once asked to borrow a pen in history.

"Fine," he told her. He slapped his glass down—after sucking it dry—and let Erin take his hand and tug him over to the little dance floor.

Erin wrapped her arms around him, pushing her

body right up against his, but somehow Jason still couldn't keep his mind off Sienna.

"You like the party?" Erin murmured, smiling up at him.

"I guess," Jason replied. But it was a lie. For him, the magical atmosphere of the yacht had become toxic. What was the deal with Sienna and Brad? How could they both cheat on each other so casually?

"You're supposed to actually move your body when you dance," Erin teased.

Jason jumped, and realized he'd just been standing still, gazing off into space. "Sorry," he said quickly. "I didn't mean to space."

"A little tipsy, new boy?" Erin asked, her green eyes sparkling. She did a little shimmy down his body and back up again.

"A little," he agreed. *And what's wrong with that?* he asked himself. After all, it was a party, he didn't have to drive, he could just crash somewhere, and everybody else was drunk too. Why shouldn't he have fun? Sienna and Brad and their relationship was just none of his business.

The music changed to a slower song, and Erin twined her arms around his neck. Jason slid his hands down her back. The sheer summer dress she wore felt silky under his fingers. Feeling bold—and drunk—he moved on down to her butt and squeezed.

He almost expected her to slap him, but she didn't. Instead, she just lifted her eyebrows with a smile and grabbed his butt right back.

Jason was so surprised that he just laughed.

Erin laughed too, then moved in and began kissing his neck. Jason closed his eyes and enjoyed the sensation. Her lips against his skin sent little tingles up and down his spine. Now she was nibbling on his earlobe like it was chocolate. Did she have a thing for him? Maybe she had some wild crush on him like he had on Sienna. True, she hardly knew him. But then, Jason hardly knew Sienna either.

I'm not thinking about that right now, he told himself. He kissed Erin's eyelid, her nose, her cheek, until she gave up her lips, her tongue. He gave a half groan as her mouth moved off his mouth and down onto his throat, warm and wet. Jason felt his body go liquid. He couldn't tell where he stopped and Erin started. He felt he could stay in the moment forever and never want anything more.

The song changed again, got faster, but they didn't break apart. They swayed together, ignoring the new tempo for a minute or so. But then Erin's hips began to move faster, and she stepped away a little, her body going with the music. Soon she was dancing again, their entwined hands her only contact with Jason. He felt a little cold without her body pressed against him, but then the beat of the music seemed to seep into him and he found himself dancing. He barely even noticed when Erin let go of his hand. He closed his eyes and let his body move with the pulsing rhythm.

"I'm going to get another drink. You want?" Erin shouted over the loud music.

Jason opened his eyes and saw her already moving away. "No thanks," he called back.

She gave him a little wave and boogied off the dance floor. Jason wandered over to the sofa and dropped down onto it. His head was—ha!—it was swimming. He was a swimmer and his head was swimming, even though there wasn't any water! Or maybe there was some water in his head. Not too much, because water on the brain sounded like something bad. But you had to stay hydrated to keep your neuronians firing. Neuronians? Neu-somethings. Jason chuckled. Neuronians sounded like the name of some alien species on *Star Trek*. *Star Trek* was for nerds.

Jason closed his eyes and leaned his head back, thinking it over. Although *thinking* wasn't really the word for it. He felt more as if he were floating. The room spun around him, but pleasantly, like a carousel. The music seeped into his muscles and he felt himself relax.

Then the sofa cushions shifted under his body. He cracked open his eyelids and found Sienna sitting next to him. Beautiful Sienna. He smiled at her.

"Nice moves out there on the dance floor," she commented. She took a sip of her drink. "You ever considered working with a pole? You'd be a natural, and I hear the tips are good."

Jason took her drink and finished it, then grimaced. "What was that?"

"O.G.B., Original Gangsta Bull." She took her empty glass back. "Bull, gin, and o.j."

"I was drinking vodka," Jason complained.

"Sorry, I was actually planning on drinking *my* drink myself," Sienna teased, like nothing had changed, like she was still . . . Jason couldn't find the word.

The music changed again. Jason could feel it pulsing through him. He laughed.

"What?" Sienna asked.

"I just like this song. It feels good," he answered.

"Well, good," Sienna said. Her long hair swayed with the music. He wanted to touch it. He wanted to wrap his hands in it and let the silken strands slide through his fingers. "Want to dance?" he asked. "Experience my moves for yourself?"

Sienna smiled. "Tempting," she said. "But I should go see what Brad's up to."

"He's up to no good. Just like you," Jason told her, feeling insanely happy. "I saw you up there with Kyle. Dirty!"

"Dirty?" Sienna frowned. "I'm sorry. Have you ever even said hello to Erin before today?"

"No. But I don't have a boyfriend." *Wait.* Something was wrong with that sentence. *Oh.* He laughed again. "I mean *girlfriend.* You're the one with the boyfriend." He reached out and touched Sienna's face. "Did you want me to wait for you? I wanted it to be you, but I didn't know if you'd have time to get to everybody. Every body." Jason chuckled. He was so witty.

Sienna pushed him away and jumped to her feet. Her eyes were cold as she stared down at him. Ice cold. He hadn't known dark eyes could look so cold. Then she turned and stalked away from him.

The music slid out of Jason's body as he realized that he'd just kind of called Sienna a whore. Or, at least, a slut. He had to go after her. Try to explain. He shoved himself to his feet, but all the bones in his legs had gone . . . somewhere. He wobbled, then slid down onto the floor, missing the couch. He'd totally fallen on his ass!

Somebody nearby began laughing at him, and Jason laughed along. The soft vibrations from the yacht's motor tickled him, and the music slithered back into his boneless body. Jason couldn't remember ever feeling this way before—so . . . ecstatic!

The yacht was a fantasy world again, and this was the best party ever. Jason just kept laughing as the fantasy world spun around him.

EIGHT

"He lives!" Dani commented when Jason staggered into the living room the next afternoon. "You should be very happy that Mom and Dad went to go look at wallpaper all day."

"You lecturing me, miss . . . miss liar?" He sat down, grabbed the box of Cocoa Puffs off the coffee table, and shook some into his mouth. "These things are loud," he said as he chewed.

"Not so much if you use milk," Danielle said, taking a bite of cereal. She looked as spent as he felt. And, judging by the cereal on the table at three in the afternoon, she'd slept pretty late herself. "The spoon actually feels heavy," she complained.

"After last weekend, I thought you'd be smart enough to cut back on the drinks," Jason commented.

"All I had was o.j.—all night." Dani yawned. "Do you think somebody could have slipped me something?"

"Maybe a bartender. At *your* request," Jason suggested. "You didn't really go the whole night with no alcohol?"

"Yeah, I did," Dani countered. "And you should be

glad I did. Because it meant I was sober enough to drive you home!"

"You don't have a license," Jason reminded her.

Dani lifted her hands up and down like she was weighing something. "Sober and no license, or wasted with license? Hmm . . ."

She had a point. "Thanks. I guess," Jason managed. He ate another mouthful of Cocoa Puffs, then decided the *CRUNCH, CRUNCH* wasn't worth it. "Great party, huh?"

"The best. I'm wiped, but I felt really blissed out, even without the drinking," Dani answered, smiling happily.

"Me too. No wonder everyone wants to do the DeVere Heights parties."

"Who wants to look at the new hall wallpaper we picked out?" their mother called as she and their dad came into the house.

Jason and Dani both groaned.

"You go," Jason said. "You owe me for not ratting you out."

"Well, *you* owe *me* for the . . ." Dani made a steering motion. But she stood up. "Coming," she called.

Jason stretched out on the living room floor and stared up at the ceiling. The room made a slow rotation. The position felt familiar. An image of Sienna ripped through his mind. Sienna walking away from him. His stomach turned over, and a sick feeling flooded his body as another image exploded in his brain: Sienna looking at him coldly. Like she hated him.

Why? Jason couldn't remember. He ran his hands briskly through his hair, trying to think. The sensation brought up another memory: other hands in his hair—gentle fingers sliding though it—and a wet mouth on his throat. Erin. Dancing with Erin. Sliding his hands over her ass.

Jason sat up suddenly, hot bolts of pain stabbing into him. Shards of memory from the night before came flooding back. Kyle running his hands over Sienna's body. And Jason himself calling Sienna a whore! Did that really happen? He climbed slowly to his feet. He had to get some air. He had to figure out what he'd actually done—what he'd done to turn Sienna into an ice queen.

An hour and two bottles of Evian later, he was jogging along the top of the bluffs overlooking the ocean. He was so tired that each step felt like swimming through quicksand, but he didn't allow himself to stop. He needed to sweat out the alcohol. How much had he drunk last night? Too much, that's all he knew for sure.

His legs felt like they were made of rubber. Really

heavy rubber. But he pushed himself to go faster, to outrun the disturbing, insistent images of Sienna. And yet they kept pace with him. He saw her walking away with every step, saw her face with every breath. Miles and miles later, Jason allowed himself to slow down, to rest.

Jason climbed down a pathway from the bluff to the beach. He pulled off his sneakers and walked into the surf up to his calves, letting the cold water of the Pacific ease the strain on his muscles. Running usually invigorated him, but he still couldn't shake his exhaustion from the night before. Slowly, he walked toward home, ignoring the cries of the seagulls and the laughter of beachgoers drifting over the dunes. The sun hung low in the sky now, making his shadow stretch out a long way to his left.

As he neared the stretch of beach near Brad's house, Jason spotted the last thing he wanted to see: a group of people from school. More specifically, a group of girls from DeVere Heights, spread out on blankets and beach towels. He'd bet Sienna was one of them. And maybe Erin. Jason slowed down, squinting into the sun to get a better look at who was there. Did he want to see Sienna? Or Erin, for that matter? It would be awkward with either one of them.

He hesitated, wondering if he should climb back up the bluff so he wouldn't have to walk right by them.

But then it occurred to him that if he could see them, they could see him. And he didn't want them to see him scurry off like a puppy with his tail between his legs.

So Jason kept walking. His heart began to pound when he got close enough to actually pick Sienna out of the crowd. She and the others had begun packing up picnic stuff, a volleyball net, and some surfboards. They were clearly leaving. Maybe she'd just go. . . .

But, no, she came heading right toward him. Obviously the potential for awkwardness didn't bother her. Maybe she wanted to yell at him.

Jason sucked in a deep breath and walked over to meet her. "Hi," he said.

"Hi." Her voice was flat and emotionless, giving him nothing. Well, he deserved that.

He glanced at the boards. "I didn't know you surfed," he said.

"You don't really know that much about me at all," Sienna countered.

"True," Jason acknowledged. He wanted to reach out and touch her, just to break through the barrier he could feel between them. But he knew that would be a bad idea.

"Sienna, come on. We're heading up," Belle called.

"I'm going to walk home," Sienna shouted back. "Stow my stuff for me, okay?"

"No way, carry it yourself," Belle said, tossing her a towel with a grin. "Lazy girl!"

Sienna smiled back at her, but the smile never reached her eyes. She was not happy. Without a glance at Jason, Sienna started to walk away. Again.

"Can I walk with you?" Jason asked.

Sienna shrugged. "If you want," she replied.

The sun was sinking as they made their way across the velvety sand in silence. Jason suddenly realized they were only about a hundred feet from Sienna's house. He didn't have much time left. "Look, I'm sorry," he said softly.

"For what?"

"I said some horrible things last night," Jason answered. He couldn't remember exactly what he'd said, but he knew he'd hurt her.

"The word I'd use is '*dirty*,'" Sienna corrected. She stopped and turned to face him. "I'd call them *dirty* things."

I saw you up there with Kyle. Dirty! The words sliced into Jason's brain. Suddenly, he could hear himself saying them to Sienna. But the words brought back something else: the memory of Sienna and Kyle together on that couch, Kyle's hands sliding over her curves. Jealousy crashed over Jason, like one of those waves that knock you to the ocean floor.

"I shouldn't have said that," he told Sienna.

"But you meant it. You still feel that way. I can see it on your face," Sienna accused, her eyes darkening until they were almost black. "As if you weren't doing exactly the same thing with Erin."

"Yeah, okay. But I wasn't cheating on anyone," Jason said.

"Right," Sienna snapped back. "So when you saw me with Kyle, you were thinking about Brad? How I was treating Brad so badly?" she inquired, wrapping her arms around herself.

"No," Jason admitted with a sigh. "No, I wasn't thinking about Brad at all. And what I said . . . it was because . . ." But he couldn't continue. How could he tell her that he'd said what he had because the sight of another guy's hands on her had made him insane with jealousy? Jason knew that Sienna was right: He really didn't know her. Yeah, she was beautiful. But so was Belle. So was Erin. Malibu was filled with beautiful girls. What made Sienna so different? It was like she could reach into his chest and touch his heart. "I was an idiot," he said helplessly.

"Yeah, you were," Sienna agreed, but she smiled and took a step closer to Jason. "You wanted some time with me last night. You've got time now. Are you finished?"

She stood so close, he could smell that apple-ocean-vanilla scent of her. "No," he murmured. "No,

I'm not finished." He reached out, wanting to touch her face. But hesitated, his fingers inches away from her, close enough to feel the heat of her skin.

Sienna turned her head slightly, closing the distance between his hand and her cheek.

He was touching her. That was all the invitation Jason needed. He took her face in his hands and kissed her, tasting her, taking her in. Sienna's mouth responded to his, and she ran her hands up his chest to lace them around his neck.

And then . . . Jason forced himself to pull away. They stared at each other for a long moment before Sienna wordlessly turned toward her house on the cliff above them. Jason watched her climb the steep stairs cut into the bluff. Then he turned and raced down the beach, his body alive with heat and passion and hope.

He veered toward the water, picking up speed, needing it, needing the motion to channel all the emotion and energy those few minutes with Sienna had created. Fast, faster. His arms pumping, his heart pounding with the rhythm of his feet on the wet sand. Spray from the ocean hit his face as he ran along the shoreline. It cooled his skin, which still burned with the memory of Sienna's touch. Now he was sprinting, running flat out—so fast that he had no chance to stop when he saw it.

Jason's bare foot hit the chilly flesh and sent him sprawling onto the cold, wet sand. His mind spun, shock filling his body. What had he tripped over? It couldn't have been . . .

He scrambled up and turned around, praying he'd been wrong about what he'd seen. But the girl's body still lay there. Facedown. Her flesh cold and blue.

CPR, Jason thought frantically.

He dropped to his knees next to the girl and tried to roll her onto her back, but she felt heavy, waterlogged. A wave splashed onto the shore, its undertow pulling her out of his grasp. Jason felt the setting sun hot upon the back of his neck as he reached for her cold arm again.

He waited for the next wave and used the thrust of the water to help him roll her over. Carrie Smith's blank eyes stared up at him.

It was too late for Jason to help her. Too late for anyone.

She was dead.

NINE

Jason climbed out of the police car and headed up his driveway. His mom, his dad, and Dani were waiting for him on the front lawn. Mrs. Freeman wrapped him in a tight hug and didn't let go. He hugged her back, then pulled away, trying to muster up a reassuring smile for his mother. It didn't work—the concern remained in her eyes. He had the feeling she was imagining *him* lying there on the sand, with blue lips and fingernails. Cold. Dead.

"Mom, it's okay. I'm okay," Jason said. His mother slowly nodded, and his dad took over, giving Jason the father-patented rib-busting special.

"You're not going to have to hug me too, are you?" he asked Dani when his dad let go.

"No. Don't worry. I'll let you off," she teased, but her gray eyes were serious.

"When the police called . . ." Mrs. Freeman shook her head. "I knew we were right not to let Dani go to that party. I shouldn't have let you go either. Where were the parents? That's what I want to know. They just waved from the dock as a bunch of teenagers and enough alcohol to kill a—"

"Mom," Jason interrupted her, "not now."

"I can't even imagine how that poor girl's mother is feeling. Did either of you know her?" his mother asked.

"A little," Jason admitted.

"We talked about surfing once," Dani said. "She promised to show me the best boards." Jason suspected that that conversation had taken place at the party, hours before Carrie died. But he wasn't going to rat out his sister. "She was only a year older than me," Dani added, her voice choked with tears.

Now Dani got the parental hug treatment. "You see why we didn't want you at that party?" Mr. Freeman said.

"Yeah," Dani answered quietly. "You were right."

"Well, we were going to fire up the grill and have a barbecue," Mrs. Freeman announced, clapping her hands together. "We have those steaks."

Jason appreciated the change of subject, even though he doubted he could eat. His own emotions weighed pretty heavily right now: guilt over not telling his parents that Dani had been on the yacht, horror over the memory of Carrie's dead body, and just a basic queasiness over the realization that he'd been making out with Erin and obsessing about Sienna when Carrie had fallen overboard to her death. "Barbecue sounds good, Mom," he said.

"We'll do the corn, too," their mother said, "and a salad."

Dani and Jason stood in silence as their parents disappeared into the house. "Thanks for not telling," she said when they were out of sight.

"You think I want to kill our mother?" Jason asked. The joke landed with an almost audible thud. Right now it was way too easy to imagine any of the people he loved being snatched away from him. The world suddenly felt dangerous.

Dani just looked at him, her big gray eyes still serious.

Jason looped his arm over her shoulders. "Let's go inside."

"Was she . . . like, deteriorating?"

With the school day less than half over, this was the eleventh time someone had asked Jason about finding Carrie's body. The morbid curiosity disgusted Jason. He probably would have gotten twice as many questions, except that Zach Lafrenière had chosen today to reappear at school, and that was also a big topic of conversation. Almost as big as a classmate washing up dead onshore.

For the first time, DeVere High struck Jason as being a pretty twisted place. Somehow, with all of its sunshine and beauty, it had seemed above this type of sordid gossip. But it obviously wasn't.

Jason slammed his locker shut and turned around. A tall girl with long, golden brown hair stood there looking at him, biting at her lip, eager to hear the details of what he'd seen. It took a moment for him to realize that she was Harberts's friend, Maggie, from the girls' swim team. He'd met her at the party.

Do you want to hear about the crab that had eaten off part of Carrie's left little finger? he thought. He didn't say the words out loud. He was afraid Maggie might say yes. "I didn't really look that closely," he told her.

"You'd have to be completely out of it to fall off the yacht. I mean, the rails are *rails*," Maggie said. "How much do you think she'd had to drink?"

"No idea. Got to go," he replied, and pretty much racewalked away from her toward the cafeteria, even though the last thing he wanted to do was eat. His stomach had been doing a slow roll every time he'd looked at food since yesterday. He grabbed a smoothie from the juice bar, figuring he could deal with that without puking, and a peanut butter sandwich that he thought he'd be able to choke down before swim practice.

"Zach, here's somebody you should know. This year's new guy." Jason didn't have to look to know it was Sienna speaking. Her voice alone made his pulse quicken.

"That's me," Jason said as he turned around, cafeteria tray in hand. "Jason Freeman, new guy until the next one comes along."

"Jason's on the swim team with Brad," Sienna added. She stood next to a tall guy with short, kinda spiky black hair. Clearly the famous Zach Lafrenière.

Zach nodded. He didn't say anything. But he seemed to take in everything about Jason with one sweep of his dark brown eyes. His expression wasn't exactly unfriendly. It was more like . . . impenetrable. Jason stared back. He'd been hearing about Zach since day one at DeVere High; people talked about him constantly, and today, especially. Jason couldn't help feeling curious about him.

The most popular guy in school—here he was at last—possessed an almost tangible intensity. He seemed to radiate energy and life.

"Line. Not moving," Van Dyke called cheerfully from a couple of people down.

Jason nodded to Zach and Sienna, quickly paid for his food, and then headed to what had become his regular place. He was surprised to see Adam sitting there. He'd been MIA in history this morning, but he clearly hadn't used the free time to shower or comb his hair. His clothes looked slept in, while Adam himself looked as if he hadn't slept in days.

Adam stood up before Jason could grab a seat. "Take a walk with me."

"Okay," Jason said. They didn't walk far, just over to the edge of the cafeteria terrace.

"You doing all right?" Jason asked as they stared out at the surfers dotting the ocean.

"She's never going to be out there again," Adam said grimly, and his words hit Jason like a punch to the gut. He'd been thinking about Carrie's body pretty much constantly, unable to force the vision of her dead eyes out of his head. But he hadn't gotten as far as thinking about *her*, and the things she'd never do: surf, graduate from high school, turn twenty-one, have any kind of life.

"Did you see anyone doing drugs at the party?" Adam asked.

"What?" Jason tripped over the sudden change of subject. "No. I wasn't really looking or anything, but no."

"Me neither. But that's what the police are thinking. I heard my dad talking about it on the phone with one of the deputies. They don't think she got drunk and took an unplanned dive. They think that she shot up and—" Adam pressed his palms together and made a diving motion.

"Shot up? Why shot up?" Jason asked.

"Needle marks on her arm," Adam replied. He glanced over his shoulder, then pulled a photo out of the front pocket of his backpack. "I snagged this from my dad. There were a bunch in the file he brought home. He probably won't miss it."

Jason lifted an eyebrow.

"What?" Adam asked defensively. "Don't worry—I'll put it back tonight. I just wanted to show it to you." He handed the photo to Jason. It showed a close-up of a girl's arm—Carrie's—with two small red marks, not much bigger than pinpricks, on the smooth, pale skin inside her elbow. A little bruising surrounded the punctures.

"Needle marks. Hardcore," Jason commented, running his finger lightly across the picture of the wounds as if that would tell him something.

"I didn't see anything like this on Carrie when I was with her last week. She didn't seem like she was on anything the night of Belle's party, either, even though it *was* a party." Adam shook his head. "But what the hell do I know? It's not like we were even friends."

Not true, Jason thought. Maybe Adam and Carrie hadn't been exactly exclusive. But they had definitely been friends.

"I keep thinking it could be something else," Adam continued. "I keep thinking . . . I could be crazy here, but I've seen some things. If I'd put it all together faster. If I'd had the balls to actually accept the truth, maybe I could have saved her."

Jason didn't know what Adam was talking about. But he knew one thing. "This isn't your fault," he told his friend, gently but firmly.

Adam turned away from the water and faced Jason. "I want you to look at something with me."

"Sure. Now?" Jason asked.

"No. The video editing suite is full of Tarantino wannabes during lunch. But meet me there after school. Oh, but I guess you have practice?"

"I can get out of it if this is important," Jason told him.

"It is," Adam said. His eyes glittered and his cheeks were flushed, almost like he had a fever. He turned his face away for a moment, and Jason saw his jaw clench. When he looked back, his expression was grim—and filled with pain. "That footage I shot at the party?" Adam muttered. "I think it might prove what really happened to Carrie."

Jason stepped into the dim video editing suite after his last class of the day. He spotted Adam at the station in the back corner, hunched close to a monitor. Had Adam really caught something revealing on film? he wondered. Or was this just a reaction to Carrie's death?

"Hey," he said as he pulled up a chair next to his friend.

Adam's body jerked in surprise. "Didn't hear you come in," he muttered.

"Got here as fast as I could," Jason replied. "What you got for me?"

"It could be dangerous for you to see," Adam said, his voice so low, Jason almost couldn't make out the words.

"I don't give a crap. Show me," Jason told him. He was a lot more worried about Adam than about anything he might see on the film. His friend was acting pretty crazy.

Adam brought his hands to the keyboard, then hesitated. "You know how I've been making this movie. . . ."

"Yeah?"

"Well, for a while—since before you got here—it mostly hasn't been a movie. It's been . . . well, research, I guess you'd call it," Adam went on. "Because while making the movie, I started noticing things. . . ." He stared at the monitor. An image of Carrie and Scott Challon was frozen on the screen, Carrie and Scott on the bed in one of the *Moulin Rouge*'s cabins. "Things somebody like me shouldn't see," Adam finally added.

"What's that supposed to mean? Somebody like you?" Jason asked. He wanted to cover the image of Carrie and Scott with his hands. Adam was in even worse shape than Jason had thought. He didn't need to be looking at that right now.

"There are two groups at DeVere. Everyone knows it," Adam said. "I don't know why it took me so long to see exactly what they were . . . I suspected, made lists, took notes, and kept filming. But I didn't say anything. I should have told Carrie, warned her."

"Look, maybe it would be better if you just showed me what you want to show me," Jason suggested gently. Once he had facts, maybe he could figure out how to help Adam. Right now, he had no idea what was going on in his friend's head.

"Okay." Adam's fingers flew over the keyboard, and a new image appeared on the screen: Brad and Lauren stretched out on one of the lounge chairs on the foredeck of the yacht. Both dripping with water, clearly just out of the hot tub.

"I saw the coming attractions for this. Didn't make me want to see the movie," Jason said uneasily. The joke was limp, and he knew it, but he had to say something to hide the wave of humiliation that crashed over him as he remembered what a fool he'd been scolding Brad like some wrinkled-up prude while Sienna was—

Focus! Jason ordered himself. *This isn't about you.* "What am I supposed to be seeing?" he asked Adam. Because it couldn't be Brad hovering over the base of Lauren's throat, which is all Jason saw on the monitor. The action crept forward, frame by frame, on super slo-mo.

"Wait," Adam said. "It's coming up. Right . . . here." On the screen, Brad raised his head. "Look at his mouth and her neck," Adam instructed, hitting a button on the keyboard to freeze the scene.

Jason leaned closer to the monitor. Something dripped from Brad's mouth—something red—and Lauren's throat was smeared with crimson. "Is that blood?" he asked.

"You see a ketchup bottle anywhere?" Adam replied. He grabbed the police photo of Carrie's arm from a folder on the table and shoved it into Jason's hand. "You tell me. Don't you think those marks could have been made by teeth instead of a needle?"

Jason suddenly wished he hadn't had that smoothie at lunch. It was trying to come back up. He swallowed hard. "You . . . you think Brad *bit*—"

Adam didn't let him finish. "There was blood on his mouth and on Lauren's neck. You saw it."

"Yeah, but . . ." Jason found all this a bit too bizarre. "Why would Brad want to bite someone? That's crazy."

Adam hit a few keys, and the scene replayed itself: Brad at Lauren's throat; Brad glancing up with blood on his lips. "Look at it," Adam insisted. "Just *look*." He replayed the scene again.

Jason stared at the monitor, leaning in close to make sure he was getting a good look at Brad and

Lauren. There was definitely blood—on *her* neck and *his* mouth. "One more time," Jason muttered.

Adam replayed it, pausing the image when Brad faced the camera, Lauren's blood on his mouth. Jason's stomach clenched. Adam was right: Brad had definitely bitten her.

Jason pushed his chair back, wanting some distance between himself and the image on screen. He felt a wave of revulsion toward Brad. "You've got to show this to your dad," he said quickly. "Brad's some kind of twisted freak. You think he killed Carrie after he bit her? Maybe she freaked and he knocked her out and—"

"No. You're not getting it," Adam interrupted. He ran his hands through his already messy hair, leaving it standing straight up. "I didn't get it, either, at first. It's too weird. It's hard to take in."

"Just tell me," Jason demanded impatiently. He was getting freaked out. He could tell something messed up was going on here, but he couldn't find the connection Adam wanted him to make. "What's the deal?"

Adam took a deep breath, his eyes fixed on the picture of Carrie. "That other group at school I was talking about—the rock stars of DeVere Heights? Brad is one of them. And so is whoever—whatever—killed Carrie." He shifted his gaze to look Jason straight in the eye. "They're vampires."

TEN

Jason laughed. He didn't mean to, but he couldn't stop himself. The horror of finding Carrie's body, the anger of having to describe it over and over to morbidly curious people all day, and now Adam going totally off the deep end. It was all too much. He felt a little hysterical.

"Vampires?" He couldn't even say the word without laughing harder.

"Go ahead. Get it out of your system," Adam muttered.

"Sorry, sorry, sorry." Jason managed to get himself under control. "I agree that Brad is . . . There's something wrong with the guy, definitely. And maybe he did even have something to do with Carrie's death. But he can't be a . . . vampire. I mean, come on. You've seen too many movies, man. There are no vampires in real life."

"I spent months telling myself the same thing," Adam answered. "If I'd just accepted the truth a little earlier, Carrie might still be alive." He shut off the monitor. "So what's it going to take to open your mind?" He stabbed his finger at the police photo of Carrie's arm. "How about two little puncture marks like these, on Lauren's neck? Because she has them. I guarantee it."

"I admit that would be pretty damning evidence," Jason agreed slowly, mostly to humor his friend, who was clearly losing it. "Um, in fact, we should confirm it. If Lauren does have the marks, that will show a connection between Brad and Carrie. Essential info. Not about vampires, but still essential. Any thoughts on where to find Lauren?"

"Yeah. She has—and this isn't all that uncommon among DeVere High students who live *outside* the gates—a job," Adam answered. "I'll show you the way. You can follow me."

"If I can keep up with your superfly Vespa," Jason said, glad to hear Adam sounding more Adam-like. It was the first time all day that he'd made a rich kid–poor kid joke.

Less than ten minutes later, Jason found himself in front of Under G's, a lingerie store.

"We're going in there?" he asked.

"Just remember they only carry European labels," Adam advised.

"I don't really need a new bra anyway," Jason said as he opened the door and stepped inside, to be greeted with an astounding array of bras and panties and other items he didn't want.

"Can I help you?" asked a frighteningly thin

woman with slicked-back hair. She looked the boys up and down and wrinkled her tiny nose as if she smelled something bad.

"Is Lauren around?" Jason asked.

The woman frowned. "She's not allowed visitors at work."

Adam slapped Jason on the shoulder. "This is her cousin from Michigan," he said firmly. The thin woman looked dubious, but before she could say anything, Lauren bustled over.

"Cousin Jason," she said, putting on a big fake smile for her boss. "I thought we were going to meet up after I got off work."

"Change of plan," Jason said. His eyes immediately went to Lauren's throat, but a necklace with large painted beads blocked his view.

The boss woman gave the three of them a warning look and moved away.

"You guys are going to get me in trouble," Lauren whispered. "What are you even doing here?"

Jason said the first thing that sprang into his mind. "I just wanted to apologize for being such a idiot at Belle's party this weekend."

"Oh, okay." Lauren frowned. "Honestly, I don't even remember talking to you that night."

"You didn't. I meant that scene while you were in the hot tub with Brad," Jason explained.

Lauren smiled. "That explains it. You don't really expect me to remember anything that happened while I was in the hot tub with him, do you?"

"You don't remember when Jason—," Adam began.

"She said she doesn't remember," Jason interrupted. He really didn't want to hear a replay of his bad behavior, especially since Lauren didn't even recall it. Maybe she'd had too much to drink. Jason knew *he* had. He'd had to practically squeeze his memories of the party out of his brain. Even Dani had been fuzzy, and she was still sticking to the not-drinking story.

"So I accept your apology. And don't do it again, whatever it was. Now please get out of here," Lauren said in a rush.

Jason shot a look at Adam. How were they going to—

Adam took action before Jason could finish the thought. "We're gone. But you gotta tell me where you got that necklace. My mom's birthday is coming up, and she loves stuff with beads."

Lauren didn't have a chance to answer. Adam slid one finger under the necklace and, a half a second later, beads were bouncing all over the floor. Lauren dropped to the ground and frantically began trying to gather them up. Jason knelt down next to her as if to help, but he ignored the beads. His attention was firmly focused on Lauren's neck. . . .

And there, without a doubt, were two tiny red marks. Marks identical to the ones on Carrie Smith's arm.

Jason scrambled backward and felt something crack under his foot: a bead. "Sor—"

"I don't need any more help. Or apologies. Just leave," Lauren hissed. Jason and Adam bolted out of the door and practically ran over to their vehicles.

"See. You saw them, right? The same marks. The bite," Adam said.

"I saw the marks," Jason confirmed. "I'm not sure what made them. But I saw them." And he knew that meant that there was a connection between Brad and Carrie.

Jason felt like his head might explode. Brad had always seemed like such a decent guy. But it seemed he was sick enough to want to get girls drunk and then bite them—maybe *kill* them! Jason couldn't believe he'd been trying to stay away from Sienna out of loyalty to Brad. Hell, he should be warning her. . . .

I have to warn her! Jason thought with a jolt. If Brad was dangerous, then Sienna was probably in danger. And, for all he knew, Sienna was with Brad right this very second. He had to get to her.

"Adam, I think you should take this to your dad," Jason said urgently.

"I can't even get *you* to believe me," Adam burst out

in frustration. "And my dad's a lot less open-minded than you are. If I say the word 'vampire,' he's going to have me climbing a mountain at one of those camps for troubled boys!"

"So don't use the V word," Jason said, pulling his car keys out of his pocket. "Just show him the tape. And tell him what we saw on Lauren. Show him the link between her and Carrie and Brad."

"No way. The second there's even a hint of legal trouble involving anyone from DeVere Heights, the celebrity lawyers come out, it gets hushed up, and it goes away," Adam protested. "I need time to get proof that no one can laugh at."

"Okay. Fair enough. You know this place a lot better than I do," Jason said. "But, look, I've got something I have to do right now. We'll talk about this some more another time, right?"

"Fine," Adam said. "Where are you going?"

But Jason didn't answer. He didn't have time. He dashed over to the VW and jumped in. The tires squealed as he pulled out of the parking lot. Sienna didn't live far away—nothing was far away in Malibu—but it felt as if it took hours to get up the hill, through the gates, and round to her house. He drove all the way up the driveway, getting as close to the door as he could.

A woman who was clearly Sienna's mom—same

dark hair and eyes—opened the front door before he could knock.

"Is Sienna here?" Jason demanded.

Mrs. Devereux didn't answer. She just looked Jason up and down as if deciding whether or not to call security.

Jason did a fast backpedal. "I'm Jason Freeman. My family and I just moved into the Heights. I'm in a couple of classes with Sienna. Is she here, please?"

"Sienna didn't tell me she was expecting anyone," Mrs. Devereux said slowly.

Jason forced himself to smile. To try to look a little less like a lunatic. "She isn't. I just thought I'd stop by. In Michigan, that was okay. I'm still trying to figure out the rules for California."

Mrs. Devereux finally cracked a smile and stepped back, allowing Jason into the house. "Sienna's out by the pool. Straight through the house and out the glass doors," she instructed.

"Thanks." Jason kept himself to a walk as he made his way through the house and out of the French doors. The day was hot, and there was no breeze to cool things down. The water in the pool stood perfectly still, reflecting the cloudless sky and the unforgiving sun. Sienna lay on a wooden lounge chair with a plush pillow. Just the sight of her made Jason's heart leap.

Sienna looked surprised to see him. She pushed herself up onto her elbows. "Jason!"

"Is Brad here?" he asked. The last thing he wanted was for Brad to come walking in on them.

"You came to *my* house to see Brad?" Sienna pulled off her sunglasses and put them on the marble table in front of her. A pitcher of water and a glass sat on the table, bleeding condensation onto the marble.

"No. I came to see you," Jason said in a rush. "Is he here?"

Sienna shook her head. "What's going on? You're hyperventilating. What's the matter?" she asked, her voice warming up with concern. She pointed to the chair next to hers. "Sit." Jason sat. "Okay. Now talk."

"I think Brad killed Carrie Smith. Or that he has something to do with her death, anyway." The words tumbled out of Jason's mouth so fast that he wasn't even sure what he was saying.

"Whoa!" Sienna held up a hand. "You've got to slow down. Say that again."

"Sorry." He took a deep breath and forced himself to speak more slowly. "I think Brad may have done something to Carrie. I think he may have killed her."

Sienna's mouth fell open. "I have known Brad Moreau my whole life," she said. "You're crazy. What would make you say something like that?"

Jason hesitated, trying to figure out how he could

make Sienna listen to him. "Look, I know after, uh, what happened on the beach, this could seem like some pathetic attempt to—"

"To get me away from my boyfriend so you can have a shot?" Sienna offered.

"Yeah," Jason said. "I mean, no. That's what it could seem like. Not what I'm doing. I'm here because I'm worried about you. Carrie had these marks on her arm. Lauren Gissinger has them too—on her throat. And I think I saw Brad put them there. I mean, I know I did. At Belle's party. I saw Brad with blood on his mouth right after he'd been kissing Lauren's neck."

Jason knew he was talking too much, saying too much at once, but he couldn't stop. "Well, obviously not kissing, because that wouldn't have made Lauren bleed," he rattled on. "Adam thinks Brad bit her, but ... I don't know. I don't know what's going on. But I think Brad may be dangerous. You've got to stay away from him."

Sienna stared at Jason as if he'd been speaking in a language she'd never heard before. "You *saw* this? You just stood there and—"

"No," Jason interrupted. "I wasn't there. Not right when the biting happened, anyway. I saw it on tape. Adam's been shooting all this footage. He's convinced that Malibu is being taken over by vampires."

"Vampires?" Sienna repeated. She stood up.

"Yeah. Insanity, I know," Jason said. "But something is going on. And you have to promise me you'll stay away from Brad until—"

"Stop," Sienna ordered. "Just . . . stop." Slowly she sank back down onto her lounge chair. Her dark eyes betrayed concern.

"I know you love Brad, but—"

"Seriously, Jason. Stop talking," Sienna ordered. She took a shaky breath. "Okay. Okay." Jason thought it sounded more as if she was talking to herself than to him. But then she lifted her eyes to his and stared at him for a moment. "There's something I have to tell you," she whispered. "I'm trusting you here, all right?"

"Of course," Jason assured her. "I'd never . . ." The words died in his throat as he noticed Sienna.

She'd been sitting there the whole time, of course, but suddenly he really *saw* her, and his breath caught in his chest.

Sienna's dark hair was glossier than he'd ever seen it; her skin clear and creamy, almost luminous; and her lips glowed a deep rose red. She was stunning, spectacular—*impossibly* beautiful.

Jason realized he was staring. "What is it?" he asked. "Sienna, you can tell me anything."

And then Sienna smiled, slowly revealing a pair of very white, very sharp, and very real fangs.

ELEVEN

"Adam is right: Brad is a vampire," Sienna told Jason quietly, her voice shaking a little.

Jason couldn't respond. He felt like he was caught in a particularly weird and vivid dream.

"And so am I," Sienna continued.

Jason's brain finally managed to get a message to his body, and he stood up so fast, he knocked his chair over. He couldn't take his eyes off Sienna's fangs. They were perfectly shaped to make the marks on Carrie and Lauren. He took a step away from her as his mind reeled in shock.

"Jason." Sienna reached for him, but he whipped his arm away from her. And suddenly the confusion in his mind vanished to be replaced by fear. Total, overwhelming fear. Sienna was a vampire. A monster. A killer.

And so was Brad.

"Which one of you killed her? Which one of you killed Carrie Smith?" Jason managed to ask, clamping down on the fear that engulfed his entire body.

"Neither. We didn't. It's not *like* that!" Sienna replied desperately, moving toward him. Jason's muscles tensed. But all she did was set his chair back on its feet. "It's not like that, Jason. My whole life—the whole time my parents have lived in Malibu—there's never been a death. Not from a vampire."

"So you're saying you've never bitten anyone?" Jason asked doubtfully.

"No. I have. We all have. We have to feed to stay alive," Sienna told him.

"You *all* have?" Jason cried. "You mean there's more than just you and Brad?"

Sienna dropped her head into her hands. "Oh, God," she said. "Yes. It's . . . it's hereditary. There are several of us. But we don't kill people. We only feed because we have no choice."

"And that's supposed to make me feel better? You haven't actually *killed* anyone, but you drink human blood?" Jason exclaimed.

"Do you think I should allow myself to die instead?" Sienna asked, her eyes bright with emotion. "It's not like you're thinking, Jason. It's . . . it's pleasurable. It's good for both of us, both sides. It's not even that I haven't *killed* someone to survive—I've never even *hurt* anyone."

Jason sat down. Mainly because he wasn't sure his legs were going to be able to keep him upright. Sienna returned to her seat next to him. "How can you say you haven't hurt anyone?" he finally asked. "Do you get permission? Do the people you . . . you *drink* from, say, 'Sure, go ahead, I've got more blood than I need'?"

Sienna swallowed hard. Jason could see the muscles in her throat working. "You're talking to me like I'm a monster. Like I'm a stranger. Like we've never kissed." She met his gaze steadily. "Like you don't know me at all."

"I don't," he snapped. "You told me that yourself, remember? And you were right! I obviously don't know anything about you, because you've been hiding the truth."

"Well, I'm telling you everything now. I'm trusting you. Not just with *my* secrets, but with the lives of every single person that I care about. And we're not monsters." She leaned closer to Jason, and strangely, she was so beautiful that even knowing what he did, Jason didn't want to draw away.

"Think about it. Think about that film of Adam's that you watched," Sienna urged. "Did Lauren look like she was in pain? Did Brad have her overpowered? Did she look like she wanted to get away from him?"

Jason pictured Lauren and Brad on the monitor. The truth was that Lauren had looked like she was having the best damn time of her life. But he wasn't ready to hear more rationalizations. "Has it happened to me?" he interrupted. "Has anyone . . . drunk from me?"

She just stared at him, her eyes big and worried.

"I deserve to know," he told her.

"Yes," she said softly. "But it wasn't me."

He felt a single second of confusion, and then he knew exactly who she was talking about: Erin. Jason remembered the ecstasy he'd felt while dancing with her. He hadn't even known her, but he'd been beyond happy during their make-out session.

"Erin," Sienna agreed.

"And that's why I couldn't remember much the day after the party!" Jason guessed. "Because somebody drank from me. Is that part of the whole experience—the victim doesn't remember it?"

"You remembered having a good time," Sienna pointed out.

A new thought slammed into Jason, making him feel sick. "So that means my sister, too?" He remembered Dani telling him that she'd had the best time in her young life after Brad's beach party.

Sienna nodded. "But she's fine. You know that. You can see it."

The idea of a vampire gorging itself on his little sister's blood nauseated Jason. It couldn't be true. None of this could be true—it was beyond ridiculous. Maybe he'd been out in the sun too long. And that made him think of something else. . . .

"You're out in the sun!" he cried, glancing up at the

perfect yellow ball in the cloudless blue sky. "You can't be a vampire. The sun kills vampires."

"Watching *Buffy the Vampire Slayer* doesn't mean you know anything about what we are," Sienna replied. "The sun doesn't bother us, not anymore. We've adapted."

"Fine," Jason said grimly. "Then what does bother you? What kills you?"

Sienna bit her lip. "You want to kill me?"

"No." Jason forced himself to dial it back. He was feeling a little crazy. This whole conversation was too surreal. "No. Of course not. I just meant . . . what else is true about vampires? What's true and what's just made up in the movies?"

"Well, we can change our appearance somewhat," Sienna said, and gestured to her supernaturally beautiful face. "This is what I look like naturally. I usually tone it down a little bit on purpose. We all do. We want to blend in with regular people."

"So you can actually alter your appearance?" Jason asked. "You can shapeshift?"

"No," Sienna said quickly. "Nothing so extreme. We can just . . . modify ourselves to a degree."

"Modify." Jason jumped on the small fact, wanting to understand. "So no morphing into bats or wolves or fog, then?"

"No. And no sleeping in coffins. I'm sure that was

going to be your next question." She actually sounded a little hurt. Absurd.

"And crosses, stakes through the heart, garlic?" Jason asked.

Sienna raised one eyebrow. "I thought you *didn't* want to kill me."

He didn't. He absolutely did not want to kill Sienna. But he did want to know how to protect himself from the ones who clearly could kill him. "Do any of those things work?" he demanded.

"Well, I think a stake through the heart kills pretty much everyone," Sienna said. "But, crosses? No. And the only thing garlic does is ruin your social life." She smiled, and Jason almost smiled back. But he wasn't ready to let the subject drop.

"How old are you? Will you live forever? How long have you been in high school?" he asked, the questions tumbling out more quickly than he'd intended.

"I'm the same age as you," Sienna replied, amused. "And I won't live forever, but most . . . of us . . . do live longer than humans. We age the same way you do, until we're adult. After that, we age much more slowly."

"So, how many of you are there? Brad, you, Erin . . . Zach?" he added, suddenly picturing Zach's cold once-over at school the other day. He was clearly the leader of Sienna's group of friends. Chances were good that he'd be a vampire too.

"Jason, I can't . . . ," Sienna began.

"What about Van Dyke?" he rushed on, suddenly remembering Van Dyke's miraculous recovery at the first swim practice. He'd gone into the locker room— with Simkins, the assistant coach—and his body had been weak and pale. He'd emerged just a few minutes later, full of energy and raring to go, while Simkins had come out pale, but looking completely blissed out. Jason suddenly understood how Van Dyke had recovered so quickly: He had fed on Assistant Coach Simkins.

"There are several of us," Sienna said. "Several families in Malibu. But no one will ever hurt you. I promise."

"Oh, yeah? What about Carrie?" Jason shot back. "Someone sure hurt her." He felt anger rising in him again. Carrie was the whole reason he'd come here, and he'd almost forgotten in the midst of this shock. "I found her body. That girl did not enjoy herself with someone from one of these families and go home happy."

Sienna wrapped her arms around herself, as if she'd suddenly gotten chilled. "No. She didn't. Poor Carrie."

"'Poor Carrie?'" he repeated. "That's it? She gets murdered by a vampire and that's all you've got to say?"

She grimaced, and he was relieved to see that her

teeth had gone back to normal. No fangs. "There's something called 'bloodlust,'" Sienna said quietly, seriously. "It's kind of an addiction—to blood. If a vampire's in the grip of bloodlust, he doesn't stop drinking. He can't."

"So the human dies," Jason concluded. "The vampire keeps drinking until the human has lost too much blood to survive."

"It hasn't happened here in decades," Sienna said. "It's forbidden by our families. It's against everything we believe in. You have to trust me on this, Jason. We all have tight control over our urges."

He gave a short, humorless laugh. "Obviously not all of you."

Worry filled Sienna's face. "Zach is furious about what happened to Carrie," she said. "He's going to take care of it. Don't worry. He'll bring down whoever killed her."

"Zach. Zach will take care of it," Jason repeated. He pictured the dark-eyed guy he'd met at school. He hadn't looked as if he cared much about anyone on the face of the earth except himself. But Jason had to admit that he *had* looked capable—more than capable—of taking care of things. Zach gave the impression that he was in charge of just about everything that crossed his path. But he was still a vampire. And Jason saw no reason to trust a vampire—especially one he barely even knew. "And Zach cares why?" he asked.

"We *all* care," Sienna snapped. "Because Carrie didn't deserve to die. The same way you would care if some human had murdered her. We care even more *because* it's one of us and that's unacceptable. That makes it our responsibility, and that's why it *will* be taken care of—by us, by Zach. Because he's the strongest. Believe me, Jason. Whoever killed Carrie won't go unpunished."

"Sienna, dinner!" Mrs. Devereux called, stepping out into the backyard. She glanced at Jason and smiled graciously. "Would you like to join us, Jason?" she asked.

"No. Thank you." Jason stood up and tried to smile. But the idea of eating with a family who liked to feed on humans turned his stomach.

"Are you sure? We're having the most delicious risotto," Mrs. Devereux said. "Our cook is world-class."

"No," Jason said abruptly. Usually he was good with parents. But usually those parents weren't also vampires. He couldn't help wondering how Mrs. Devereux felt about him. Would she want him hanging around Sienna?

"I, uh, my parents will be looking for me," he added. He tried to force a smile, but his upper lips stuck to his dry gums, and he was afraid it had come out looking more like a sneer.

Sienna walked him to the front door. She touched his arm lightly. "Hey," she said quietly. "You okay with all this?"

He stared into her gorgeous eyes and felt his heart beat faster, the way it always did in her presence. *She's not human,* he told himself. How could he be having these feelings for a vampire? It was so wrong. He tried to rein in his body, to stop the automatic attraction he felt for her. But he couldn't. His body didn't care what his brain thought. His body wanted Sienna whether she was a vampire or not. "No. I'm not okay," he admitted.

Sienna looked upset, and Jason realized he'd hurt her again. Maybe even more than he had that night on the boat. But she'd asked, and the truth had come out.

"I just need to think about all this," he said gently. That got a tiny smile, but Jason wondered if he was lying. His body seemed to have made a judgment about Sienna. But his brain still wasn't sure that he could trust her.

It was too much. He had to get out.

He hurried to his car and peeled out without a backward glance. The sun beat down, bathing the whole of Malibu in a cosmic spotlight. Maybe it was all a dream. Yeah, that made sense. More sense than anything else. A place like DeVere Heights couldn't really exist, Jason thought. It was too extreme. Too dazzling. Too weird. It couldn't be real. Any minute now, he would wake up in Michigan, where everything was normal. Where the weather wasn't always sunny. Where the girls were a little less magnificent but a lot more human.

Where your friends didn't turn out to be vampires.

TWELVE

"I'm sorry, is that a *vegetable* sandwich?" Adam asked at lunch the next day. "Have you gone so native that you're a vegetarian now?"

Jason peered at the grilled mush in his pita. "I'm not in the mood to eat anything that bleeds," he muttered. He forced himself to meet Adam's gaze. "I talked to Sienna yesterday."

Adam swallowed hard. "And?"

Jason glanced around. He'd purposely led Adam over to a deserted table inside the cafeteria, rather than going out to their usual spot. He couldn't chance their constant tablemate, Luke Archer, overhearing this conversation. Luckily, almost nobody ever ate inside. They had the place to themselves.

"And . . . you're right. She says there are vampires in the Heights. She's one of them. And Brad, like you thought." Jason said.

"I'm sorry, but . . . *what*?" Adam cried. "Are you telling me that you just went up to Sienna and asked her if she was a vampire?"

"Uh, no. I told her that you thought Brad was a vampire," Jason said.

"What?" Adam practically shrieked. His skin turned even paler than usual.

"Well, maybe I didn't say that exactly," Jason replied quickly. "I just said that you thought . . . that you thought there might be vampires. In DeVere Heights."

"Oh, my God," Adam said, looking shell-shocked. "They're going to kick my ass all the way to the loony bin!"

"No, they're not," Jason assured him. "I mean, Sienna didn't even seem surprised. She just showed me her fangs and basically said you were right."

"Oh." Adam thought about that for a moment. "*Oh*. So I'm right. I'm not crazy. There are vampires."

"Yes," Jason confirmed.

"Good. Cool. I mean, not good. But, you know, good." Adam took a deep breath and seemed to calm down a little. "Sienna and Brad. How many others?"

"A lot of them. For all I know, everyone in DeVere Heights is a monster," Jason spat.

"No way." Adam shook his head. "I've known Sienna since first grade. Brad, too. They're not monsters."

"She *told* me she's a vampire," Jason said. "She had fangs, for God's sake. Fangs in a human head—that equals monster, right?"

"I've been thinking about that a lot," Adam answered. "When I started to piece things together, I kept getting back to a basic truth: Malibu is a spectacular place to live. If vampires were monsters, then it wouldn't be. People would be turning up dead every night, no one would go out after dark, and the real estate prices would be much, much lower."

"I can't believe I'm hearing this." Jason dropped his sandwich back onto his tray. "You're the one who told me that a vampire *killed* Carrie. If that's not the behavior of a monster, I don't know what is!"

"It is," Adam agreed. "So *one* vampire is a monster—not the whole lot."

"So it'll be like *The Wizard of Oz*? We'll all go around asking, 'Are you a good vampire or a bad vampire?'?"

Adam shrugged. "You have to understand, man. Everyone who made my list of . . . of vampire suspects, I guess you'd call it, came from a family that is important to this town. Every single charity in Malibu has a Devereux or a Moreau or a Lafrenière on the board," Adam explained. "And the DeVere Center—that big brick building up on Cliffside Court? They're doing research into blood replacements, real cutting-edge stuff. Obviously they're trying to find a way to free themselves from having to drink human blood."

"You're telling me these vampires are out in the open, researching blood, and nobody cares?" Jason had a hard time believing that.

"Nah. They usually do things anonymously," Adam said. "But when I started to suspect that they were . . . well, *unusual* . . . I checked into their company holdings and their bank records. My old man would be proud to know I inherited his research skills. I found all kinds of links between the DeVere Heights families and charities, museums, hospitals. Basically— everything good in Malibu? Funded by vampires!"

Jason just stared at him.

"I know what you're thinking. Adam Turnball, freak with too much time on his hands," Adam said. "But you gotta believe me. I've done my homework."

"But one of these philanthropists killed Carrie!" Jason declared. He just couldn't let it go.

Adam ran a hand through his hair and shook his head. "This is the first death I've ever heard of that has a vampire feel to it. You have to understand—they're not all bad. I mean, most of them aren't bad."

"Tell that to Carrie," Jason said.

"Please, just stop saying her name, okay?" Adam asked. "I have nightmares about her. Sometimes even when I'm awake. Those shots I got of Brad and Lauren—they were what totally convinced me my theory was right. If I'd just had the *cojones* to accept the truth a little earlier, I might have saved her."

"What were you going to do?—rent a van with speakers and blast the news all over town?" Jason said, and then realized he wasn't helping. He lowered his voice. "I just mean, it's not your fault. You didn't kill her. A vampire did. Let's focus on that."

"Okay. Well, whoever killed her isn't like Sienna or Brad," Adam said. "The vampire that killed Carrie is evil. Sienna and Brad simply aren't."

Jason sighed. "That's what Sienna said. She thinks whoever did it is some kind of rogue vampire. One that's gone feral. She said it was called bloodlust."

"Bloodlust?"

"Yeah. It's like an addiction. When vampires have bloodlust, they can't stop drinking. They keep going until they've drained so much blood that the human dies."

Adam's face went even paler.

"She said it hasn't happened in decades."

"Well, we can't let it happen again," Adam replied. "My dad told me that the cops picked up Scott Challon—you know, the guy who was making out with Carrie at the party?"

Jason nodded.

"Well, lots of people saw them together. I guess they told the cops. And, of course, I even have video footage of it," Adam said. "The cops figure Scott might know what happened to Carrie. He might be the last one who saw her alive."

"So they think he might've killed her," Jason translated.

"He's the only suspect they have," Adam answered. "And I think they're right."

"So Scott's a vampire?" Jason asked.

"I think so. I've been filming everybody, trying to get proof." He shook his head and smiled faintly. "You know, it never occurred to me to just go ask one of them. You're not bad for a novice."

"Glad I could help," Jason said wryly. "So the cops have Scott. Will they charge him?"

"Doubtful," Adam said. "And his family is so rich, he'll be sprung in no time. But that doesn't matter. I'm going to find out if he did it. And if he killed Carrie, I will personally make sure he never kills again."

Jason took in his friend's frame. Adam looked like he'd never lifted a weight in his life. But his eyes were deadly serious. "You're talking about a murderous vampire," Jason reminded him. "How are you planning to stop him?"

"I don't know yet," Adam admitted.

"Look, Sienna said Zach is pretty pissed off about this whole Carrie thing and he's going to take care of it. And *you* said the police are circling Scott," Jason pointed out. "Let them handle it."

"I don't trust Zach, and the police aren't going to be able to make anything stick," Adam said flatly. "At the moment, they think somebody gave Carrie the drugs that killed her. But pretty soon they'll find out that there weren't any drugs in her system and then they'll drop the case. We're the only humans who know Carrie's murderer was a vampire."

Jason frowned. The guy had a point. He eyed Adam, who was drinking Yoo-Hoo through a curly plastic straw. *Drinking it* ironically *through a curly plastic straw,* Jason corrected himself. Adam was a good guy. He was smart, he noticed things, and he knew his way around a camera. Clearly, he'd also picked up a lot about investigating from his dad. But in a fight, he'd be butchered, and Jason couldn't let that happen. He sighed.

"If you're really going to go after this vampire," Jason said, "then I'm going with you."

THIRTEEN

"**H**eads up!" Adam yelled the next morning. Jason glanced up from his locker to see a piece of paper folded into a triangle flying at him through the air. He caught it right before it hit his eye.

"What's this?"

"The list." Adam lowered his voice as he came closer. "I've been working on it for a couple of months, ever since I started to suspect . . ."

"Oh." It was Adam's list of suspected vampires, then. Well, Jason knew a few who should definitely be on there. Starting with Sienna.

Sienna. As if to taunt him, a wisp of her perfume reached his nose. Incredible how he could pick out her scent even in a crowd of people. His body reacted to her, as usual, with a rush of adrenaline. He glanced up as she walked by, to see her chatting with Belle as if nothing were wrong. She didn't even look in his direction.

He hadn't spoken to her in the two days since she told him her secret. He didn't know if he wanted to. Didn't know if she wanted him to, either.

His body ached to go after her, to go talk to her, to hold her in his arms.

But his mind couldn't shake the image of those fangs. Maybe she wasn't evil. But she also wasn't human.

Jason forced himself to turn away. He closed his locker and began walking in the opposite direction. His first class was on the other side of the school. Adam walked with him. Jason unfolded the list and glanced at it as he went. Moreau. Challon. Devereux. Lafrenière. There was a line drawn underneath those four, then the names Henry and Van Dyke.

"Those top four are also the names of the top contributors to every charity and cultural resource in Malibu," Adam said. "Sienna's mother just hosted a gala to raise money for the hospital. Brad's father's company just committed to sponsoring a year-round Malibu symphony series on the beach, free to the public, with free barbecue and all. Scott's parents—"

"I get it," Jason said. "This list . . . it's a who's who of the Heights. There isn't anybody on here who doesn't live behind the gates."

"Hey, it takes a big pile of dough to live forever," Adam said as he dodged a big guy barreling down the hall. "If they do. Live forever, I mean. Did you ask Sienna that?"

"Yes, and they don't—although they do live longer than humans. She also confirmed that she can't turn into a bat, or smoke. Oh—and no sleeping in coffins,"

Jason added. He glanced down at the list again. "So this is a Heights thing. No outsiders."

"You and your family might be the token humans. Congrats," Adam agreed. Jason didn't love the idea of being trapped in a small gated area with who knew how many of the beautiful and bloodthirsty.

"The families, they created the Heights," Adam continued hurriedly as Jason veered over to his classroom door. Adam's first class was three rooms away. "And lots of those families have French roots—consider the surnames: Devereux, Lafrenière, Moreau, et cetera. The Devereuxs still own vineyards in France and in the Napa Valley. They're one of the oldest families in this area—where do you think DeVere Heights gets its name? The Devereuxs and the Lafrenières have been here the longest—well over a hundred years—but it's been almost as long for the other families. And in California time, that's forever. Pretty much nothing in L.A. is over fifty years old."

"Is everyone on this list a confirmed V?" Jason asked, pausing outside the classroom.

"Well, I was pretty sure Brad was when I saw that blood on his mouth. Sienna outed herself and confirmed him," Adam said, "as well as Erin Henry and Michael Van Dyke—or, at least, she didn't say no when you brought them up. I don't have proof about Scott, but . . ."

"But he was all over Carrie, and she got bitten," Jason finished for him, leaving out the dead part; it wasn't like either of them could forget that not-so-minor detail. "What about Dominic, that guy I had the run-in with at Brad's party?"

"You mean the Dominic who would have beat you into the ground if Brad hadn't come to the rescue?" Adam countered.

"Please. I was holding my own."

"True. You lasted a lot longer than Matt," Adam agreed. "I'm just busting on you."

"But that was a weird situation," Jason said. "I wonder if superstrength is a vampire thing. Because there is no way that kind of power should have been coming out of Dominic's runt body."

"You've got a point. Although 'runt' might be exaggerating a tad," Adam said. "His dad's a partner in a high-powered law firm, and his mother's on the school board of governors. I guess he goes on the list."

"Maybe that's why Sienna freaked out when I tried to take Dominic down," Jason said, suddenly seeing the fight in a whole new light. "She knows he's a vampire and she was terrified he'd kill me."

"'Cause it would have ended the party early," Adam said. "If we add Dominic to the list, does that mean we automatically add Belle?"

"Can you be the best friend of one vampire *and* the

girlfriend of another and not be dentally enhanced yourself?" Jason asked. "Do they let humans that far into their circle?" *Would Sienna ever let someone like me in that far?* he couldn't help adding to himself. *And what would happen if she did?*

"Doubtful." Adam took the list away from Jason and started adding names, including Belle's. "And, besides, Belle's surname is Rémy—that's very French." He hesitated, looking up at Jason. "Should we consider that Carrie could have been killed by Belle or Erin or someone of the female persuasion?"

"I think the last few days have proven that pretty much anything is possible," Jason said.

"Point, got one, you have," Adam answered. He narrowed his eyes at Jason. "You have seen a *Star Wars* movie, I assume."

"A what?" Jason asked blankly.

Adam's eyes went wide.

"I'm from Michigan, Turnball. Not the Amish country. Of course I've seen *Star Wars*," Jason said, and laughed.

"Well, I don't know," Adam protested. "Who knows what kind of deprivation you've suffered, living in the middle of the country all your life? Michigan *is* in the middle, right?"

Jason rolled his eyes. "Let's get back to the list," he

said. "What do you think of Maggie? I don't know her last name. She's on the girls' swim team."

"Maggie Roy? Huh. Well, she's from the Heights, but that's the only thing I'd call suspect about Maggie," Adam answered.

"I'm pretty sure she's been feeding on Aaron Harberts," Jason told him. "Somebody definitely drained him at Brad's party—he was still tired at swimming practice a day and a half later. And I know he and Maggie got friendly at that party. I heard them talking about it."

Adam added Maggie's name to the list, then put stars by the names of people who had been confirmed. "Anybody else?"

"Not that I know of. But until a few days ago, I didn't believe in vampires," Jason said. "So I guess anything's possible. What's the plan?"

"I figure we talk to people who were at the party the other night," Adam said. "See if anybody noticed Carrie talking to anyone on this list. That's how we narrow down our suspects."

"But your eye is on Scott," Jason said.

"It is. I mean, you saw them on the bed." Adam squeezed his eyes shut as if that would block out the memory. "But I've been thinking about it. There's no actual proof against Scott. I don't want to miss something by focusing exclusively on him."

Jason nodded. Made sense. "Aren't people going to wonder why we're so interested when we start with the questions?" he asked.

"I'll tell everyone I'm making a documentary about Carrie's death," Adam said. "You tell them you're helping me. People are morbid—they'll want to talk about it."

Jason had seen *that* for himself. "All right. I'll do what I can." And maybe, just maybe, he thought, this investigation would keep his mind off Sienna.

"Anything?" Jason asked Adam on Thursday at lunch.

Adam shook his head. "The usual. Everyone loved the party, no one remembers a thing about it. You ask them for specifics and their eyes glaze over."

Jason didn't know what to say. The truth was, he had a hard time remembering anything specific from the yacht party himself. And everyone he'd talked to about Carrie's death said the same thing: They saw her making out with Scott Challon. And nothing else. "What about Scott? He still seems to be our number one suspect. Did your dad tell you anything new?"

"Yeah. The cops released him. The only evidence against him is circumstantial: He was the last one seen with Carrie." Adam looked pretty wrecked. Jason wondered if he'd been sleeping at all this week. "And it's just as we expected," Adam went on. "Carrie's drug tests came back, and of course they were all negative. So the police have ruled her death an accident, not murder. They're going to close the case today."

Jason put down his pizza. Suddenly he didn't feel hungry anymore. This was so unreal. He knew Carrie had been murdered, and yet the police couldn't even prove it. Hell, they didn't even suspect murder anymore. "I wish we could tell the police about the vampires," he said. "They're working without all the info."

"Yeah, but I'd like to go to college next year," Adam said. "'Gee, Dad, I'm pretty sure Carrie was killed by a vampire' is like a one-way ticket to a lovely padded cell."

"Did Scott say anything to the cops?" Jason asked. "Anything we can use?"

"Actually, he said Carrie went off with Luke Archer toward the end of the party," Adam said.

"Luke?" Jason frowned in thought. He did remember having seen him there, but Luke had seemed solidly committed to his alone-time with Luke. "Did the cops talk to him?"

"Nah. My dad said they tried to, but they couldn't find him."

"Why not?" Jason asked. "He's been in school."

Adam shrugged. "Don't know. It's weird. But now that they've decided her death was accidental, they don't even care about talking to Luke. Nobody else saw Carrie with him, anyway."

"Maybe Scott was just trying to shift the blame to someone else. Easy to blame the quiet loner," Jason said thoughtfully.

"So Scott is still our prime suspect," Adam surmised.

Jason nodded. "We think he's a vampire and we definitely saw him with Carrie."

"The police report puts Carrie's time of death around twelve thirty," Adam said. "And the timestamp on my film has Carrie making out with Scott at twelve fifteen."

"That doesn't give her much time to have gone off with Luke, or anybody else," Jason pointed out.

"It was Scott—it had to be," Adam said grimly. "The police have just released a bloodlusting vampire. How long do you think it's going to take for him to kill someone else?"

FOURTEEN

"Let's hit the pool, guys!" Coach Middleton yelled into the locker room after school.

Jason grabbed his towel and slammed the locker shut. Usually swim practice was his favorite part of the day—a chance to relax, work his muscles, feel the water. But, today, he dreaded it. He'd managed to avoid Brad all week. In fact, he'd avoided all the friends of Dracula, at least the ones he knew about.

Does Brad know Sienna told me the truth? Jason wondered. *Is he going to be pissed?* And what about the exchange they'd had at Belle's party? Jason wondered if he should apologize, maybe say he'd been drunk?

"Freeman! Let's go kick some ass," Brad called, rounding the row of lockers. "I'm going to set a fast time today." He whipped his towel at Jason, hitting him in the arm, and let out a whoop. Some of the other guys picked it up, howling as they charged out to the pool.

Jason followed more slowly, not sure what to think. Brad was acting as if nothing had happened between them. Was it possible Sienna hadn't told him about her conversation with Jason?

Or did Brad just not care that Jason knew he was a vampire? Because why would he? It's not like Jason was DeVere's own Van Helsing.

"Warm up," Coach Middleton ordered.

The guys plunged into the pool and began with some easy laps. Jason wandered over to where Brad was about to jump in.

"So what up?" Brad greeted him. "Haven't seen you all week. I mean, I've seen you, but you know. I can't believe it's already Thursday. I haven't even started to study for this French quiz I've got tomorrow."

"Feels like it was Monday about three minutes ago," Jason agreed.

"I hear ya," Brad agreed. "The first few weeks of school are always cake. But then the homework sets in and the freedom comes to an end. Sucks." He gave Jason a grin and dove into the pool as Van Dyke climbed out, shaking water from his ear.

"Yo, Freeman!" Van Dyke bellowed, lifting Jason in a bear hug that almost crushed his ribs. Van Dyke dropped him back to the ground and ambled away.

Jason chuckled, but felt a little guilty. Van Dyke had always been affable, but now Jason had a hard time looking at him the same way.

And with Brad, it was even worse. He'd been nothing but a friend to Jason ever since they first met. In return, Jason had accused him of murder. Great.

It's more than that, a little voice whispered in Jason's head. With Brad, it went beyond the vampire issue. It was the Sienna issue. Jason felt guilty just watching Brad in the pool, knowing how he felt about the dude's girlfriend.

Sienna. How did he feel about her, anyway? Attracted to her? For sure. Disturbed by the casual way she talked about drinking blood? Also, for sure. Under the circumstances, Jason reflected, it probably wasn't safe to have feelings for her at all.

"You're up, Freeman," Brad called. Jason started. Brad was already climbing out of the pool.

"Thanks," Jason said. He shoved the thought of Sienna out of his head and plunged into the water.

Swimming focused him. It always did. It blocked out hot girls and vampires and murder mysteries. There was only Jason and the water. Practice ended too soon. He wished it could last for days, long enough to let him finally get rid of all the stress the past week had generated.

But shortly, he was out of the water and heading for the parking lot. Dani had gotten a ride today, so he would be driving home alone. And he was alone when he heard Sienna laughing. Jason didn't have to look up to know it was her, probably there to pick up Brad.

His stomach clenched into a knot. He didn't want

to see Sienna, but he couldn't avoid her. His eyes just couldn't resist taking a look at her. Without meaning to, he stopped and glanced over.

Sienna sat leaning against the adobe wall of the front stairway, laughing as Brad told her some kind of story. Jason felt his face grow hot. She never laughed that way with *him*.

"Hey, Jason. Our relay team's getting good, don't you think?" Brad called.

Great. Now Jason had to go over and join them. Had to watch as Brad slipped an arm around Sienna and she rested against him, reaching up to kiss his cheek. Whether Sienna was a vampire or not, Jason felt a surge of jealousy.

"We should be able to shave off a few more seconds in another couple of practices," Jason said, trying to get his mind off Brad and Sienna.

"I was thinking we should make another run to Eddie's for those fish tacos," Brad said. He glanced at Sienna. "Can you believe this guy ordered a beef taco there?"

Oh, don't even think about asking me to third-wheel with you and Sienna, Jason thought. "I've never been such the fish guy," he replied.

"Okay, but you and Adam and I should definitely hang out again," Brad said. The line sounded a little rehearsed to Jason. "Maybe we could even convince

Adam to show us a little of his movie. Since we're all the stars and everything."

That one came out even more rehearsed. *Got it,* Jason thought. Sienna must have told Brad about her conversation with Jason. Which meant Brad knew that Adam was onto them, that his movie was about the vampires, and now Brad worried that Adam might tell other people what he knew.

Just like the first day we hit Eddie's, Jason realized. Brad had seen Adam filming the big guy that Dominic had pulverized. He knew that it was totally fishy that Dominic had beaten up a guy the size of a house, so he didn't want Adam talking to Matt. That explained Brad's sudden change of plan and his sudden interest in hanging with Jason and Adam. Jason chuckled. He was finally starting to understand a lot of things.

"You think Adam would be up for that?" Brad asked. Even Sienna looked a little anxious about the answer. Jason decided to tell them what they really wanted to know: whether Adam was against them or not.

"I doubt he'd be willing to show the masterpiece until it's done," Jason replied. "But I know he'd be up for a taco run. He's always telling me how long he's known you—you and Sienna and everyone. He's a fan."

The unasked question had been answered. Brad smiled. Sienna relaxed.

"Cool. I'll text you," Brad told Jason. He slid his arm from Sienna's shoulders to her waist. "Catch you later."

"Bye, Jason," Sienna said, giving him a long, serious look as she headed off with Brad. But it wasn't enough. A few words and a meaningful look was just not enough of Sienna.

I've got to see her alone, Jason thought. *Even if she is a vampire.*

"Red alert," Adam said, coming up to Jason in the walkway at the end of Friday afternoon. "I got a tip."

"Yeah? What?" Jason asked.

"I followed Scott into the bathroom after physics. Heard him making plans to go out tonight. I'm going to trail him, see if he tries to pick up a girl."

Damn, Jason thought. He'd been planning to go to Sienna's after school, but he didn't want to tell Adam that. He'd never admitted to his friend that he had a thing for Sienna, even though Adam must have noticed by now.

"You think you'll be okay without me?" he asked Adam. "I have plans tonight."

"Oh. Yeah, sure," Adam said. He didn't sound all that confident, though.

"Listen, all you're going to do is follow him, right?" Jason asked. "You're not going to try to fight him or anything."

"Right," Adam said.

"If you need me to play Robin the boy wonder, call me on my cell and I'll get your back," Jason told him as they walked out to the parking lot.

"You know it." Adam split off toward his Vespa, while Jason headed for the VW.

Dani was waiting for him. "Thank God it's the weekend," she said as soon as he got in the car. "I am so sick of getting up when it's still dark out."

"Yeah," Jason murmured, pulling out of the lot.

"Kristy and I are going to this barbecue tomorrow— Alexa Vassard is throwing it. Apparently Alexa's parents have the biggest hot tub in Malibu," Dani said.

"Uh-huh." Jason tuned out while Dani talked about her plans. He was just happy to hear her back in social mode. Maybe she would like it in California after all. He let her chatter on while he thought about what to say to Sienna.

He knew it would be a little weird to just show up at her house like nothing had happened. Still, they hadn't exactly had a fight. . . .

"Is that Scott Challon's brother?" Dani asked.

The mention of Scott's name caught Jason's attention. "Huh?" he queried, looking around. He'd stopped at a red light, but he hadn't noticed the car that had pulled up beside him. Dani nodded toward it, trying to be subtle. "You know, Scott, the guy the cops thought—"

"Yeah, I know Scott," Jason interrupted. He leaned forward so he could see past Dani into the vintage Mustang next to them. Luke Archer sat at the wheel, lost in his own world, as usual. He didn't even glance in their direction.

The light changed, and Jason hit the gas. "That was Luke Archer," he told Dani. "He's not Scott's brother."

"Are they cousins or something?"

"No." Jason squinted at his sister. "Why?"

"They look so much alike," Dani commented as she pulled her bag onto her lap and began digging through it for something. Obviously she was done with the conversation. But Jason was stuck on the Scott and Luke thing.

"They don't look anything alike," he said. "Scott's a jock, and Luke's a . . . I don't know, a loner."

Dani rolled her eyes. "That has nothing to do with what they look like."

"I know, it's just that they're really different. Luke's thin and pale and stuff."

"They have the same hair," Dani said. "Same basic chin and cheekbones."

"If you say so," Jason replied doubtfully.

"Obviously you spend way more time looking at guys than I do."

Dani swatted at him and he laughed.

After he'd dropped her off at home, Jason headed straight over to Sienna's house. He wanted to get there before he chickened out. If he was going to see her, he had to do it now. He had to know what was up between them. Did she feel anything for him? Did he pull at her heart the way she did at his? And did that even matter? Did anything matter other than the harsh fact that she used his kind for food?

Jason leaped out of the car, strode to the door, and rang the bell. He hoped Sienna would answer, but he figured he could deal with her mom again if he had to.

He wasn't expecting Zach Lafrenière.

"Freeman," Zach said, sounding less than thrilled. He looked Jason up and down with his cool dark eyes, radiating a faint air of disapproval. Even so, Jason wanted Zach on his side. Something about him demanded attention. He was all coiled energy, like a snake ready to strike.

"Hey, Zach," Jason said. "I'm looking for Sienna."

Zach didn't move. He held Jason's gaze for a moment, his dark eyes boring into Jason as if he could read his mind. *He knows,* Jason realized. *He knows Sienna told me about them.* But he didn't break eye contact. Even though his heart had begun to race, he didn't want Zach to know he was on edge.

This guy is a vampire, Jason thought. But the idea was still too Sci-Fi Channel to feel real.

"Sienna!" Zach called suddenly. Then he nodded briefly to Jason, turned, and walked away, leaving the door open. Not exactly an invitation, but not a get-the-hell-out-of-here, either. Jason stepped inside and followed Zach toward the backyard.

Sienna was just getting up from her chaise when Jason reached the glass doors. His heart sank as he took in the scene: not just Zach, but Brad, Van Dyke, Belle, Dominic, and Erin. They all sat around the pool, just hanging out like normal people. Except that they were all vampires. Sienna hadn't confirmed his suspicions about Belle and Dominic, but Jason was pretty sure that this group had more in common than just money and social status.

Jason was alone in a house full of blood-drinkers, and something primal inside urged him to run. But Sienna came walking toward him, a smile playing on her lips, her dark eyes as intoxicating as ever. Jason could feel that she wasn't evil.

He forced himself to act normally as he stood by the doors, waiting for Sienna to reach him.

"Jason," Sienna said. "Hi. Do you want to join us?"

He took a deep breath. "Maybe. What are you doing?"

Belle and Zach exchanged a look. Van Dyke suddenly got up and jumped into the pool, swimming furiously.

"Nothing," Sienna said. "Just hanging."

But everyone was quiet and tense. Clearly, Jason had interrupted something. He glanced at Zach again, who didn't look away. "No thanks," Jason said. "I just wanted to drop by and say hello. So, hello, and now I'll let you get back to . . . hanging."

He turned back into the house, and Sienna followed him to the front door.

"What was that all about?" he asked her quietly.

She sighed. "Look—"

"Did I interrupt some big vampire conference?"

"We're trying to figure out what happened to Carrie," Sienna murmured, glancing over her shoulder. "I told you, Zach wants to take care of it."

"Well, good luck." Jason reached for the doorknob.

"Wait," Sienna said, stepping closer to him. "I'm glad you came. I didn't expect to see you here again."

The closeness of her made his head swim. "I didn't expect to be here again," he admitted, smiling in spite of himself. "But I had to see you."

Sienna smiled back and took another step toward him, and immediately Jason felt himself swept away— by her apple-vanilla scent that reminded him of the ocean, the wild, vivid beauty of her face, and the incredible sweetness of her smile. If he didn't touch her, he thought he might go crazy. Without thinking, Jason reached out and slipped his arm around her waist, pulling her close. Before he could stop himself, his mouth was on hers.

He felt Sienna's body tense in surprise, but then slowly her arms moved up around his neck. She opened her lips, inviting him in, deepening the kiss, her tongue, briefly, meeting his.

Then, abruptly, she pulled away. Her dark eyes troubled now, confused.

Jason smiled, turned, and left the house. He felt Sienna watching him as he walked to his VW and got in. And he couldn't stop himself from grinning; it was nice to know that he could confuse Sienna that way.

Too wired to head home, he went for a drive. He loved living in a state where he could actually make use of having a convertible even in the fall. The sun sparkled on the ocean as he sped along the Pacific Coast Highway. In the water, he could see a few surfers making the most of the late-afternoon sunshine.

Jason breathed in the salty ocean air and felt himself begin to unwind. There'd been a weird vibe over at Sienna's, no doubt, but no one had threatened him. No fangs had made an appearance. It was probably just like Sienna said: The vampires were talking about their rogue member, whoever he was. Trying to figure out what to do. Trying to help. But they clearly didn't want an outsider like him getting involved.

By the time Jason turned back toward DeVere Heights, the last rays of the sun were turning the sea to gold. Jason's cell rang. He glanced at the number: Adam.

"How's it going?" Jason asked as soon as he hit talk.

"We've got a problem." Adam sounded freaked.

"What?"

"It's Scott. He just went into The Dreamhouse."

"Where?" Jason asked.

"It's a club in town. But that's not the problem. Jason, he had a girl with him. What if he's going to kill her?"

FIFTEEN

Jason pulled over to the side of the road. He needed to concentrate. "Calm down," he told Adam. "How do you know she's not some friend of his—another vampire, even?"

"I've never seen her before," Adam said. "And, besides, he just picked her up on Santa Monica Pier. That's where he went after school. He met her there, they started flirting, then they went to The Dreamhouse together."

Jason's throat felt tight. "If he wanted to kill her, why wouldn't he just take her to an alley or something?" he asked.

"I don't know, maybe he likes the thrill," Adam spat. "He didn't kill Carrie in some dark alley."

"Good point," Jason acknowledged. He figured The Dreamhouse was probably pretty dark and crowded, just like Belle's yacht had been. Nobody had noticed Carrie's death there, and nobody would notice another girl's death at the club. "All right, look, we don't know for sure that Scott is the rogue vampire," he said, as much to reassure himself as Adam. "I'll meet you at the club and we'll watch him together. If it seems like he's going to bite anyone, we'll stop him."

"How are we going to get in?" Adam asked. "We're not legal."

"Don't worry, neither is he," Jason reminded him. "Just wait for me."

He hung up and pulled the VW back out onto the road. He didn't plan to drink tonight, but he figured he'd better leave the car home, just in case. Luckily, his parents were out at a business dinner for the evening, so he didn't have to explain where he was going in such a rush.

"Dani!" he yelled as he tossed the car keys onto the counter.

No answer.

"Danielle?" He glanced around and spotted a giant pink Post-it on the fridge. He grabbed it and read, "Gone to Kristy's to study. May sleep over. Dani, XOXO."

"Huh. That better be the truth," Jason muttered. He didn't want to think about her out at some party, being a nice snack for a vampire. At least he knew she'd be nowhere near Scott Challon. He called a cab, changed into jeans and a black T-shirt, and ran back outside just as the cab arrived.

It took ten minutes to get to The Dreamhouse. Adam was waiting out front. "How are we going to get in? I don't have a fake ID," he said anxiously.

"I'm not sure. Let's just go check it out." Jason strode confidently to the door. At every club he'd ever been to, he'd found that if you just looked like you knew what you were doing, they'd let you in. Hopefully it would work the same here. "Hey," he said to the bouncer, his eyes already roaming the inside of the club to show that he wasn't nervous about being carded. "Two of us. What's the cover?"

"Hey, Freeman. Ten bucks each." Jason looked up, surprised. The bouncer was Luke Archer.

"Luke, thank God," Adam said. "I was worried we wouldn't get in."

Luke cracked a smile and glanced around. "No worries," he said. "You do still have to pay, though."

Jason handed over a twenty, taking in Luke's muscular arms. He'd never noticed before how built the guy was. Luke wasn't on any sports teams, so Jason just assumed he wasn't athletic. But obviously he worked out—maybe so he could keep this job. After all, you couldn't be a bouncer unless you were big enough to be intimidating.

"Thanks, man," he said. Luke nodded.

The club was packed, but with a different crowd from the parties in DeVere Heights. Mostly college-age kids. The lights were dim. House music pulsed through huge speakers on the walls, and writhing bodies crowded the tiny dance floor. Deep booths lined the sides of the place, big enough for six or seven people to sit. In the back room there was a pool table—though nothing close to the museum piece at Brad's—and a few dartboards.

Jason pushed his way through the crowd, scanning the faces for Scott Challon. Adam followed, peering at the people in the deep booths. At the back of the room, Jason spotted a wide double door. It led out onto a huge deck over the beach. People hung around in little clumps out here, smoking and talking away from the loud music inside. He did a quick check for Scott, but saw no sign of him.

"Let's go back inside," Adam said. "Scott's not out here."

"Yeah." Jason went back in and led the way over to the other side of the room.

"There he is," Adam murmured.

Jason followed his friend's gaze and spotted Scott. He sat in a corner booth, all the way at the back, his arm around a pretty, red-haired girl. A few other guys sat toward the front of the booth, playing some drinking game. Jason thought he recognized them from school, but it was hard to see them clearly in the dark of the club.

"Grab that table," he told Adam, pointing to a small table about fifteen feet from Scott's booth. "We'll hang here and keep an eye on him."

"What are we going to do if he attacks her?" Adam asked. "He's got friends with him. We can't take them all."

"Buffalo, buffalo, buffalo!" the guys at Scott's table began to chant.

"Hopefully he won't attack her," Jason said, raising his voice to be heard over the buffalo boys. "If he does, we make a scene, get everybody looking in his direction. He won't do anything public."

Adam nodded. "I wish I had my camera," he said. "Then I could get proof."

Jason laughed. "I don't think the club owners would appreciate you filming a high school kid hanging out in their place." He stood up. "I'm going to get some beers so they don't come kick us out." He made his way back through the crowd to the long wooden bar near the entrance. He glanced over at Luke to nod hello. But Luke didn't notice—his attention was focused somewhere toward the back of the place. Jason turned to follow his line of sight and noted, to his surprise, that Luke was watching Scott Challon.

"Help you?" the girl behind the bar yelled over the music.

Jason turned, taking in her platinum-blond pigtails and her pierced eyebrow. "Yeah, uh, two Super Bocks."

She grabbed a couple bottles, opened them, and

handed them over. Jason dropped some cash on the bar and picked up the beers. He glanced back at Luke, but some other beefy dude now stood guard at the door. *Must be Luke's break time,* Jason decided as he elbowed his way through the crowd. But at the edge of the dance floor, he spotted Luke again. Not dancing, not even talking to anyone, just standing there—and still watching Scott Challon.

"Check it," Jason said, setting the beers on the table. He nodded over his shoulder to Luke.

"What?" Adam asked.

"Luke's been eyeballing Scott the entire time I was gone," Jason told him. "You think he's suspicious too?"

Adam shrugged. "Could be. He may not suspect Scott's a vampire, but Scott did try to shift the blame for Carrie's death onto Luke. Maybe Luke heard about that and wants to make sure Scott gets taken downtown."

"Yeah. Or maybe he's seen Scott here before," Jason said grimly. "Maybe he's seen him pick up other girls—or hurt them."

Luke suddenly turned away and headed toward the back of the club.

"I'm going to follow him," Jason said. "Maybe he can tell us something useful."

"You're not going to say anything about vampires, are you?" Adam asked anxiously.

"No, I'll just see if I can get him talking about Scott," Jason said. "If he's suspicious of the guy, he might mention something we don't know."

"Sounds good. I'll stay here and keep an eye on that girl. And the vampire she's sitting with." Adam took a swig of his beer and settled into his seat.

Jason headed toward the back of the club again, peering through the bodies for any sign of Luke. How could he lose sight of such a big guy? But Luke was gone. Jason glanced out onto the deck. No sign of him. He wasn't near the pool table, either. The only other place was the men's room. Jason pushed open the swing door and went in.

It was even darker in here—two out of three lights were broken—but it only took Jason a few moments to realize that the room was empty, except for Scott Challon.

Jason was so surprised to see Scott that he just stared.

"Hey," Scott said, catching his eye in the mirror.

Jason recovered quickly. "Hey," he said, making sure to sound bored. He ambled over to the sinks, where Scott was checking his hair in the mirror. Jason turned on the water, splashed some on his face, then ran his hand through his own hair. He glanced at the stalls, just to see if Luke had gone into one of them, but no one was there.

He gave Scott a nod and went back out into the club. Immediately, he scanned the crowd for Adam, expecting him to have followed Scott over. He noticed a thin, sandy-haired guy playing darts, but when he turned toward the dim lights, Jason could see it wasn't his friend. Where was Adam?

A sudden fear struck him: What if Scott had jumped Adam? It would've been easy enough for Scott to spot Adam watching him.

How long does it take a vampire to kill someone? Jason wondered frantically. Sienna hadn't told him that. He shoved his way through the crowd, desperate to get back to his table. If Adam wasn't there . . .

But Adam *was* there. Converse sneakers up on the neighboring chair, drinking his beer as if nothing was wrong. Jason let out a sigh of relief and dropped into his chair.

Adam gave him a once-over. "You look like crap, my friend," he commented.

"Why are you still here?" Jason asked. "You were supposed to be following Scott."

"I *am* following Scott." Adam raised his beer toward the corner booth. "He hasn't moved."

"What?" Jason squinted across the room at Scott Challon, who remained sitting exactly where he'd been when Jason left. Scott's arm was still around the redhead, and now they were kissing.

"So far, it's been pretty tame," Adam said. "He hasn't gone anywhere near her neck. Or arm. Or looked like biting her at all. The second he does, I figure I'll hurl my beer bottle at him. That should get everyone's attention."

"But . . ." Jason stopped, baffled. "Are you sure he didn't get up at all?"

"Of course I'm sure," Adam said. "I never took my eyes off him."

SIXTEEN

Jason had begun to wonder if he was losing his mind. He'd just been in the bathroom with Scott, not Luke. He was certain of it. And yet, here was Scott, sitting where he'd been sitting all evening and Adam said he hadn't moved! Jason glanced across to see that Luke had returned to working the door. So confusing.

Dani said Scott and Luke look alike, he reminded himself. *Guess she was right.*

"Here we go," Adam said. "Scott's getting up."

Jason spun back toward the corner booth. Scott was inching his way along the bench to get up. His friends were already standing, waiting for him. The redhead slid along the bench behind him.

"We've got to follow them," Adam said, moving to get up too.

"Wait a sec. I don't think the girl's going with them," Jason replied. "Look." The red-haired girl was writing on Scott's hand with a ballpoint pen. *Probably giving him her number,* Jason thought. She stood on her tiptoes and kissed Scott, then wandered off into the crowd.

Scott and his buddies headed for the door.

"Still, we have to go after him," Adam insisted. "He might go pick up another girl somewhere else."

Jason nodded slowly. True enough. But his confusion between Scott and Luke bothered him. "You go ahead," he told Adam. "I'm going to stay here. I want to keep an eye on Luke."

"Luke?" Adam repeated. "Why? He's not a suspect. He's not even a vampire!"

"I know, but there's something strange going on," Jason said. "I can't explain it."

"If anything, Luke's on our side," Adam pointed out. "He seems to suspect Scott too."

"You're going to lose Scott if you don't go now," Jason said.

"Okay." Adam gave him one last, confused look. "You sure you want to stay here?"

"Yeah. Call me if anything bad happens."

Adam nodded and went off after Scott. Jason saw him slap hands with Luke on the way out. Luke looked perfectly relaxed.

Jason went over to the bar and found a seat. He ordered another beer and settled down to watch Luke, feeling like an idiot. Adam was right: Luke had always seemed like a pretty normal guy, and Jason had no reason to suspect him of anything. In fact, he didn't even know what he *did* suspect. But he had an uneasy feeling in his stomach, and it had something to do with Luke.

"When's last call?" he asked the pigtailed bartender.

"Two," she answered. "Why? You in it for the long haul?"

"I think so," he replied, glancing at his watch. It was only midnight, and Luke probably had to work the door until closing.

Jason turned on his stool to look out over the whole club. The redhead who'd been with Scott was now dancing with a group of girls on the dance floor. Luke leaned against the door frame, taking money and checking IDs. Jason sighed and took a sip of beer. It was going to be a long night.

At one thirty, the red-haired girl brushed past him, heading for the door. Jason watched her go, hoping she didn't plan to meet up with Scott. He pulled out his cell and checked for messages. Nothing. No word from Adam since he'd left.

When he looked up again, Luke was gone.

Jason leaped off his stool and rushed over to the door. Just outside, he could see Luke talking to the other bouncer. The other guy nodded, then they banged fists in farewell and Luke took off toward the parking lot.

Surprised, Jason followed him. *How am I supposed to trail him without a car?* he wondered. Jason smiled wryly. He wasn't so hot at this detective stuff. Guess he'd never grow up to be a private eye. But he could at least see what direction Luke drove off in.

He kept back twenty feet or more, not wanting Luke to notice he was being followed. Luke walked all the way to the edge of the parking lot, where there were no lights, and faded into the darkness behind a huge H2.

Jason broke into a jog, trying to catch up. When he reached the SUV, he stopped and inched his way around it, using it for cover.

There! Luke was leaning against a Toyota—who knew they allowed Toyotas in Malibu?—five feet away. But he wasn't alone. The redhead from the club was with him, keys dangling from her hand as she laughed at something Luke said.

The Toyota must be her car, Jason thought. *But what is she doing with Luke?*

Their voices were low, so he couldn't make out the words, but the tone was clearly flirtatious. Jason shook his head. So *this* was why Luke had been watching Scott—Scott was hitting on the girl he liked. It didn't explain the men's room confusion, of course, but then it *had* been dark in there. Jason decided he'd just made a mistake—and he felt like kicking himself. He'd wasted all night here watching a guy who was just jealous.

He almost felt like laughing. Between Sienna telling him about the vampires and Adam getting so caught up in his investigation of Scott, he'd seriously started imagining things. Like Luke turning into Scott Challon in the bathroom.

I'm going to call a cab to go home, he decided. *Enough Van Helsing for one night.*

"Come on," Luke's voice broke into his thoughts. "The view is great from there."

Jason plastered himself against the H2, hoping they wouldn't see him. He didn't want to have to explain to Luke why he was hanging out in the middle of a deserted parking lot.

"From the alley?" the girl sounded skeptical.

"No. The entrance is in the alley," Luke said. "There's a gate that leads to the beach."

"Okay. Sounds delicious." The girl giggled, and Jason heard their footsteps moving away toward the service alley that ran behind the club. He peered around the other side of the SUV, waiting for them to move out of sight so that he could show himself.

The moon had come out from behind a cloud, and it shone down onto the lot. He could see the girl clearly now, see her smile as she adjusted her purse on her shoulder.

And he could see the guy, too—which came as a shock. Because it wasn't Luke Archer.

It was Scott Challon.

SEVENTEEN

"Let's go," Scott said. He took the girl's hand and led her toward the alley.

Jason had to remind himself to breathe. What was Scott doing back at the club? Where had he come from? Jason scanned the parking lot, looking for Adam. Surely his friend would have called him to say Scott was heading back to The Dreamhouse.

But it was Luke *with that girl,* a voice whispered in Jason's head. He had been certain that it was Luke. How could the girl be with Luke one second and with Scott the next?

She couldn't be, Jason thought. *Unless Luke made himself look like Scott!*

And, with that thought, Jason yanked out his cell and called Adam, who answered on the first ring.

"Adam, where's Scott?" Jason demanded. "You still following him?"

"Yeah. He's at Duke's Burgers. Been here for more than an hour," Adam complained. "Just him and his friends. I wish they'd go home if they're not going to commit any crimes."

Jason's heart began to thump so hard that he was

surprised Adam couldn't hear it. "You're sure he's there right now?"

"Yes. He's eating French fries and telling jokes. His boys are laughing. I'm looking right at him."

"So am I," Jason murmured. "Scott and that red-head he was with earlier have just disappeared around the side of the club."

"*What?*" Adam cried.

"Just stay on Scott. Don't let him leave your sight," Jason said. He hung up the phone and ran toward the alley. He knew what was going on now, and it was very, very bad. If Scott was sitting in a burger bar, then it *was* Luke holding hands with the redhead. And if Luke had made himself look like Scott Challon—he had to be a vampire.

Jason raced around The Dreamhouse and into the dark alley. The two-story building blocked the moon, and there were no lights. The sound of the surf drifted up from the beach behind the alley, but Jason didn't see any beach access from back here. The alley was filled with Dumpsters for the club and some old rusted barstools. Besides The Dreamhouse, the nearest building was three hundred yards away. There was absolutely no reason for anyone to come into this alley unless they were here to drop off supplies at the service entrance to the club, or to pick up the garbage. Why would anyone bother putting in an access path to the beach?

He's going to kill her. Jason knew it with absolute certainty. Soft laughter drifted toward him from somewhere up ahead. He hurried forward, running softly to keep from being heard. Finally he spotted them, up against the concrete wall of the club, making out. Luke's hands were in her red hair, and his lips were on her neck. He opened his mouth, and Jason saw the moonlight glint off vicious fangs.

Jason shouted, "Hey!" and the vampire looked up.

He still looked like Scott Challon in almost every way. But his eyes met Jason's. Green eyes shone in the darkness as if lit from within. There was no humanity there, only evil and uncontrolled desire: bloodlust. Just what Sienna had described—pure, pulsating hunger for human blood, an unnatural need. But of one thing Jason was completely certain: They were Luke Archer's eyes.

Jason actually felt a momentary sense of relief as everything finally added up. It had been Luke all along. He'd been impersonating Scott the whole time—even at Belle's yacht party—and so Scott had gotten arrested, not Luke. No one had even seen Luke near the dead girl. Well, except Scott, Jason remembered, but nobody had believed him.

Luke stared at Jason now, his fangs still sunk into the flesh of the girl's neck.

"I think we've got some things to discuss," Jason said firmly. He took a step toward the vampire.

Luke lifted his head and released the girl's neck. Blood dripped from the corner of his mouth, black as oil in the darkness. The redhead swooned, falling back against the wall of the club, almost unconscious. She raised her hand to her neck, smearing blood all over herself. But when she saw it on her fingers, she only laughed as if it were the funniest thing she'd ever seen.

"Get out of here!" Jason told her. "Run. *Go!*"

The girl looked up at him, still smiling vaguely as if she'd had too much nitrous oxide at the dentist's surgery.

"Run!" Jason yelled.

She blinked, confused, then turned to Luke. "Scott, what's going on?" she asked.

Luke smiled, his razor-sharp fangs showing white against the darkness. His eyes still glowed with lust. "It's your lucky day," he hissed at the girl.

Finally she seemed to snap out of her trance. Staring at the atrocity that was Luke's mouth, she backed away. Jason grabbed her arms and shoved her toward the entrance of the alley. Tears streaking her face, she stumbled into a run. He watched her until she disappeared around the corner of the building. Then he turned to face the vampire.

Luke licked his lips and smiled a bloody smile. "It's

nice of you to take her place," he growled, his voice at least an octave lower than normal. "I generally prefer female blood, but if it means so much to you, I'll be happy to drink yours instead."

EIGHTEEN

Jason felt a thrill of fear as he stared at the creature before him: a vampire. A feverish nightmare come to life.

Luke chuckled. The sound was grating, like metal scraping against metal. And somehow it cleared through the fog of fear in Jason's brain. No matter *what* the guy was, he'd killed an innocent girl. And he intended to kill again. Jason intended to defend himself at any cost.

"Sorry. I'm not up for getting drained by a blood-lusting freak tonight," he said grimly.

Luke's laughter echoed off the walls of the building as he began to change. His face twisted, losing any hint of Scott Challon's features. Gradually, the face of Luke Archer emerged. The same face that Luke wore when he sat at Jason's lunch table in the school cafeteria. But then his body began to change, as well. The muscles of his arms expanded, growing to twice their normal size. His legs and torso lengthened. Even his neck seemed to stretch as he grew half a foot taller, so that he now towered over Jason.

Finally, Luke stood still—impossibly strong,

improbably massive. His upper lip curled and he let out a low snarl.

Jason's neck spasmed as if his body remembered the last fight he'd had with a vampire—Dominic—who had been kind of thin, and not very muscular. But he'd almost squeezed Jason's throat closed before Jason had managed to defend himself. His strength had been entirely out of proportion to his size.

But Luke was huge. Jason couldn't even imagine the extent of his strength. He swallowed hard and balled his hands into fists. He saw no way to escape. All he could do was fight.

Jason went on the offensive, dropping into a fighting stance and then springing forward with a series of jabs to Luke's torso. He got in a few solid hits, but the guy barely seemed to notice. He grabbed Jason's hand in mid-swing and jerked him forward, toward those flashing fangs.

Jason ducked, still going forward, using the force of Luke's own move against him. Luke stumbled backward, thrown off balance. Jason took advantage of the vampire's confusion to get in a roundhouse kick to the chest. Luke stumbled farther back.

But then he laughed.

In one move, he lunged forward and backhanded Jason across the face. The blow was so strong that Jason's head snapped to the side and he fell.

Luke jumped on him immediately, pinning Jason to the ground. He bared his fangs. "Did you really think you could stop me?" he snarled.

"No . . . but I can," a cold voice replied.

Luke leaped off Jason and scanned the alley.

Jason whipped around too, as he scrambled to his feet. No one was there; no one had entered the alley. And yet, by the time he turned back to Luke, Zach Lafrenière was standing between them.

Jason glanced up at the roof of the club. Zach must have jumped down from there. Insane. The roof had to be almost thirty feet high. It became increasingly obvious to Jason that he knew very little about vampires.

Jason watched the two as they faced off.

Luke didn't bother talking to Zach. He just hurled himself at the other vampire. But Zach leaped straight up into the air, tumbling over Luke's shoulder to land behind him. Immediately he wrapped his arm around the bigger guy's neck and squeezed.

Jason backed away, trying to get out of the range of Luke's flailing legs. Luke struggled, twisting back and forth, but Zach held on. Finally Luke threw all his weight back against the wall of the club, slamming Zach into the concrete.

Zach let out a strangled cry, and Luke laughed and jerked away from Zach's grasp, turning to attack head-on. But Zach was faster. He ducked and rolled to the side so that Luke's fist smashed harmlessly into the wall.

Behind his opponent once again, Zach jumped into the air, shooting six feet straight up. He kicked Luke in the back of the neck, snapping his head forward. Then, on the way down, he caught hold of the guy's head and twisted it savagely to one side, trying to break his neck. Watching, Jason felt as if he'd slipped into *The Matrix*. Evidently the laws of physics didn't apply to vampires.

Luke spun with the move and grabbed Zach's legs, using the force of Zach's jump against him. Zach flew through the air and landed in a heap ten feet away.

Jason expected him to stay there, but Zach leaped right back up and charged at Luke, slamming him back against one of the Dumpsters. The thick metal crumpled where he hit it. Thick. Metal. Crumpled. Jason couldn't believe what he was seeing.

Luke bellowed like an enraged animal. He pummeled Zach with his fists, his eyes burning like green fire. Zach blocked most of the blows, but he was slowing down.

He hasn't drunk as much blood as Luke, Jason realized. *All that blood consumed in bloodlust has made Luke stronger.*

Zach ducked a blow and jumped to the side, grabbing one of the rusted bar stools. He held it in front of him for protection, but Luke caught hold of the metal legs and pulled with all his strength. Zach flew forward, stumbling to the ground as Luke tore the stool from his grasp.

In one move, Luke snapped a metal leg off the stool and hurled himself on top of his enemy. Pinning Zach down with one arm, he raised the metal leg over his head like a spear. In just a moment, Luke would plunge the metal stake into Zach's heart, and Jason remembered Sienna saying that that was fatal for humans and vampires alike.

He had no choice. He ran at Luke and threw himself at the vampire with all his strength.

Caught off guard, Luke tumbled off of Zach, just as he had started to bring the metal stake down. He hit the ground hard, and Jason heard the stake clatter to the pavement. He breathed a sigh of relief; he'd saved Zach's life—for the time being. But right now was not the time to celebrate.

Hold him down, Jason told himself, driving Luke's shoulders into the ground with every ounce of strength he possessed. But in a few moments, Luke had managed to free one arm. He reached up and threw Jason off. Jason felt himself flying through the air and then he slammed into the blacktop—hard. The wind rushed from his lungs and he lay still for a moment, just trying to breathe.

Meanwhile, Luke rose to his feet, reached down, and grabbed Jason by the throat. He lifted him off the ground with one hand and slammed him back against the wall. Jason kicked out, hoping to connect with a vulnerable part of Luke, but there didn't seem to be one.

Jason couldn't think of another plan of attack while suspended several feet above the ground and slowly running out of air. He struggled to stay conscious, but blackness clouded his vision.

All he could see was Luke's blazing green eyes as he bared his fangs and went for Jason's jugular.

Then there came a sickening thud, followed by a hideous sucking sound. Luke's eyes widened in surprise and he looked down. Jason followed his gaze— just in time to see the metal stake emerge from Luke's ribcage and shoot straight into the wall beneath his own armpit.

Luke stared at the metal stake as if confused. Then he slumped forward, dead.

Over Luke's hunched shoulders, Jason met Zach's eyes. His gaze was cool and steady, in spite of the fact that he had just stabbed Luke through the heart.

Was he trying to stab us both? Jason wondered.

Zach jerked the stake backward, and Luke's body tumbled to the pavement. Jason fell with him, landing in a crouch over the vampire. But he didn't take his eyes off the body, because it was changing. The crazed vampire who'd been ready to kill Jason a few seconds ago was gone. Luke was . . . Luke again. A thin guy, not especially tall, not especially muscular.

But Jason noticed something else different about him now: His features seemed sharper, his bone structure more perfect, his skin completely unblemished. He'd never been this remarkable-looking at school. Clearly he'd been toning down his appearance the same way Sienna did, in order to blend in.

His clear green eyes were open, but the crazed glow of the bloodlust had died with him. His mouth bore traces of blood, but the fangs had vanished. He looked entirely human.

"Freeman." Jason looked up to see Zach holding out a hand. He grabbed it, and Zach pulled him to his feet. "You okay?"

"Yeah." Jason's voice came out hoarse. He looked down at himself, searching for signs of injury. Everything hurt, but nothing seemed to be broken. "I'm fine." He looked at Zach. "How about you?"

Zach laughed, but there was no humor in it. "I'm great," he said. And Jason could see that he was. The guy looked as if he were going clubbing, not as if he'd just survived the fight of his life. No bruises, no blood, not a hair out of place.

"What were you doing here?" Jason asked.

"Looking for him." Zach glanced down at Luke. "We couldn't let him kill again."

"You knew?" Jason demanded. "You knew it was Luke?"

"Not until tonight," Zach said. "He didn't grow up with us, so we didn't know he was . . . one of us. But there's a certain feeling we get. I've had suspicions about him for a while now."

"And you didn't do anything about it?" Jason said, disgusted.

"I didn't know he'd go rogue," Zach replied flatly. "Bloodlust is dangerous. It's forbidden. We're taught that from infancy. None of us would ever give in to it. The very idea is unthinkable."

Jason sighed. "Sorry. I know you're not all . . . like him. I'm just—"

"It's all right," Zach cut him off.

Jason studied him. Sienna and Brad were so friendly, so *normal*. But Zach was different. Aloof. Yet he'd done the right thing tonight. "You saved my life," Jason said. "I guess I owe you one."

"No. You saved my life too," Zach said. "You don't owe me anything."

Jason smiled. "Okay. We're even."

For the first time, Zach smiled back. For an instant, then it was gone. "No, not even. You shouldn't have been here. It wasn't your problem," he said. "Go home. I've got some cleaning up to do."

Cleaning up? Jason thought. Weren't they going to call the cops? What the hell was Zach going to do with a dead guy who'd been staked through the heart? He opened his mouth to ask, but the look on Zach's face silenced him.

I don't want to know, Jason decided. He already knew more about the ways of vampires than he wanted to. "Okay. Good luck," Jason said.

Zach just raised an eyebrow.

"Right. No luck necessary," Jason corrected himself. He turned and walked away. Zach obviously knew what he was doing.

When he got back to the parking lot, Jason pulled out his cell and called Adam.

"Jason? What's going on?" Adam greeted him.

"You still following Scott?" Jason asked, picking his way through the cars toward the road.

"Yeah."

"Well, you can stop," Jason said. "We found the killer—"

"We?" Adam interrupted.

"It's a long story. I'll tell you tomorrow." Jason reached the edge of the parking lot and stepped out onto the sidewalk. It was late, and only a few cars whizzed by on the Pacific Coast Highway.

"So it's not Scott?" Adam asked.

"No—our very own Luke Archer. He was a vampire," Jason said. "But he's dead."

A long silence on the other end of the line. "Jason," Adam finally said. "Did you . . ."

"No." Jason took a deep breath. "Look. It's all taken care of. I'll explain in the morning."

"Wanna meet at Peet's Coffee?"

"Yeah. I'll see you there at ten." Jason hit end, then began scrolling through his phone book for the number of the cab company he'd used to get here. He felt drained, both physically and mentally, as if he'd been through a fifteen-round boxing match and the SATs all at once.

"Need a lift?"

The unmistakable voice of Sienna. Jason looked up slowly from his phone, unable to stop himself from smiling at the sight of her. The exhaustion vanished from his body the instant his eyes met hers.

She sat in her Spider, which was idling on the side of the road. "What are you doing here?" he asked, walking over. He leaned in through the passenger-side window.

"I was at the The Dreamhouse," Sienna said.

"Not while I was in there, you weren't," Jason replied.

She shrugged. "Maybe you just didn't see me."

He squinted at her. Had she changed her appearance too? Or was she just teasing him? "Did you come with Zach?" he asked.

Sienna switched her attention to the CD player and changed the disc.

Jason sighed. Obviously he'd asked too much. He couldn't expect her to tell him all her secrets. Not yet, anyway. He straightened up and looked around at the road, the beach, the moon on the water. He should call a cab to take him home. He should leave these vampires to themselves.

"Are you coming or not?" Sienna asked, her voice like velvet in the night.

Who was he kidding? Let Sienna drive off by herself? Please. As if he could keep away from her.

"Yeah, I'm coming." Jason opened the door and climbed in beside her.

As she pulled out into the California night, he smiled to himself. When he left Michigan, he'd been hoping for less of the ordinary, and more of the unexpected. Malibu had delivered in style.

So had Sienna Devereux.

VAMPIRE BEACH

INITIATION

For LA's finest writing group—Chris, Drew, Emily, Kathy, and Matt

Special thanks to Laura Burns and Melinda Metz

ONE

"Hey, Freeman! Wait up!"

Jason Freeman grinned as his friend Adam's voice carried across the wide-open courtyard of DeVere High. He turned, and found himself staring into a camera lens. Adam Turnball jogged toward him, jostling his ever-present camcorder as he filmed.

"I haven't been getting the handheld-camera effect I want in my film," Adam explained. "The camera's not shaking enough, so I'm thinking I must walk very smoothly. I'm extremely graceful, you know."

"Hence the jogging?" Jason asked.

"Yeah." Adam turned off the camera and bent over, sucking in a long breath. "I tell you, bro, I suffer for my art. Running is not my strongest subject."

Jason chuckled. He rarely understood what Adam was talking about, but he always found him amusing. "I don't even think that thing's switched on half the time," Jason teased him. "You've been making this movie ever since I met you, and so far I haven't seen squat."

Adam fell into step beside him as they made their

way toward the parking lot with the rest of the juniors and seniors who could drive. "Let me guess: You think I use the camera as a shield between myself and the harsh realities of high school society. That I don't feel safe without a camera. That I'm only comfortable viewing the world at a distance, through a sanitizing camera lens."

"No, actually, I think you just like to freak people out by pretending to film them all the time," Jason replied.

"Damn, you got me." Adam grinned. "But you know I always like footage of you. The Michigan farm boy wholesomeness, the all-American blond good looks. Why, you could be the next Brad Pitt, my friend."

"I've never set foot on a farm in my life," Jason said. "I'm from a suburb of Detroit."

"Details." Adam waved his hand dismissively in the air, his hazel eyes twinkling.

As they passed through the tall arch over the entrance to DeVere High, Jason took in a lungful of the warm California air. The scent of flowers mingled with the smell of the ocean half a mile away. It had been several months since his move to Malibu, but the place hadn't lost its ability to impress him. "I can't believe it's November and I'm still wearing Tevas," he commented. "Do you have any idea how cold it is in Michigan right now?"

"Too cold for me," Adam said. "Anything below sixty-five qualifies as freezing as far as I'm concerned."

"Hey, Freeman," Brad Moreau called as they passed him. "Turnball."

"What's up?" Adam replied.

Jason nodded at Brad, his best friend on the swim team. But he didn't head over to the carved stone bench where Brad sat. Because Brad wasn't alone; he had Zach Lafrenière with him. And Zach was radiating "no humans allowed" vibes that could probably be felt on Mars.

"What's with the vampire conference?" Adam asked, lowering his voice. "Something going down I should know about?"

"You shouldn't know about any of it," Jason muttered. "And neither should I." That was the single most astonishing thing about Malibu so far: the fact that the in-crowd wasn't just your average love-to-hate-them group.

They were vampires.

Most days, Jason expected to wake up and realize that half his new friends being vampires was just a bizarre dream. But so far it hadn't happened. Adam was the only other person he knew who understood the truth about Zach, Brad, and the rest of that posse. And Adam didn't seem to find it nearly as freaky as Jason did.

But then, Adam had grown up with the vampires. And Jason had only met them a few months ago. Maybe over time, he'd get used to knowing such a massive secret. Maybe.

"Let's just go," he said gruffly, wanting to change the subject. The way Zach looked at him made him nervous. Of all the vampires, only Zach put Jason on edge. The others mostly acted like normal—normal for SoCal—people. But Zach was different. More powerful. More reserved. And definitely more unwilling to befriend Jason—and probably any human.

"Aren't you going to wait for Brad?" Adam asked.

Jason shook his head. "We don't have swim practice today. Coach Middleton said since it's a holiday week, we could have the time off. He figured nobody was going to be at their best two days before Thanksgiving."

"Sweet," Adam said appreciatively. "Hey, that means we can hang after school tomorrow, right? I've been meaning to force you to watch the entire oeuvre of Stanley Kubrick, a subject in which your knowledge is sorely lacking."

"Hey, I've seen *The Shining*," Jason protested.

"That's not enough," Adam told him. "What do you say—a DVD marathon *chez moi* tomorrow?

"Sure," Jason told him. They'd reached the parking lot. He nodded toward his 1975 Volkswagen bug, parked under a palm tree to the right. "I'm that way."

"And I remain in the bike parking section," Adam said ruefully. "Not that I don't love my Vespa. I just wish it had, you know, four wheels and a backseat to make out in." He held up a fist, knuckles out toward Jason.

Jason bumped fists. "Later."

Adam took off for the Vespa with a wave, and Jason headed for his car. He wondered where his younger sister, Danielle, was. He'd forgotten to tell her there was no practice today. He could've driven her home. But a quick scan of the parking lot revealed no sign of Dani. She must have caught a ride or taken her usual bus.

"Guess I'm flying solo," Jason murmured, unlocking the car. He began to lower the roof; it was way too sunny and gorgeous to ride with the top up.

"Want some help?" a voice asked from behind him.

Jason recognized that voice: *Sienna.* He felt a rush of nervous energy—*that* was just one more thing he'd got used to. Sienna Devereux made him hot, she was a vampire, and she was taken. Strangely, perhaps, he was having the most trouble with that last one.

He didn't turn around. "I've got it, thanks," he said.

Sienna didn't leave. He laughed and glanced over his shoulder. "You're not really here to offer help, are you?"

"Nope," she said, her plump lips curving into a smile. "I'm here to ask for some. Can you give me a lift home?"

Jason finally turned to look at her full-on. Man, she was sexy. Her dark eyes were gleaming with amusement, and her long black hair was pulled into some kind of messy knot on top of her head. Jason longed to pull out the pins that held it up and let her silky hair spill down over his fingers. He shook the thoughts away. She was Brad's girlfriend. He was Brad's friend. That meant that most interesting thoughts about Sienna had to be banished from his mind.

"What's wrong with the Spider?" he asked. Sienna's imported Alfa Romeo always seemed to be out of commission.

She shrugged. "I think it hates me."

"That's impossible," Jason replied. She raised one perfect eyebrow, and he realized that he sounded like a complete dork. "Cars don't have feelings," he added quickly. "Unless you know something I don't."

"I know *lots* of things you don't," she said lightly. She opened the passenger door and folded her long legs into the VW.

"So I guess I'm giving you a ride home." Jason laughed. He hooked the folded top into place and climbed in beside her. "Why don't you just get a new car? Your parents have the money."

Sienna turned in her seat to look at him. "Really now, Michigan," she purred. "If I had a new car, I wouldn't need rides home, would I?"

"My point exactly," he told her.

She shook her head, smiling. "Well, where would be the fun in *that*?"

Jason grinned and found himself gazing directly into her beautiful dark eyes. Then he realized he'd been staring at her for just a bit too long.

Sienna leaned toward him. Close. So close, Jason thought she was about to kiss him. . . .

In fact, she gave his Michigan State key chain a casual flick with her finger. "I think you have to use the little metal thingy on the end of this in order to make the car go," she teased.

Jason turned the key in the ignition, trying to shake off the feeling that something had just very nearly happened between him and Sienna. "Ha! Like you'd know," he retorted jokingly. "Your car *never* goes."

As he pulled out of the parking lot onto the Pacific Coast Highway, he caught a glimpse of Brad and Zach still sitting on the bench outside school. "Why didn't you just wait for Brad to take you home?" he asked Sienna.

She didn't answer, and for a moment he wondered if she'd even heard him. He shot a glance at her, and she was frowning.

"He had to ... do something with Zach," she finally replied.

Jason nodded. He'd suspected as much. Brad and Zach were busy with some vampire-related business. Sienna didn't want to be specific about it, and that was okay with him. When he'd first found out about the vampires living in his gated community of DeVere Heights, he'd gotten pretty involved, pretty fast. One rogue vampire had killed a girl from school. Jason had ended up tracking him down and fighting him all alone in an alley, trying to prevent a second murder.

If Zach Lafrenière hadn't turned up at the last moment, Jason knew he would probably have ended up dead. The whole experience had taught him everything he needed to know about the vampires: They were outrageously strong, they could change their physical appearance, and they knew some seriously freaky fighting moves.

He wasn't anxious to get that up close and personal with vampire business again. Being friends with some of them was enough—Sienna and her best friend, Belle; Brad and his oldest friend, Van Dyke. Even Zach was okay. Jason knew that they were good people whose parents did a lot of charity work in the community. Beyond that, he didn't want to know much about the day-to-day vampire activities. His own private don't-ask-don't-tell policy.

A light turned red in front of him, and Jason eased to a stop. To the left, the Pacific Ocean spread out to the horizon, its gray-blue water calling to him. Maybe he'd slip on his new wet suit and try some surfing this evening. With winter approaching, the sun went down early. But he'd discovered that surfers stayed on the water until the very last drop of light was gone. He would definitely have time to catch a few good waves. He'd only taken three lessons so far, but he already knew enough to go out on his own.

The late afternoon sun glinted off the water, and a warm breeze ruffled his hair. Hard to believe it was almost Thanksgiving. Warm sun, clear blue sky, crashing ocean surf—life just did not get any better.

"You are seriously zoning," Sienna commented.

The light was green. "Sorry," Jason replied as he hit the gas. "Sometimes the whole Malibu thing still distracts me."

"What 'whole Malibu thing'?" she asked.

"You know, the unrelenting incredibleness of the place." That was the best way he could describe it.

"Yeah. I've been to a lot of places, and Malibu is still the most beautiful," Sienna agreed.

Jason glanced at her in surprise. Sienna's family—in fact, all the vampire families—had more money than he could even imagine. When she said she'd been to a lot of places, he believed her. The Devereuxs vacationed in Europe, Asia, Australia. He'd seen the photos scattered around their house. It was nice to know that California still held up, even with that kind of competition.

"Any big plans for Turkey Day?" Sienna asked as they turned off the highway and headed up the hill toward DeVere Heights.

"The usual: food and football," Jason told her. "My aunt Bianca is coming in from New York. Danielle has about thirty outfits lined up to run by her. She approves of Bianca's fashion sense."

"Well, who wouldn't?" Sienna said. "The woman knows how to dress."

Jason's eyebrows shot up. "You know my aunt?"

"Sure." Sienna gave a languid shrug. "I mean, it's not like we're best friends or anything, but I've met her. Her husband was on the hospital board with my mom."

"Oh." Jason knew that Aunt Bianca had helped his father land his new job at the Los Angeles advertising firm—the new job with the huge raise that had led to their moving out here to Malibu. And he knew that Bianca had suggested they buy a house in DeVere Heights. But somehow he hadn't realized that Bianca knew Sienna and her parents. "I guess Bianca's husband was really involved in all the Malibu charities and stuff, huh?" he asked.

"Yeah." Sienna glanced over at him. "Didn't you know that?"

"I never really thought about it," Jason said. "Aunt Bianca was only married to him for four years before he died. And it's not like they spent much time in Michigan. They were always off to New York or L.A. or Paris or some other exotic locale. I met him at their wedding and maybe one or twice after that."

"So he wasn't exactly Uncle Stefan," Sienna guessed.

"I guess he was, technically," Jason said. "I just never thought of him that way. We've seen a lot more of Bianca since he died than we ever did before. I think my mom is happy to have her sister back."

"Makes sense," Sienna said. "But you should be glad Bianca married Stefan, or you wouldn't be living in DeVere Heights."

"What do you mean?"

"Bianca used his contacts. You know, pulled some strings for you guys," Sienna explained. Then she grinned. "We don't let just anyone live up here, you know," she teased.

"So if it weren't for Uncle Stefan, I never would have met you," Jason said. "I guess I do owe him one, then." *Was that too much?* he wondered the second the words left his mouth. Sienna always seemed to be flirting with him, but he didn't usually flirt back. He mostly figured that she was just kidding around.

Sienna didn't answer, but she gave him a long sideways look that sent the blood racing through his veins. Jason turned into the driveway of her ultramodern house and stopped the car.

"Thanks for the ride," she said casually, climbing out and closing the door behind her.

"No worries." Just having her out of arm's reach made Jason relax a little. It took serious concentration to remember that they were only friends when she was so close by. He reached for the gearshift, but suddenly Sienna turned back to the car.

"Did I drop a pen in there?" she asked, leaning in over the door. Her hair, loosened by the wind on the drive, slipped out of its knot and fell forward around her face.

Jason's pulse sped up. *Friends!* he thought. *Who am I kidding?* She soon found her pen and looked up. Jason stared at her lips, slightly parted, then raised his eyes to meet hers. She held his gaze and didn't move away. Without meaning to, Jason found himself leaning toward her. . . .

His lips were barely an inch from hers when the phone rang.

Jason jumped in surprise as a Backstreet Boys song played out from his cell. "Dani's idea of humor," he explained to Sienna. "She's always changing the ring-tone." He searched for his phone, eventually managing to extract it from a pocket, but he didn't recognize the number on the screen. He hit talk. "Hello?" he barked into the mouthpiece. Whoever it was had seriously bad timing.

Too late. The caller had already hung up. Jason shrugged and turned back to Sienna.

But she was gone.

TWO

Not even the perfect Malibu sunshine could cure Jason's bad mood as he drove home from Sienna's house. He'd been so close to kissing her. He could practically feel her lips on his.

What kind of idiot answers the phone at a time like that? he thought, pulling to a stop in front of his house. *Why didn't I just ignore it?*

He pulled in a deep breath, trying to achieve calm. Sure, he'd been stupid to go for the cell. If he hadn't, he could have done what he'd been wanting to do for months—kiss Sienna. But, then again, the call had saved him where his self-control had failed, and Jason didn't want to be the kind of guy who would make out with his friend's girlfriend. It would have been wrong. And obviously Sienna thought so, too, or she wouldn't have taken off.

Maybe she was insulted that instead of kissing her, I answered the phone, Jason thought. *Maybe that's why she left.* But he didn't think so. He figured she'd realized what they had come so close to doing, and so she'd left. She didn't want to hurt Brad any more than Jason did.

With a sigh, he climbed out of the car and made his way into the house. Their Malibu home dwarfed the house they'd lived in back in Michigan. Sometimes it didn't seem possible that this was home now. But the delicious scent of his mother's pumpkin pie wafting from the kitchen made the place smell like home. Mrs. Freeman had been making it every Thanksgiving since Jason could remember.

"Hey, Mom, I'm back," he called, making his way into the kitchen.

"Good, you can help me," his mother replied. "I can't reach the good china—it's up on the top shelf."

Jason shook his head. "It's only Tuesday. Why are you getting the good china out now?" he asked. His poor mother looked ready to drop from exhaustion. Her blond hair was a mess, and flour obscured the MR. BUBBLE on her T-shirt.

"You know I need to feel like everything's ready," she replied. "Just because it's a new house doesn't mean the Thanksgiving rules change."

"Yeah, and the rule is that Mom has to be completely freaking out for the entire week before Thanksgiving," Dani put in from her perch on one of the stools at the breakfast bar. "Why are you home so early?" she asked Jason.

"No swim practice today," he replied, reaching over his mom's head and pulling down a stack of china plates. "Sorry I forgot to tell you. I would've given you a ride, but you were already gone."

"Maria drove Kristy and me home. She got her license last weekend," Danielle said. "Isn't that awesome?"

"Sure. It means less time as the Danielle taxi service for me." Jason took down the gravy boat and handed it to his mother.

Dani ignored him. "Anyway, on the way home we stopped at Peet's Coffee and ran into Maggie Roy. She said Zach Lafrenière is having a huge party Friday night. It's his eighteenth birthday."

"Huh," Jason said. He realized that that was probably what Zach and Brad had been talking about at school. He had to smile, thinking how he'd assumed some top-secret, hush-hush vampire business was going down when they were really just planning a party.

"You're going, right?" Dani asked.

"I guess. First I've heard about it," Jason said.

"Well, Jason might be going, but you aren't," his mother told Dani.

Danielle's mouth dropped open. "You are *not* going to keep me away from the best party of the entire year!"

"Oh yes, I am," Mrs. Freeman replied. "You know how I feel about DeVere Heights parties. The kids here seem to have a new one every week, and you tell me every time that it's going to be the best party ever."

"Yeah, but this one really will be," Dani argued. "Tell her, Jason."

Jason shrugged. "Zach is the most popular guy at school," he told his mom.

"Then I'm sure he won't miss you at his birthday party," Mrs. Freeman said. "He'll have plenty of friends to help him celebrate."

"But—"

"No, Danielle. It scares me too much. I don't even really like Jason going," Mrs. Freeman said. "Not since that yacht incident."

Dani fell silent for a moment. Jason knew she'd been as freaked out as he was by what happened at Belle Rémy's yacht party a few months back. A girl, Carrie, had fallen overboard and washed up on the beach the next day, dead. Jason remembered it all too well—he'd been the one to find the body.

Mrs. Freeman had pretty much changed her party-going rules a minute later. And she didn't even know the truth about what had happened at the yacht party. If she did, she wouldn't have stopped at keeping Dani home from the parties, Jason thought. Even locking Dani in her room for a few years wouldn't be enough—she'd probably drag the whole family back to Michigan without second thought. Because the dead girl hadn't drowned the way everybody thought: Carrie had been the rogue vampire's unfortunate victim.

That was Jason's introduction to the vampires—a murderer on the loose, filled with a bloodlust that drove him mad. Sienna had told Jason that the vampire community strictly forbade its members to take the life of a human. And Zach had ended up killing the rogue to stop him from murdering again. Jason had believed them when they said there would be no more murders, when they said the DeVere Heights vampires only took a little blood from their human friends.

But that didn't mean he was okay with it.

Every party he'd gone to in DeVere Heights had hosted an orgy of vampire feeding. The vampires supplied plenty of alcohol and some seriously upscale surroundings. And then they seduced their human peers with their glamour and charisma. In the process, the vampires drank human blood. But the humans never remembered. They barely even noticed. All they knew was that they'd had an amazing time—partying.

Jason knew how it felt—he'd been bitten by a vampire. It hadn't hurt, and he'd been deliriously happy for hours afterward. A little chemical bonus. If that feeling could be put into pill form, the world would be addicted. He also knew that the vampires had to feed in order to live. He understood all of it. But he still didn't want to be a vampire's dinner, and he didn't want his sister to be either.

"Jason, are you going to help me out here?" Danielle asked, breaking into his thoughts.

"Uh . . . no," he said. "Sorry. Those parties do get wild." *And you might get bitten,* he added silently.

Dani rolled her eyes. "I can't believe this. You've all turned into a bunch of conservative little grannies."

"Well, that doesn't sound like much fun," said a gravelly voice from the hallway. Jason turned to see his aunt Bianca pulling a rolling suitcase in from the front door.

"Bee!" Mrs. Freeman squealed, sounding just like Dani when she greeted one of her friends. She ran over and threw her arms around her sister.

Dani laughed, and Jason knew why: Aunt Bianca was definitely not a "Bee." Bee was a cute little girl with pigtails. And Aunt Bianca was, well, stunning. Tall and slim, she had straight dark hair that hung down her back, and big, deep blue eyes. While Jason thought his mom was pretty—in an all-American-mom sort of way—he knew Bianca was the real beauty of the family. Her all-black designer outfit with a knee-length trench coat and high-heeled black boots didn't hurt. She looked like she'd stepped out of a fashion magazine. Maybe if his mom put on those boots . . . but Jason couldn't even imagine it.

"Hey, big sis," Bianca said, hugging Mrs. Freeman. She pulled away and looked her up and down. "You look exactly the same." Bianca glanced over at Jason and Dani and gave them a grin. "But these two have gone California on us! Jason, I've never seen your hair so blond."

He went over to kiss her hello. "It's the sun," he said. "It's *always* sunny here."

"So you like Malibu?" she asked.

"Definitely."

"He fits right in," Danielle added, coming to greet Bianca. "He's already learning to surf."

Bianca laughed. "And how about you?" she asked Danielle. "Are you adjusting?"

Dani shrugged. "I have a few friends."

"You have about twenty friends," Jason corrected her.

"Yeah, but who knows how long I'll be able to keep them if I'm never allowed to leave the house!" Danielle replied, with a pointed look at their mother.

Bianca raised her eyebrows. "Does this have anything to do with the old-grannies comment?"

"You showed up in the middle of a battle. Clash of the generations," Mrs. Freeman explained.

"She won't let me go to a party—," Dani began.

"But we're not going to bore you with the details,"

Mrs. Freeman interrupted. She turned back to Bianca. "How long are you in town?"

"A week or two," Bianca replied, taking a seat at the breakfast bar.

"Are you going to see any movie stars?" Dani asked. Aunt Bianca worked as a casting director and frequently dealt with big-name actors. Even though she lived in New York City, her job required her to fly back and forth to Los Angeles several times a year. She kept an office in L.A.

"I might," Bianca said, her eyes twinkling. "In fact, it would be helpful if you could come along and act as my assistant at some of the meetings."

"Oh, my God! I would *love* to," Dani cried. "Thank you." She threw her arms around Aunt Bianca, and Jason felt himself relax a little. Two minutes with Bianca, and Dani's foul mood had evaporated. Jason was glad their aunt would be with them all weekend— it might even mean he would manage to get to Zach's party without a major scene from his sister.

"So when do I get the grand tour?" Bianca asked when Dani released her. "I hope you guys like the house. Stefan always said DeVere Heights was the only place to live in Malibu."

Mrs. Freeman smiled sympathetically. "It's your first Thanksgiving without him," she said softly. "How are you holding up?"

Jason knew that Bianca and Stefan had fallen in love pretty much at first sight. Even though Stefan had been a good twenty years older than Bianca, she had been completely and genuinely devoted to him. Jason had to admit that the few times he had met Stefan, the guy certainly hadn't behaved like a sixty-something. He was handsome, intelligent, and witty, and Bianca had taken his death—in a nasty traffic accident—pretty hard.

Bianca's smile faltered. "It's tough, Tania," she admitted. "But being here with all of you really helps."

Mrs. Freeman nodded. "Well, let's show you around, then."

Jason grabbed his aunt's suitcase. "I'll put this up in the guest room," he said. "I don't need the tour." *What I need is some time to get over my idiotic behavior with Sienna,* he thought as he headed for the stairs. He had a feeling it wouldn't be easy. He might have to start with a nice lobotomy.

"I'm going to start you off with the worst one, just to get it over with," Adam said after school the next day. "Now I want you to be prepared. It's bad. It's very, very bad."

"Then why do I have to see it at all?" Jason asked. He swung his locker door shut and took a moment to silently appreciate the lack of textbooks to drag home.

Thanksgiving weekend equaled no homework. Nothing but relaxation for the next four days. And food.

"Even the worst Kubrick is better than ninety percent of the crap that most people like," Adam replied. "Besides, there's an orgy in *Eyes Wide Shut*."

"Why didn't you just say so?" Jason joked. "There's no such thing as a bad orgy." He led the way out to the front courtyard. A few guys were playing Frisbee on the lawn, and a mini traffic jam choked the road near the gates from the parking lot. Everybody wanted to get out of school and start enjoying the holiday weekend.

"Freeman!" Michael Van Dyke came charging past, smacking Jason on the shoulder as he ran. "See you Friday."

"Zach's birthday soirée?" Adam asked, watching Van Dyke sprint for his Hummer. "You going?"

"I guess," Jason replied. "Brad and Sienna both told me I *had* to go." In fact, that was the only thing Sienna had said to him at all today. She hadn't exactly avoided him, but she also hadn't made eye contact even once. Was she thinking about their near-kiss from yesterday? Was she *relieved* that it hadn't happened—or disappointed? He couldn't tell. But if he went to Zach's party, at least he'd have another chance to talk to her.

"You think it'll be a typical vampire-fest?" Adam asked, lowering his voice.

"I'm expecting a little more from Lafrenière."

"Fair enough." Adam grinned. "But I don't need anything fancy. Cold beer and hot girls, that's it!"

Jason knew the vampire parties could be relied upon to provide all that in style. And this being Zach's eighteenth birthday bash, who knew what other amusements might be served up?

Although, Jason reflected, he'd be even more psyched for the party if he didn't know that the humans would be part of the buffet. He still found it unsettling. Even with the whole no-harm—no-foul setup. And even though Sienna and Zach had assured him that no other vampires would succumb to bloodlust, he had a hard time letting go of his suspicion. Who knew what made a vampire cross the line? Maybe it was like becoming an alcoholic. One day a couple of drinks just weren't enough. One day just a taste of blood would lead to more and more and—

"Jason, look out!" Adam cried.

A strong arm wrapped itself around Jason's neck.

THREE

Instinctively, Jason grabbed the guy's forearm, yanked it down, and threw his own weight forward. The guy stumbled to the side, releasing Jason to regain his own balance.

Jason crouched, prepared to fight. He remembered all too well what it was like to fight a vampire with superhuman strength. He had to be ready. . . .

"Dude, chill!" his opponent cried.

Jason squinted into the bright sunshine, trying to make out the guy's face. "Tyler?"

"This how you say hello in California?" Tyler laughed, holding up his hand for a high five.

Jason laughed in amazement to see his old friend standing there. "What the hell are you doing here?" he demanded, slapping Tyler's hand.

"Visiting. Duh," Tyler said cheerfully.

Jason shook off his surprise and reached out to hug his friend. He hadn't seen Tyler in months.

"Somebody want to explain all this male bonding?" Adam asked.

Jason stepped back and grinned. "Adam Turnball, Tyler Deegan."

Adam held out a hand. "First friend in Malibu," he said.

Tyler shook. "First friend in kindergarten," he replied.

Adam whistled. "You totally win. Although Jason and I don't throw down every time we see each other."

"Yeah, what was that about?" Tyler asked, rubbing his arm as he turned back to Jason. "You're pretty jumpy for a mellow California dude."

"Sorry," Jason said. "I was just thinking . . . well, I, uh, got into a fight a while ago, and when you grabbed me . . ."

"Say no more. I will not try the sneak-attack hello on you ever again." Tyler glanced around, his brown eyes wide. "The guy in the 7-Eleven gave me directions to the school, but I thought he must be wrong. This place is awesome!"

"You're not kidding," Jason agreed. "The cafeteria has an ocean-view terrace."

"You mean you don't have that in Michigan?" Adam teased. "Do you at least have a *glacier*-view terrace?"

Tyler snorted. "It's cold, but it's not *that* cold. Can't compete with this, though." He glanced around again, and Jason took the opportunity to check out Tyler's jeans and well-worn Detroit Pistons T-shirt. He had a dark blue hoodie tied around his waist, and his curly dark hair was longer than Jason had ever seen it. He also had at least three days' worth of stubble on his chin.

He looks like crap, Jason thought with a twinge of concern for his old friend.

Tyler turned and caught him staring. "Admiring my new tat?" he asked, lifting his arm to show off a fake tattoo of Tweety Bird in garish yellow.

Adam laughed. "What'd you do, hit the gumball machine jackpot?"

"You know it," Tyler said. "This was my prize. And there was a little kid watching, so I had to put it on." He rubbed at the temporary tattoo with his finger. Tweety's face didn't budge. "I can't get the damn thing off."

Jason had been friends with Tyler long enough to know when he was putting on an act. And right now, he going all out for an Oscar in "funny and normal." But the stubble and the long hair and the showing up randomly in California—not so normal.

"Where's your gear? Let's get it in my car. Or did you drive out here?"

Tyler held out his thumb.

"You *hitched*?" Adam yelped. "All the way from Michigan?"

"Yep. I caught a ride with this one dude I know who took me through three states—a trucker," Tyler said. "Then I just hitched the rest of the way. I'm short on cash, so no first-class flights for me."

"You're here. That's what matters," Jason answered.

"I figured I'd crash your Thanksgiving. I couldn't stop thinking about your mom's pumpkin pie. It's like I could smell it from home and it just lured me out here. Think your parents will mind?"

"They'll probably kick me out of my room and give you my bed!" Jason said, slapping Tyler on the back. "They love your ass." Jason knew why Tyler didn't want to do the holiday thing in Michigan. His parents had gone through a nasty divorce a year or so before. Now it was just Tyler and his dad in the house, and Jason knew things weren't too happy. No pie there, to say the least. "There's plenty of room," Jason added. "Our new place is pretty big."

"Understatement. His house is ginormous," Adam volunteered. "He's just being modest."

"That's my boy," Tyler replied. "Freeman has always been impressively self-deprecating."

Adam waved his hand dismissively. "It's all an act," he joked. "What I find impressive is thumbing your way across half the country. That's a lost art, my man. Very Kerouac of you."

Tyler shot Jason a questioning look, and Jason laughed. "Pay no attention to the Adam-isms. Half the time nobody really knows *what* he's talking about."

"And that's just the way I like it," Adam agreed. "It keeps people off-guard. So listen, Jason and I were heading to my place for a movie-viewing-plus-pizza-snarfing party. You in?"

"Sounds good," Tyler said. He clapped Jason on the back and headed off with Adam as if they'd been friends for years.

It's good to see him, Jason thought, smiling as he watched his old friend. He realized Tyler hadn't said anything about gear. He didn't even seem to have a backpack. Jason figured he must have left in a hurry. He hoped it wasn't because things were bad—well, worse than usual—at home.

"You wanna tell me what the hell that movie was supposed to be?" Tyler asked on the way home from Adam's that evening.

"Who knows?" Jason replied. "Adam says Stanley Kubrick is the greatest director of all time and that his movies are required viewing, even the bad ones."

"Huh." Tyler thought about it for a moment. "People in L.A. are clearly bizarre."

"Can't argue with that," Jason agreed. *And you don't know the best part,* he thought ruefully. The image of Sienna's face leaped into Jason's mind, and he shoved it away. He'd gotten used to doing that since he'd met her. But it was harder than usual today, because of the memory of the kiss that didn't happen. "Hey, when did you leave Michigan?" he asked, forcing his mind away from Sienna. "Why didn't you call me before you came?"

"I did," Tyler said. "I thought you Californians all had your cell phones surgically attached to your ears, but you didn't even pick up."

Jason took the turn through the tall iron gates of DeVere Heights. "When did you call?"

"Just yesterday," Tyler said. "Thought I'd give you a heads up, but when you didn't answer, I figured I'd just surprise you."

I can't believe it, Jason thought. *Tyler is the one who called when I was about to kiss Sienna.* Somehow, everything seemed to come back to Sienna. "I didn't get to my cell in time, sorry," he said. "And I didn't recognize the number. It wasn't the Fraser area code."

"Yeah, I got a new cell," Tyler told him. "It's from where my mom lives now, in Chicago."

"You've been staying with your mom?" Jason asked, surprised.

"Nah. I went to see her a couple of months ago, but she was mostly busy with her new boyfriend." Tyler drummed his fingers nervously on his lap, and Jason could hear the bitterness in his voice. Tyler still hadn't forgiven his mom for leaving. "But hey, she sprang for a brand-new phone and I don't have to pay the bills. So it's all good."

Jason didn't know what to say. Obviously it wasn't all good. But they were Tyler's issues to deal with, and he didn't want to make things any harder on his old friend.

Tyler let out a long sigh and leaned his head back against the seat.

"How long have you been on the road?" Jason asked. "It must've taken days to get here."

"Only two days," Tyler said. "I got lucky. Guess I don't look so much like a serial killer that people won't pick me up."

"You look more like a serial killer than usual," Jason told him with a grin. "I know Coach Salzman isn't letting you in the pool with that hair."

"Nah, I quit the team," Tyler said. "The relay was lame without you, anyway."

Jason was too surprised to answer. He and Tyler had been on the swim team together since seventh grade. Despite Tyler's new situation, Jason wouldn't have guessed he would change so much. Although . . . Jason couldn't stop himself from thinking about what had happened the last time he saw his friend. When the Freemans had left Fraser, Tyler was pretty messed up.

"I know what you're thinking," Tyler said.

"What are you, psychic now?" Jason joked.

"No, I just know you. You're thinking about what happened," Tyler said. "At your going-away party."

"Yeah." Jason slowed as they approached his street. "Well . . ."

"Look, I screwed up," Tyler said. "I know I did. But I didn't think . . . I mean, I thought I could still show up and you'd be happy to see me. Am I wrong?"

"Of course you're not wrong," Jason replied. "But you took my *car*, man! And you drove around stoned. You could've totaled it—or, even worse, yourself or somebody else."

"I know, but I didn't," Tyler said. "The car was fine, and nobody got hurt. It was a stupid thing to do and it will never happen again. Okay?"

"Okay," Jason replied, feeling relieved to have gotten that little issue off his chest. He pulled to a stop in the driveway and turned off the engine. The house glowed welcomingly in front of them, its lights shining brightly against the dark November sky. Dani was pacing back and forth on the porch, talking on her cell phone. None of them got very good reception inside. "This is it. *Mi casa es su casa* and all that," Jason said with a smile.

Tyler reached for the car door handle, then hesitated. "I just want you to know . . . I don't hang with those guys anymore—the ones I brought to your party. And as for the drugs? Well, let's just say I could do one of those public service announcements and be all 'my life is perfect now that I'm clean.'"

Jason laughed, but he doubted "perfect" accurately described his friend's life. He knew Tyler wouldn't have shown up in Malibu without a single change of clothes otherwise. He couldn't help wondering if Tyler was hiding something.

"Holy cow, is that Danielle Who Smells?" Tyler suddenly bellowed. He bolted from the car and rushed toward the house.

"Oh, my God!" Jason heard Dani squeal. "Kristy, gotta go." She hung up her cell and flung her arms around Tyler. "Ty the Spy!"

Jason laughed as he headed up the driveway. Dani and Tyler had given each other dumb nicknames when they were all little kids. Tyler picked Dani up and spun her around, and Dani laughed like a maniac. Jason knew Tyler had been her very first crush when she was little. And though she had long grown out of that, she still looked psyched to see him again. He was kind of like a second big brother to her, and Tyler had always treated her like his kid sister.

He's probably missed the whole family since we moved, Jason realized as he watched them. After his parents' divorce, Tyler had spent a lot of time at the Freemans' house. They were more of a family to him than his real one. So it made sense that he'd want to come to them for Thanksgiving. Maybe it was as simple as that, Jason thought, running up to the porch to join Tyler and Dani. Maybe Tyler didn't have anything to hide at all.

FOUR

"Get out of the bathroom!" Dani yelled the next morning. "Jason!"

Jason pulled open his bedroom door, blinking against the bright morning sunshine, to see his sister waiting near the bathroom at the end of the hallway, yawning. Her hair was in a messy ponytail, and she wore her baggy Paul Frank pajamas with the monkeys on them. "I'm not in there," he called to her.

Dani glanced at him and frowned in confusion.

"It must be Tyler," he said.

Dani's eyes widened in horror and her hand flew to her hair. Without a word, she turned and ran back into her own room, slamming the door behind her. Jason chuckled. His sister was not a morning person—in her tired haze, she'd obviously forgotten Tyler was even there. He figured she'd be perfectly made up, washed, and blow-dried by the time she made another appearance.

Tyler stuck his head out of the bathroom door. "You need to get in here?" he asked Jason.

Jason stared at his friend. He looked seriously pale, with deep circles under his eyes. "Nah, I can wait," he said. Tyler nodded and disappeared back into the bathroom.

Shaking his head, Jason retreated into his bedroom. Whatever was going on with Tyler, a good night's sleep hadn't solved it. The dude still looked like crap.

But by breakfast time, Tyler seemed to have rebounded. He was busy helping Mrs. Freeman mix pancake batter when Jason came into the kitchen.

". . . and Mr. Ruck tripped and knocked over the whole podium," he was saying.

Jason's mom dissolved into laughter. "I always hated that guy," she remarked. "Ever since we were on the same PTA committee, when you and Jason were in third grade."

"'Morning," Jason said, heading to the fridge for some OJ.

"Happy Thanksgiving," his mom replied. She grabbed his arm as he passed her and spun him away from the refrigerator. "We're all sitting down to eat together this morning. I don't want you doing your typical orange juice and banana on the run."

"She's showing off for Aunt Bianca. I'm even supposed to put out the good coffee cups," Danielle said from the dining room, where she was setting the table. As Jason had expected, she was fully dressed and looking perfect.

"I am not showing off," Mrs. Freeman said, handing Jason a basket full of muffins and pointing to the table.

He dutifully carried the muffins over and set them down. "Yes, she is," he murmured to Dani.

"Totally," Dani laughed.

"Your aunt Bianca is here?" Tyler asked from the counter. "How come I didn't see her last night?"

"She had to go to the office for some last-minute thing," Mrs. Freeman replied. "She didn't get back until almost midnight."

"Weird," Jason said. "Doesn't everyone try to cut out early the day before Thanksgiving?"

"Not in her job," Dani put in. "Dealing with all those high-powered, demanding Hollywood peeps."

"My ears are burning," Bianca said, appearing in the kitchen. "Are you talking about me behind my back?"

"Only good things," Jason assured her. "I think Dani wants to have your job after college."

"Oh, I hope not," Mrs. Freeman said. Aunt Bianca gave her an arch look, and Mrs. Freeman shrugged. "No offense, Bee, but wrangling celebs isn't exactly—"

"Boring?" Dani interrupted. "I'd love to be a star-creator like Aunt Bianca. With one place in New York and another in California. Traveling all over." She sat down at the table and grabbed a muffin.

"That's my girl," Aunt Bianca laughed. "Be adventurous."

"Do you have a place out here?" Tyler asked, coming to sit next to Dani.

"I don't, actually," Bianca replied. "My late husband had a home in Malibu, but I sold it after he died. It made me sad to be there."

Tyler nodded sympathetically. "That's tough."

"Besides, I don't need a place here anymore. I can always stay with my big sis," Bianca said, grinning at Mrs. Freeman. "And if she gets sick of me, my company will put me up in a hotel."

"I'd take the Beverly Hilton over our house any day," Dani commented.

"Me, too, if somebody else is paying," Jason's dad called from the stairway. "Did I miss breakfast?"

"Nope. The pancakes are ready, so everybody sit," Mrs. Freeman replied.

Jason and his father sat across from Dani and Tyler, and his mom and aunt took the ends. Looking back and forth between them, Jason noted again how different the two women were. Somehow he'd never noticed it before. It was more than just their looks, though Bianca's dark hair was nothing like his mother's short blond bob. They also had strikingly different attitudes toward life. His mom was, well, a *mom*—in a good way, of course. But Bianca always acted like she was still just a kid herself. *Well, she is a bit younger than Mom,* Jason thought.

He took a look at Bianca's sweater-and-jeans ensemble. The outfit would've looked normal on his mother, but on Bianca, it seemed über-stylish. It reminded him of Sienna's comment about his aunt's fashion sense.

"Hey, Aunt Bianca, do you know Sienna Devereux?" he asked suddenly.

She looked at him in surprise. So did Dani and Tyler.

"Who's Sienna Devereux?" Tyler asked. Dani just widened her eyes in her usual, gossip-detecting way.

"A girl at school," Jason said, aware of the blush slowly creeping across his cheeks. He cleared his throat. "My friend Brad's girlfriend."

"Hmm . . . The name sounds familiar," Aunt Bianca said. "Stefan knew the Devereuxs, of course. I probably met her once or twice. Why do you ask?"

"Just wondering," Jason said. "She mentioned that she'd met you. Said she likes the way you dress."

"Oh, well, in that case, I love her already," Bianca joked.

"Jason does too," Danielle teased. Jason tossed a muffin at her.

"So, Tyler, how long are you staying?" Aunt Bianca asked. "Do you have to be back for school on Monday?"

Tyler kept his eyes on the pancakes he was smothering with syrup. "Uh . . . technically. But I can skip a day or two. I'm a senior."

"When did that become an excuse for cutting class?" Mr. Freeman asked.

Tyler finally looked up, and Jason thought he saw a hint of annoyance in his friend's eyes. But it disappeared immediately, and Tyler grinned. "They're giving SAT practice tests next week. I already took the SATs, so I don't have to go."

"Sweet," Jason said. Although when he was at their old school, they certainly hadn't spent days giving SAT practice tests. Apparently, things had changed.

But as his family continued to chat with his old friend, Jason kept his thoughts to himself. Tyler had always been a favorite with the Freemans. Jason hadn't told his parents about the driving-while-stoned episode from last year. He hadn't told Dani, either.

All that was in the past, and that's where Jason planned to leave it.

"Danielle Who Smells, why aren't you up here playing?" Tyler called a few hours later. "Jason's too much of a lightweight to be any fun. Look at him all panting and stuff."

Jason shook his head. They'd only been shooting

hoops for fifteen minutes and he wasn't even out of breath. Neither was Tyler, which was a little weird. The guy had looked so exhausted this morning that Jason had figured they were in for a day of sitting in front of the TV while his mom puttered around getting everything ready for the big dinner. But Tyler had gotten a second wind.

"I'd rather lounge," Dani answered from her chaise next to the pool. She'd decked herself out in a bikini and a pair of big sunglasses. "Besides, isn't it called one-on-one?"

"Well, yeah, if you're going to get all literal on me," Tyler grumbled good-naturedly.

Danielle turned back to her reading, some chick-lit book with a drawing of a woman in a tight dress on the front.

"You're just trying to distract me from kicking your ass," Jason said. "It won't work."

"We'll see." Tyler dribbled the ball toward the hoop mounted on the pool house wall, ducking and spinning to avoid Jason's coverage. He took a shot—and scored, nothing but net. Tyler did a little victory dance, getting in Jason's face.

"I'm still winning, jackass," Jason pointed out.

Tyler laughed and passed the ball to Jason.

The pool house door opened, and Bianca came out dressed in a black bathing suit and sandals with little cherries on the toes. "Time out," she called. "I don't want to get hit by any flying basketballs."

"Wimp," Jason teased, and she made a face at him as she crossed the court. "I have to warn you," he added, lowering his voice, "that Dani's going to spend the whole day trying to convince you to talk Mom into letting her go to the party."

"I'm afraid she'll be disappointed, then." Bianca sighed. "I've never been able to talk your mother into anything."

"I can't believe you guys have a pool house," Tyler commented as Bianca made her way across the grass toward Dani. "Hell, I can't even believe you have a pool!"

"It's pretty weird," Jason agreed. "Almost as weird as being able to sit around in a bathing suit in November."

Tyler watched Bianca settle into one of the chaises. "Dude, your aunt is *hot*," he said, dropping his voice to a whisper.

Jason rolled his eyes. "She's my *aunt*, loser," he replied. "You can't call her hot in front of me."

"I'm just saying." Tyler grinned. "She's not *my* aunt."

Jason tossed the ball at him—hard. "She's, like, forty-two," he said. "I think you're a little too young for her."

"Forty-two?" Tyler repeated. "Are you serious? She looks amazing."

Jason glanced over at Bianca. She did look pretty good for her age, now that he thought about it.

"Plastic surgery?" Tyler asked.

"I don't know," Jason admitted. "Maybe. People out here seem to think it's normal to get all kinds of lifts and tucks and liposuction. And she does work in Hollywood. It's all about the image."

"Huh." Tyler took a lazy shot at the basket and missed. From inside the pool house came a loud crash. "What was that?" Tyler cried.

"Probably just the pool guy," Jason said. "Dad asked him to come by today. He wanted to give him a tip for Thanksgiving." He crossed over to the pool house door and pulled it open. Joe, the pool guy, was trying to maneuver the skimmer out of the crowded supplies closet next to the bathroom.

"Need some help?" Jason asked.

"No, I got it," Joe replied. "Sorry about the noise, I just knocked over all the vacuum hoses. I'm really out of it today."

"No problem," Jason said. "You don't need to clean the pool on Thanksgiving, though. My dad just wanted to say thanks."

"I know," Joe said. "But I figured while I'm here I might as well skim out the leaves. It'll only take a second."

"You're a perfectionist," Jason joked as the guy

headed out with the skimmer. He knocked into a palm tree with the long handle and laughed, shaking his head.

"I think he's had a few Turkey Day beers," Tyler murmured.

Jason chuckled. "Game on," he said, grabbing the ball from Tyler. He shot and scored, but Tyler was close behind, immediately making another basket. Jason played harder, and for a while, the only sounds were from the ball hitting the ground or the wall.

When Danielle and Bianca appeared nearby, Jason jumped. He'd been concentrating so hard that he hadn't even seen them get up from the lounge chairs.

"Mind if we walk through?" Dani asked, nodding toward the pool house door. "We need dry towels."

Tyler held up his hands. "I need a breather, anyway," he said.

"What's wrong with your towels?" Jason asked.

Danielle grinned, glanced over her shoulder, and lowered her voice. "Joe dropped the skimmer in the water and totally splashed them," she said, amused. "He was so busy staring at Aunt Bianca that he almost fell in the pool himself!"

Bianca nudged her toward the pool house. "Quiet, he'll hear you! And *you're* the one he was looking at, young lady."

They disappeared inside, still talking.

"Shouldn't we be helping your mother with dinner?" Tyler asked. "She's been cooking all day."

"Go ahead and try to set foot in the kitchen. I dare you," Jason said. "It's a Thanksgiving tradition: Mom cooks about twenty different things at once while Dad spends the whole day on the turkey. Every year they almost burn the house down, but they love it."

"Sounds romantic," Tyler said flatly.

Jason grimaced. He'd forgotten about the animosity between Tyler's parents. His friend probably didn't want to hear cute stories about happily married couples. "You want to play anymore?" he asked, trying to change the subject.

"I think I'm done. This sun is too strong." Tyler pulled off his T-shirt and mopped his sweaty face with it. "Besides, I'm winning," he added with a grin.

"No wonder you want to stop," Jason joked.

Dani pushed open the door and stepped out with a new towel wrapped around her waist. Bianca followed, wearing shorts and a gauzy top. "I'm going to head inside for a bit," she said. "I've got some calls to make for work." She left them with a little wave.

"Still want that job?" Jason asked his sister. "Working on Thanksgiving?"

But Dani ignored him. She was staring at Tyler's chest. "What happened to you?" she asked. "You're covered in bruises."

Jason glanced at his friend in surprise. Danielle was right. The entire left side of Tyler's rib cage was covered in the sickly yellowish marks of bruises that were starting to heal.

"Oh. It's . . . uh . . . it's nothing," Tyler replied, quickly pulling his T-shirt back on to cover the bruising.

"Did you get mugged or something while you were hitching here?" Jason asked, thinking that it would explain Tyler's lack of clothes and belongings.

"Are you kidding?" Tyler put on one of his patented megawatt grins. "Who would mug someone as sweet as me?" He jumped up and grabbed the ball, passing it to Jason energetically. "Let's go, man, game on!"

He's trying to distract us from the bruises, Jason thought. *What is up with him?* "I thought you were done," he said aloud.

"I have a few more spectacular shots in me," Tyler replied. "Unless I've hurt your pride too much already."

"No more basketball," Mrs. Freeman called from the French doors that led into the living room. "Dinner's in an hour. Everyone get ready."

"Get ready?" Tyler repeated. "Is this a dress-up thing?" He took a dubious sniff at his sweat-covered T-shirt.

"I don't know about dress-up, but it's definitely not a smelly T-shirt affair," Danielle replied, laughing.

Tyler looked dismayed, and Jason grinned. "Don't worry, I can spot you some threads."

"Thanks." Tyler followed Jason into the house. "We never do the whole big Thanksgiving thing. My dad's version of giving thanks is eating turkey in front of the tube so he doesn't miss any football games."

"How is your dad?" Jason asked tentatively. After the divorce, Tyler hadn't wanted to talk about his parents at all. Maybe he was starting to deal with it a little now.

"Who knows? I barely see the guy," Tyler replied. "I spend as little time at home as I can. I can't wait for graduation so I can get out of there."

Jason didn't know what to say. It seemed like Tyler's home life was worse than ever. He noticed Danielle shooting Tyler a sympathetic look as they climbed the stairs to the second floor. He never understood why, but girls seemed to like troubled guys.

"I'm thinking green-and-orange-striped polo shirt for you," he said, "with maybe a pair of plaid golf pants."

"You wish," Tyler replied, seeming relieved at the change of subject.

"Hey, you have no clothes. You're at my mercy," Jason warned. When they reached the upstairs hallway, he turned toward his bedroom. "Let me just grab some stuff."

Tyler and Dani headed down the hall toward their rooms while Jason pulled a pair of khakis and a blue button-down shirt from his closet. He snagged a pair of jeans and a few T-shirts, too. If Tyler was going to be here all weekend, he'd need more than just one change of clothes. He took them down to the guest room where Tyler was staying.

The door was open, so Jason went in. Tyler was standing over by the window, cell phone to his ear. Probably listening to a voice mail, Jason figured. He dumped the clothes on the bed and turned to leave. His sneaker tangled in Tyler's hoodie, which was lying on the floor near the foot of the bed, and Jason nearly tripped. He bent to pick up the sweatshirt, and a pre-scription pill bottle tumbled out of the pocket, so he swooped back down to grab that, too. "Sorry, man," he said, tossing the hoodie on top of the other clothes on the bed.

He reached out to put the pills on the dresser so they wouldn't get lost. But as Jason glanced down at the bottle in his hand, he paused to take a closer look.

The name on the label wasn't Tyler's.

FIVE

"What are you doing?" Tyler snapped, his voice tense.

Jason turned to find his friend off the phone. "Sorry," he said again. "I tripped on your hoodie and almost kicked your pills across the room." He tossed the bottle to Tyler. "I didn't want you to lose them."

"Thanks." Tyler quickly shoved the bottle into the pocket of his jeans.

"What are they for?" Jason asked. "You sick?"

"No, they're just, uh, painkillers," Tyler replied, frowning.

"For the bruises?" Jason pushed. He knew Tyler didn't appreciate the questions, but he wasn't about to back down. His friend was walking around with someone else's pills, hitching across the country with no supplies, and covered in bruises. He'd have to be blind or stupid not to notice that something was wrong.

"Yeah." Tyler clearly didn't intend to elaborate, but Jason held his gaze until finally Tyler sighed. "I got banged up a week or so ago, and the doctor gave me some pills for the pain."

"Banged up how?" Jason asked.

"Playing football," Tyler said. "You know how it is."

"Not really," Jason replied. "I don't play football. Neither do you."

Tyler just stared at him for a moment, busted. Tyler was a swimmer, not a football player. They had that in common—both liked watching a good game on the weekend, but neither one of them liked to play. "Yeah, well, that's why I got banged up," Tyler said at last. "I suck." He smiled nervously, clearly wondering whether Jason would buy it.

Jason frowned. He knew Tyler was lying about the bruises and pills being prescribed for him. But why? He'd come all the way to Malibu to see Jason—why not tell him the truth? "Look, Ty . . . ," Jason began.

"Do you seriously have a shirt from Disneyland?" Tyler interrupted, grabbing one of the T-shirts from the bed. "What are you, five years old?"

Jason stifled a sigh. Clearly, Tyler was determined not to talk about anything serious. But then, maybe that was just what he needed: a break—a vacation from his problems back home. It worried Jason that his friend was taking medication that had been prescribed for somebody else, but it wasn't any of his business—unless Tyler wanted it to be. And right now, he obviously didn't.

"They were giving them out for free at an Angels

game," Jason explained. "Besides, that shirt would be pretty big on a five-year-old."

Tyler chuckled. "Thanks for the loan. Guess I better shower before dinner, huh?"

"Good luck getting in there before Dani!" Jason laughed, heading for the door. "See you downstairs."

"Everything looks amazing, Mrs. F," Tyler said as they all sat down around the dining room table. Jason agreed. His mom had made the place look like a TV special on the perfect Thanksgiving holiday.

The table was decked out with all the new linens and china Jason's mother had bought when they moved to California. It had a less wintry feel than their dining room in Michigan had. Here, everything, in shades of light green or blue, felt summery. Even the candles in the middle of the table were blue and smelled like the ocean.

"Thank you, Tyler," Mrs. Freeman said. "I only hope the food lives up to it."

"Don't pretend to be all modest," Aunt Bianca told her sister with a smile. "You know you're a great cook."

"I'm sure it's not up to your standards," Mrs. Freeman replied. She turned to Tyler. "My little sister only eats in the best restaurants in New York and L.A."

Bianca rolled her eyes. "I just don't see the point in cooking myself when other people do it so much better."

Jason knew his mom and his aunt always bickered to some degree, but the sisters seemed to be getting on each other's nerves a little more than usual during this visit. Jason glanced at Dani, who shrugged.

"Here's the main event," Mr. Freeman said, coming in from the kitchen with the turkey on a platter. He placed it down in the center of the table. "Should I carve now or wait until everyone's had their salad?"

"No salad for me," Jason said. "I like to get right to the meat."

"Me too," Tyler seconded.

Jason's dad nodded. "Okay, I'll carve now."

"Why don't we let Jason carve?" Bianca suggested. "He's a big, strapping man now. Let him take over the carving duties."

Dani almost spit out her mouthful of water, and Tyler laughed out loud.

"'A big, strapping man'? Freeman?" he teased.

Even Jason had to laugh. "That's okay, Aunt Bianca. I don't need to carve a turkey to feel like a man," he said reassuringly.

But Jason noticed that Bianca actually looked a little put out at having her suggestion dismissed so lightly. Maybe that was why, with a slight tone of irritation, she said, "I just think it's time we stopped treating you like a child. You're almost done with school. Soon you'll have to start making your own decisions."

"Well, that's true. I guess you're right and I'd better get some practice in by carving the turkey," Jason said with a smile. He knew Tyler and Danielle would make fun of him for the rest of the weekend, but he wanted to lighten the atmosphere. He stood up, took the carving knife from his dad, and got to work.

Aunt Bianca shook her head. "Can you believe how grown up he is?" she asked Jason's parents. "Dani, too. In a few years they'll be off at college."

"Off at college," Dani repeated, nodding. "College—where there are lots of parties!"

Mrs. Freeman sighed. "Danielle—," she began.

"Mom," Dani interrupted. "Your guru, Dr. Phil, would say to let me go to Zach's. He'd say that I need experience dealing with parties while I'm still in the safety of my home, with my big brother to look after me."

Jason choked back a laugh. So Dani had resorted to invoking Dr. Phil. Well, it just might work.

"Dr. Phil doesn't have all the facts in this case," Mrs. Freeman answered.

"What facts does he need that—," Danielle began.

"End of discussion," Jason's mom said firmly.

"I'm getting flashes of us and Mom," Bianca commented lightly to her sister. "Remember how overprotective she always was? Remember how we used to have to sneak out and—"

"Looking back, I think she might have been right all along," Jason's mother said, cutting Bianca off sharply. Then her voice softened. "Maybe it's something you don't realize until you're a parent yourself. It wouldn't have hurt the two of us to listen to Mom a little more back then." She grinned. "Not that I'll tell her that anytime soon. I don't want to face an attack of the I-told-you-so's."

"You know, Stefan was friends with the Lafrenières for years," Bianca put in soothingly. "I'm sure you don't have to worry about Dani at their son's party." Jason knew Bianca was just trying to help Dani out, but he knew she had just pushed his mother a little too far.

"That's it," Mrs. Freeman snapped. "Danielle, I told you—no. Bee, this is none of your business!"

Jason glanced at Tyler. His friend looked seriously uncomfortable. The last thing he needed was a family feud at dinner—he'd had enough of that in his own house. Jason hoped Bianca would just let the party thing drop.

"You want Danielle to make friends with the right people, don't you?" Aunt Bianca pressed. "Well, the Lafrenières do more charity work than anyone else in Malibu! There are some valuable contacts to be made. You have to want that for Dani and Jason."

"Don't tell me what I 'have to want,'" Mrs. Freeman said, her voice rising. "The answer is no.

Those parties are too wild, and Danielle is not going."

Nobody spoke for a moment and Jason was afraid that the day would be completely ruined. The air held a weird energy. He didn't know where it was coming from, but everyone was on edge.

Bianca opened her mouth to say something else, but Danielle jumped in. "Don't worry. I'll just go to the movies or something on Friday," she volunteered quickly, her eyes darting between her mother and Bianca. Jason could see that she wished she'd never brought the party up at all. "It's no biggie. It's not like being refused the last scoop of mashed potatoes. They look great, by the way, Mom."

"Everything's great, Tania," Jason's dad agreed. "Let's enjoy it. It's Thanksgiving."

That was enough for Bianca to think better of whatever she'd been about to say. She nodded and fell silent.

"Well, I for one have a lot to be thankful for, this Thanksgiving," Tyler said, raising his glass of cider. "And I'd like to propose a toast to all of you, the Freemans. Thank you for including me in your Thanksgiving. You've always made me feel right at home, and today is no exception."

Jason's mom smiled, and Aunt Bianca chuckled. "You mean because we're willing to argue in front of you just like you're part of the family?"

"Exactly," Tyler said with a grin. Everybody laughed, relaxing for the first time since they'd taken their seats.

Jason shot his friend a grateful look. Tyler had always been able to charm anyone—from senior citizens to toddlers. This time he may have saved Thanksgiving.

"Okay, pass your plates for turkey," Jason announced. "And let's eat!"

"Sorry I mentioned the P word at dinner," Dani said later that night. She, Jason, and Tyler were heading upstairs for bed after they'd finished cleaning up the kitchen. "I didn't know it would set things off like that."

"You always used to go to parties back in Michigan," Tyler said. "What's the difference?"

"The parties are more out of control here. But I'll deny saying it if you try to quote me. Mom's parentnoid enough as it is," Dani answered, pulling her cell phone out of the pocket of her trendy shrunken blazer. She changed the faceplate every day, and today her cell was zebra-striped. "I'm going to call Billy. He's the only one I know who isn't going to Zach's. He'll come up with something fun for Friday night."

"Ooh, Billy," Tyler teased. "That your boyfriend?"

Dani rolled her eyes. "I still haven't picked out the lucky guy who gets to be my *boyfriend*," she answered. "But it definitely won't be Billy, because he's gay." She hit a speed-dial number on her cell. "What's up, Billy?" she asked, wandering toward her room.

"See you in the morning," Jason told Tyler. "Thanks for putting up with my family."

"You kidding? Your family should get an award for Most Functional Thanksgiving. Nobody even got close to throwing food or crying."

Jason laughed. "True. Although I think my mom might've lobbed the gravy at Aunt Bianca if she hadn't spent so much time making it." He slapped Tyler's hand and headed down the hall to his bedroom. The basketball combined with the huge dinner had made him sleepy, and he flung himself down on the bed fully dressed. He'd rest for a few minutes, wait for Dani and Tyler to use the bathroom, then go brush his teeth.

But he'd only been lying there for a minute or two when a noise at the window startled him—a soft bang, followed by silence, then another little bang. Almost like someone was tapping from outside. Jason got up and went over to peer out.

The moon, almost full, cast an eerie silver light over the backyard, reflecting up from the still surface of the pool. The carefully spaced potted trees around the back deck threw distorted shadows onto the ground. As Jason watched, one of them moved.

He leaned closer to the window, staring into the darkness as someone stepped out into the moonlight.

Silver light on sleek black hair. Pale, perfect skin, luminescent in the darkness. *Sienna.*

Jason threw open the window and leaned out.

"Hey, Michigan," Sienna called quietly. "Can I come up?"

Sienna was at his house, asking to climb up to his room. Jason felt as if he had died and gone to heaven. *Yeah,* he thought, *if heaven's like an episode of* Dawson's Creek*!* He glanced at the vine-covered trellis that rose from the back deck up to the top of the house. It ran about a foot to the left of his window and it would be pretty easy to climb, now that he thought about it. "Sure. Come on up. As long as you don't call me Dawson," he told Sienna.

She just gave him that slow, sly smile of hers, then put one slim hand on the bottom of the trellis and gracefully pulled herself up, shimmying her way toward him as if she'd done it a million times. Before Jason knew it, she was level with his window.

"Want to give me a hand?" she asked, her voice husky.

Jason put his hands on her waist to steady her as

she edged sideways and slid one long leg over his windowsill. Then the other leg.

"What are you doing here?" he asked, forcing himself to let go of her. "Not that I'm not pleased to see you."

"I need to talk to you." She raised one eyebrow. "But is your cell turned off this time?"

Her question brought him right back to their almost-kiss in the car. Sienna moved closer. As close as she'd been that day.

"I threw the thing away," Jason joked. He waited for Sienna to start talking; instead, she reached out and cupped his face in her hands, her body leaning into his.

Jason's brain was trying to tell him something—something about Brad, about vampires, about Sienna being off-limits. But his body overpowered it. He had to kiss her. Now. He leaned in, wrapping his arms around her.

Sienna tilted his head to one side, and sunk her teeth into his neck. Electric pain shot through Jason as he felt her begin to feed. He pushed her away with all of his strength.

Sienna stumbled backward. Her dark eyes had turned yellowish and they gleamed with desire. But not desire for Jason, just for his blood. And he'd seen that look before—in the eyes of the rogue vampire.

Sienna laughed as she reached for Jason again. Her fangs gleamed white and sharp in the moonlight, and her gaze was focused on his throat. Those eyes showed no sign of the girl he knew. He saw only bloodlust.

And Jason knew she was about to drink him to death.

SIX

"Get away from me!" Jason yelled, pushing Sienna away savagely. She fell to the floor. And he sat up. In bed. Alone.

He stared around the room, but there was no one there. The window was closed. "A dream," he muttered in relief. He'd fallen asleep waiting for the bathroom. Breathing hard—whether from fear or excitement, he wasn't sure—Jason got up and yanked open the door. The hallway was empty.

He stalked down to the bathroom and splashed his face with cold water. *Of course it was a dream,* he thought, beginning to decelerate. *Sienna would never come here, never come on to me like that. I've clearly absorbed too many of those* Dawson's Creek *reruns Dani's always watching.* But it had seemed so real. The feel of her in his arms.

And the look of bloodlust in her eyes.

Jason shoved the thought away and focused on getting ready for bed. But once back in his room in the dark, he couldn't shake the thoughts of Sienna. What the hell with that dream? He knew Sienna would never feed on him. He knew she'd never give in to the bloodlust. She'd promised him, and he believed her.

It's because of today, he thought. *That strange energy at dinner must've gotten into my head and into my dreams.*

He pounded his pillow into a ball and tried to get to sleep. But thoughts of Sienna kept playing on his mind, keeping him awake until well after two in the morning. At last, finally, he drifted off.

This time, he didn't dream at all.

On Friday morning, Jason was the last one down-stairs. Bianca was reading the paper at the dining room table. Dani sat yawning at the breakfast bar, and Tyler was shoveling cereal into his mouth.

"Where's Mom?" Jason asked, surprised to find his father manning the coffee machine.

"Gone already," Mr. Freeman replied. "She took the leftovers over to the town hall. They're doing a run to a homeless shelter with donated food."

"Cool," Jason said. He grabbed a bowl and sat next to Tyler for some cereal.

"I'm going to head into L.A. this morning for a lit-tle shopping," Aunt Bianca said from the dining room. "Want to come, Dani?"

Danielle's eyes lit up at the prospect of shopping. "Definitely!" Then she glanced at Jason. "What are you guys doing today?"

"Adam and I promised to show Tyler the beach," he said.

"Maybe I'll stop by after," Danielle decided. She finished her juice. "Surfrider Beach?"

Jason nodded. "Yep. Best waves around."

"Can't come to Malibu without checking out the waves," Tyler added. But he didn't sound that enthused.

Bianca stood up and stretched. "Ready?" she asked Danielle.

"Always," Dani answered, grinning as they headed out.

Jason finished his cereal. "Ready?" he asked Tyler as he stuck his bowl in the sink.

"Always," Tyler replied, but his Dani impression was weak. His voice stayed much too calm and flat, and Jason noticed that the dark circles under his friend's eyes had deepened since yesterday.

Jason walked out to the front hall and grabbed his surfboard. "We can take turns. Or we can rent you a board."

"Whatever," Tyler said as he followed Jason to the car. He got in, settled back in the seat, and didn't say a word until they arrived at the beach. Jason had never seen Tyler so moody before, not even right after his parents' break up.

"I'm going to hit the bathroom," Tyler said as soon as Jason parked.

Jason got out of the car and stared down at the beach. It was a calm day, and the water was practically still. It looked more like the Henderson Marina back in Michigan than the Pacific Ocean. He figured that the mood Tyler was in, he probably wouldn't care, but the flat water tortured Jason. He wanted his board time.

But then he noticed something else to torture him: Sienna. Well, Sienna and Brad, with Belle Rémy and her boyfriend, Dominic, Zach, and a few other kids from the Heights. A few other *vampires*. Jason's mind instantly flew to the dream he'd had last night—the dream that had kept him tossing and turning for hours. Sienna so close. That kiss about to happen.

How could he just walk over there and say hello to her as if he hadn't been thinking about her for the past ten hours?

"Let's go, bro!" Tyler boomed, jogging over from the bathroom. He smacked Jason on the back. "Show me those California sands!"

Jason stared at him. The bags under his eyes remained, but otherwise this was a whole new Tyler. He grabbed the cooler from the backseat and rushed down the wooden steps from the parking lot to the beach. Jason grabbed his board—just in case the waves got going later—and raced after him.

"Freeman!" Brad called, waving. "Over here!"

"Friends of yours?" Tyler teased as they headed over.

"Nah. I'm just kind of a celebrity around Malibu," Jason said. "The guy on the white towel is Zach. The one giving the party."

"Ah, Mr. Popularity himself," Tyler exclaimed jokingly.

"And he's very, very rich," Jason added.

"Lucky bastard," Tyler joked.

"Hey, Jason." Belle ambled over to meet them, her long, athletic legs moving easily over the sand. "Who's your friend?"

Jason shot a look at Belle's boyfriend, Dominic, who glared at them from his seat on a dark blue beach blanket. He existed in a constant state of insane jealousy, and Belle seemed to like to get him all tweaked. She was already giving Tyler one of her best flirty smiles.

"Tyler Deegan, Belle Rémy," Jason said quickly. "And her boyfriend," he added with a nod toward Dominic.

"Hey," Tyler said. Jason could tell he got the hint when he raised his voice and called to Dominic. "Hey, man."

Belle backed off, pouting a little, and Dominic relaxed enough to nod hello.

"Come sit with us," Brad called, waving them over

to a red-and-white-striped blanket set up under a huge white umbrella. An open cooler sat in its shade, bottles of water, beer, and soda spilling over the top along with the ice. Sienna lounged in the sun just next to it. As Jason approached, she sat up and pulled her sunglasses down to look at him.

"Hi," she said in the same husky voice she'd had in his dream. Jason's throat went dry. He had a bad feeling he was about to make a complete ass of himself.

His premonition came true when the *Powerpuff Girls* theme rang out from his pocket: "Dani, I'm going to massacre you," he muttered. But, glad to have a reason to turn away from Sienna, he pulled out his cell phone. "Hello?"

"Jason, it's Adam. Help me out here," said his friend's voice.

"What's up?" Jason asked.

"I'm in the parking lot. I see your bug. But where are you?"

"Adam, have you even come down to the beach yet?" Jason asked.

"No," Adam replied. "Why?"

"Because if you bothered to look, you'd see me about twenty yards from the stairs," Jason told him.

"Yeah, but that requires effort," Adam pointed out. "This way, I don't even have to look."

"Just for that, I'm not going to tell you if we're to

the left or the right," Jason said. He hung up as Adam appeared at the top of the steps. He gave a wave and bounced down the stairs, kicking off his shoes at the bottom. Then he made a big show of hopping barefoot across the hot beach.

"Oh, take it like a man," Jason called.

Adam grimaced. "That is some hot sand," he protested, flinging himself onto the blanket next to Sienna, grabbing some ice from the cooler and rubbing it on his feet.

"That's disgusting," Sienna said, but she shook her head in amusement.

Jason secretly admired how Adam had effortlessly managed to make himself right at home on Sienna's blanket. Maybe that was because he didn't have any confusing hot-but-scary dreams to contend with.

"Jason's being rude," Sienna said, glancing up at Tyler. "I heard him introduce you to Belle. I'm Sienna."

"Sienna, huh?" Tyler replied. "I've heard about you."

Her eyes immediately went to Jason, and he wanted to smack his old friend in the head.

"What did he tell you?" Sienna asked, immediately turning back to Tyler.

"Lots of mysterious things." Tyler sat right down on the blanket next to her and leaned in as if to tell her a secret.

Zach gave Jason his usual cool nod as Jason sank down on the blanket between him and Tyler. Jason had known Zach long enough to know that he wasn't the most friendly guy ever born. He was always polite, but never especially enthusiastic. Zach liked to keep to himself.

Jason leaned across Tyler toward Sienna. "My friend has only recently been released from a . . . let's call it a mental health facility," he told her in a loud whisper. "Compulsive lying is a side effect of his treatment."

Sienna gave him a light push and turned her attention back to Tyler. "So think any of what you heard about me is true?"

"You'll have to tell me," Tyler murmured, ignoring Jason.

"Okay. So what are these mysterious things you've heard?" Sienna asked, and even Adam leaned in to listen.

"Well . . . ," Tyler said, drawing it out as long as he could. "Apparently, you like the way Jason's aunt dresses."

Sienna's eyebrows shot up. "Wow, that *is* mysterious." She laughed. "What else?"

"That's pretty much it, actually," Tyler said, lying back on the blanket.

Adam and Sienna laughed.

She looked up at Jason. "You suck at gossip," she informed him.

"Well, what can I say? I don't like to talk behind people's backs," Jason replied virtuously, struggling to keep a straight face.

"Not true. I've heard you describe our history teacher as a hottie on more than one occasion," Adam put in. "He likes the way Ms. Buchanan's butt looks when she reaches up to write at the top of the blackboard," he added to Sienna and Tyler.

"Oh, really?" Sienna asked laughingly.

"Hey, Buchanan's got back. Can I help it if I notice?" Jason grabbed a beer, trying to cover his embarrassment. He knew they were just teasing him, but somehow it was always worse when Sienna was involved.

"So you can give us all the dirt on Freeman, huh?" Brad asked Tyler, admirably unphased by the fact that Tyler was practically sitting in Sienna's lap.

"Whatever you want to know," Tyler replied.

"Who was his first love?" Sienna asked immediately.

"Wait!" Adam cried. He rummaged in his backpack and pulled out his mini-camcorder. "This I have to get on camera."

"Tyler, don't you want to hit the water?" Jason asked.

"Are you kidding?" Sienna said. "I'm not letting go of him until I hear all your secrets."

Tyler shot Jason a mischievous look, then leaned in and whispered in Sienna's ear.

"Hey, share it with the rest of the class!" Adam complained.

"Sorry," Tyler said to Adam, drawing back from Sienna, but only a little. "Jason's first love, I'm sorry to say, broke his heart."

"Liar," Jason reminded Sienna.

Adam spun to focus the camera on Jason's face. Jason reached out and plucked it from his hand, turning it off.

"Broke his heart how?" Sienna asked.

"She left him for another guy," Tyler explained sorrowfully. "Unfortunately, for Jason, he just couldn't compete with me."

"You?" Sienna cried.

"You hit on your friend's girlfriend?" Zach asked.

Jason took special note of Zach's question, since he rarely deigned to join the conversation. He couldn't help wondering if Zach had somehow picked up on his feelings for Sienna.

"Nah, she hit on me," Tyler said. "That happens a lot, you know?"

"Right, because you're irresistible," Sienna said, trying to look serious.

"I'm glad you noticed," Tyler replied.

Jason shook his head. *Yeah,* he thought, laughing. *Tyler can charm anyone.*

"So she hit on you and you went out with her?" Sienna was saying, her gaze focused on Tyler even though Brad's arm was around her. "You bad boy!"

"I was only eight," Tyler replied with a wink. "All I did was sit with her at lunch one day."

Sienna and Brad laughed, and Sienna turned to Jason. "Did you forgive him?"

"I made him give me his top three baseball cards and lend me his Game Boy first. Then I forgave him," Jason said.

"Fascinating though this is," Adam put in, "I'd rather hear about the more recent adventures of our boy hero. Don't you have any good Freeman-in-high-school stories?"

"Sure," Tyler said. "Which do you want to hear first, the time Jason stole a keg from a 7-Eleven, or the time he had three different dates to the same dance?"

Sienna was still holding Jason's gaze. "The one with the dates," she said. "Absolutely."

"I don't need to hear this. I was there," Jason said. He stood up and grabbed his board. "Besides, I need to get some practice in before my next lesson with the Surf Rabbi."

"Those waves look about your speed," Adam

joked, gazing out at the ocean, which remained as smooth as glass.

"It's all about feeling the water with your soul, heathen," Jason answered. Then he ran toward the surf. The baby waves wouldn't be much of a challenge, but he had a feeling that watching Sienna as she listened to a rundown of his love life might be.

Except that the very fact she wanted to hear about said love life showed that she had some interest in him. *An interesting kind of interest,* Jason thought, grinning to himself as he splashed into the water.

When he returned to the flotilla of blankets, Dani had joined the group.

Jason dropped down on the blanket next to her. "Not going in the water?" he asked.

"Maybe later," she replied, yawning. "I think I'm going to nap first. I got no sleep last night."

"Why?" Jason asked. He was damn sure Danielle hadn't been awake for the same reason he had.

"Tyler was on the phone all night," Dani said, keeping her voice low. "The wall between our rooms is so thin. I kept waking up because he was talking so loud."

"Who was he talking to?" Jason asked.

"How should I know?" Dani said. "But he got at least four calls, and it sounded kind of serious. I heard him say he needed more time. He kept saying that two days aren't enough."

"Enough for what?"

"I don't know." Dani bit her lip. "He's been acting weird ever since he got here."

"So you noticed too," Jason said.

"Of course, I noticed. It's totally not like him," Dani said. "Tyler's usually so funny and laid-back—which he still has been, some of the time—but the rest . . ." She shook her head. "I don't know. He's been kind of hyper."

Jason didn't answer. He knew Tyler had been acting differently since before they left Michigan, but Dani didn't know that. And he didn't want to tell her. Although her crush was long gone, she still had a major soft spot for his old friend. Why ruin that?

"He sounded pretty upset last night," Danielle said thoughtfully. "I think he may be in some kind of trouble. I'm a little worried about him." She stretched out on the blanket and closed her eyes.

Jason also lay back. He wanted to catch up on his sleep. But, though he was tired, his mind refused to switch off and let him relax. Tyler had him more than a little worried, too. . . .

SEVEN

*W*as Tyler in trouble? Jason didn't know what to think. What were the mysterious, middle-of-the-night phone calls about? Why would Tyler need more time? Jason had assumed Tyler's moodiness was because of his less than stellar home life. But maybe there was more to it.

Jason figured he would try to find some time to sound Tyler out about his situation later. Now wasn't the time—there were too many people around. Eventually, he drifted off to sleep.

By the time he woke up, the sun had moved halfway across the sky. Somebody had repositioned the umbrella to cover him, and the entire group was gone. Jason sat up groggily and looked around. He spotted Tyler in the water with Brad and Dominic, Adam filming them from the shore. Belle stood with the surf breaking over her toes, watching.

Danielle was swimming nearby. Her friends Kristy and Billy had shown up.

"I think you were drooling," said a voice from behind him.

Jason quickly wiped his mouth, then turned to find

Sienna laughing. "You've caught the lying thing from Ty," he accused with a smile.

"You're definitely more gullible than I expected," she replied. "Have a nice nap?"

He stretched his arms above his head, working out the stiffness that came from lying on the sand. "I didn't get much sleep last night," he explained.

"How come?"

Because I was thinking about you, he thought. "I don't know. I probably ate too much," he said aloud, hoping his voice sounded casual.

Sienna looked at him silently for a long moment, and Jason felt a sudden pang of nerves. It was almost as if she knew what he was thinking. Or else maybe she wanted to talk about the fact that they'd come close to kissing the other day. The air between them buzzed with energy. He wasn't sure if he moved toward her or she moved toward him, but suddenly they were only a foot apart on the blanket, her long, bare leg touching his.

"Sienna! Come help me," Brad called from the water.

She turned away, and Jason felt cold.

Brad stood shaking droplets of water from his hair. "Can you bring me my goggles?" he called to Sienna. "I got salt in my eyes."

Sienna rummaged around in Brad's bag. As she stood up with the swim goggles, she reached out and ran her fingers through Jason's hair. He shaded his eyes and looked up at her.

"Your hair's a mess from sleeping," she said quickly. Then she was gone.

Danielle and Tyler passed her on their way back up from the water. Tyler bent over and shook his long hair over Jason, purposely flinging water on him.

"Ass hat," Jason commented.

"Sweet life you have here," Tyler said, dropping down onto the blanket. "The ocean is great!"

"Does it make you miss the swim team?" Jason asked, figuring that the question didn't sound too leading but might give him some info about what was going on with Tyler.

Tyler gazed out at the horizon. "If the school pool had a view like this, it would."

Dani pulled her wallet from her big straw bag. "Adam and I are going to get some bubble tea," she told Jason. "You want?"

"What the hell is bubble tea?" Tyler asked.

"It's this disgusting iced tea with big, round globs of tapioca in it," Jason told him. "The tea is fine, but when you suck up a tapioca ball, it's like ingesting a loogie."

"Oh, gross," Dani cried. "You are such a Neanderthal. It's delicious."

"I think I'll pass," Tyler said.

"Suit yourselves." Dani walked off across the sand toward the snack bar a quarter of a mile away. Adam jogged over to join her. That left Jason and Tyler on the beach.

"Only in Malibu does the snack bar serve bubble tea and lobster rolls instead of Coke and hot dogs," Jason said. "Crazy place."

"I could get used to it," Tyler replied.

"Too bad you have to leave so soon." Jason searched his friend's face. "When do you have to be back in Michigan?"

Tyler shrugged, still gazing at the ocean. "Whenever."

"Oh." Jason hesitated, then plunged ahead. "Because Dani heard you saying you only had two days."

"What?" Tyler asked, his attention snapping back to Jason.

"She heard you on your cell last night, I guess. Thin walls." Jason tried to make his voice sound casual.

Tyler grimaced. "Sorry. I hope I didn't keep her up."

"I think you did a bit," Jason replied. "And she was a little worried about you. She said you kept saying you needed more time. Who were you on the phone with?"

"Just, er, you know . . . my girlfriend." Tyler sighed. "She's the needy type. She didn't even want me to come out here, and now she wants me to get back to Michigan as soon as I can."

"Your girlfriend?" Jason repeated. "Who? I didn't even know you were seeing anyone."

"Yeah. You don't know her," Tyler said vaguely. "I'm really sorry if I bothered your sister."

Jason wasn't sure what to say. Dani had made it sound as if there was something sinister about the phone calls, and Tyler's explanation didn't really add up. But it wasn't any of Jason's business who the guy talked to on his phone, or when.

Besides, surely if Tyler was in some kind of trouble, he'd tell me about it, Jason thought. *Wouldn't he? I've given him enough openings.*

"Later, my friends. We're taking off," Brad said as he, Sienna, and Zach approached the blankets.

Jason glanced at Sienna. Her hair was wet from swimming, and droplets of water slid down her smooth, tanned skin. She was hot fully dressed and dry. Right now, she was scorching. Jason didn't want to get caught staring at her with his tongue dragging in the sand, so he dragged his eyes away.

"You're all leaving?" Tyler asked.

"We've been here for hours," Belle replied. She gathered up her stuff while Dominic shook out the blanket. "And we have to get ready for the party tonight."

"Translation: Sienna and Belle have to spend the next five hours doing their hair," Brad joked. He took down the umbrella and folded it up.

"And I have to spend the next five hours party-proofing the house," Zach put in. "My father's afraid we'll trash the place."

"See you guys at the party," Sienna said. She'd

wrapped a sarong around her waist and it clung to her hips as she picked up her beach bag.

"I don't know," Tyler said. "I haven't been invited to this infamous party."

"Infamous?" Zach queried.

Jason rolled his eyes. "Danielle is pissed because my mom won't let her go. They've been fighting about it all week."

"Why can't she go?" Zach asked, frowning. "She's always welcome."

"My mom freaked out about Carrie, and I don't blame her," Jason said evenly. He knew Zach would understand what he really meant: that maybe he didn't want his little sister hanging out in a house full of vampires.

Zach thought about that, then nodded.

"But you should come, Ty," Brad put in. "Mrs. Freeman can't tell *you* no."

Tyler shrugged. "That's up to Jason."

"Well, of course *Jason* wants you to come," Belle said. "Don't you, Jason?"

Jason hesitated. The last time they'd partied together hadn't gone so well. *It won't happen again,* Jason told himself. *Tyler said all that was behind him.*

"Sure, we'll be there," Jason said aloud. What was friendship without trust?

• • •

"Maybe just a movie," Dani was saying later as Jason pulled the VW into the driveway of the house later. She'd been on her cell ever since they'd left the beach. "Hello? Billy?" she said, raising her voice. Frustrated, she hit end. "I lost the signal," she complained.

"Why didn't you make plans with him while we were at the beach?" Jason asked. He found it baffling how much time she spent on the phone with her friends. She'd called Billy about three minutes after saying good-bye to him in person.

Danielle ignored him, shoving open her car door and climbing out. Tyler swung himself over the side of the convertible without bothering to use the door.

"It's a little cramped in the back, bro," Tyler joked. "Not enough room for me and all the beach gear."

"When I get a car, it'll be bigger," Dani said. She pulled the wet towels out of the backseat and shoved them into Tyler's arms, then grabbed her straw bag. "Straight to the laundry room," she told Tyler. "Mom hates when we leave towels around."

"Got it." Tyler took off toward the house, Dani following.

As Jason started toward the front door, a cell phone chirped from the car. He turned around and scanned the VW, finally spotting Dani's phone—gray faceplate today—on the front seat. Jason figured it was probably Billy calling back.

He grabbed it and hit talk. "Hello?"

"Time is running out," said the guy on the other end.

"To get movie tickets?" Jason asked.

There was a pause, and Jason wondered if the signal had died again. "Hello?"

"Don't try to be cute," came the reply. "You have your deadline. After that, I get really upset."

Jason rolled his eyes. "Dude, it's Malibu. What is there to be upset about?"

"Malibu?" Laughter filled his ear, and then the guy said, "Thank you. Remember, thirty-six hours."

"What are you talking about?" Jason asked. "Billy?"

But he heard only silence. Jason pulled the phone away from his ear and glanced at the screen. It was empty. The guy had hung up.

"Who were you talking to?" Tyler asked from behind him.

Jason turned and shrugged. "I thought it was my sister's friend Billy, but he was being really weird. Maybe it was a wrong number."

Tyler strode forward and snatched the phone from Jason's hand. "That's *my* phone, moron," he snapped. He hit a few buttons, calling up the phone log.

"Excuse me?" Jason said, annoyed. He and Tyler trashed each other a lot, but they were always just joking around. This time, Tyler didn't sound amused at all. "Did you just call me a moron?"

"I heard you tell him you were in Malibu," Tyler said angrily. "What the hell did you do that for?"

"Because I thought it was Billy," Jason retorted. "What was your phone doing on the front seat?"

"It must've fallen out of my pocket when I got out," Tyler said. "But I bet Danielle wouldn't appreciate you answering *her* phone either."

"She wouldn't go all psycho on me," Jason said. "What's your problem?"

"What else did he say?" Tyler demanded.

"He said something about thirty-six hours and how he'd be upset if you missed the deadline," Jason replied. "Now why don't you tell me who that was and what the hell is going on?"

Tyler looked him up and down, his eyes dark with fury. "You know, man? It's none of your business," he said. He turned and stalked into the house without another word.

Jason stayed rooted to the spot, replaying that phone conversation in his mind. Clearly the guy on the phone was threatening Tyler. But why?

Now, at least he knew one thing for sure: Dani was right. Tyler was in trouble.

Serious trouble.

EIGHT

At eight o'clock, Jason decided it was time to go talk to Tyler. His friend had vanished into the guest room after their argument out front, and he hadn't come out since. But Zach's party started in half an hour, and Jason wanted to clear the air before that. Besides, if Tyler was in need of a friend, Jason would step up—if Tyler would let him.

"Ty, you awake?" he called, knocking on the bedroom door. There was no answer, but the door swung open a bit. Jason stuck his head in. "Tyler?"

The room was empty. Glancing around, Jason spotted Tyler's prescription bottle sitting on the dresser. Except he knew that it wasn't Tyler's prescription—there had been someone else's name on it. Guiltily, he went over to check out the bottle. *Maybe I just read it wrong,* he thought hopefully.

Ryan Swank, the label read. Not Tyler Deegan. Not even close.

Jason squinted at the rest of the info, which included a doctor's name and a phone number from Detroit. And the name of the medication: Ritalin.

Ritalin. Another lie, then. Jason knew Ritalin

wasn't a painkiller. It was for ADD, but could be abused for a high.

And Tyler didn't have ADD.

Jason's heart sank. Tyler had promised that he was done with drugs. But the fact that he had a bottle full of Ritalin seemed like more than mere coincidence. Jason shook the bottle. He'd only held it for a second yesterday, but he was pretty sure it had felt heavier then. It seemed that Tyler had taken some of the pills. *Well, that explains his ability to go from exhausted to manic in sixty seconds,* Jason thought grimly. He sighed and put the bottle back down.

Out in the hallway, Jason went over to the bathroom door and pounded on it. "Tyler, you in there?" he yelled.

"In the shower!" Tyler called back. "Be out in five."

Jason hesitated. He'd been worried about taking Tyler to Zach's party before, but now he *really* didn't want to. If Tyler was still taking drugs, there was no telling what he'd do at one of the wild DeVere Heights blowouts.

"Listen, you want to ditch on this party tonight?" he called through the door. "Maybe hang with Dani and her friend?"

"No way," Tyler replied. "Sounds like this party is a primo event."

Like Tyler would ever turn down a party. Jason

couldn't come up with a solid reason why they shouldn't go. He wasn't ready to confront his friend about the drugs. He needed to think of a game plan for tackling that one without alienating Tyler. In the meantime, he decided he'd have to hope for the best. But he was *not* looking forward to partying with Tyler tonight.

"Have fun," Dani said, twenty minutes later.

"You could not sound more insincere if you tried," Jason told her with a grin.

"Don't worry, we'll pour one out for you," Tyler said as Jason pushed open the front door and stepped out into the cool California night.

"Have two. I'd have two if I were there," Dani shouted after them.

"Be good at the movies," Jason called back as she closed the door.

"Why doesn't she just tell your mom she's going to the movies and then come with us?" Tyler asked.

"She did that once," Jason said. "And that was the party where someone died."

"Ouch," Tyler replied.

"Yeah. I think she's too spooked to try that again." They got into the bug, and Jason pulled out. He drove slowly down to the main road in DeVere Heights, taking as much time as possible to get to Zach's.

"These parties really as good as Dani says?" Tyler asked, a hint of nervousness in his voice.

"Yeah. It can get pretty wild." Jason glanced sideways at his friend. "We can still blow it off, if you want."

"You don't want to take me to your precious party, do you?" Tyler suddenly snapped. "That's why you're talking about skipping out, right? You're still stuck on that one time I took your car. Just get over it already!"

"Look, you told me you were done with the drugs, but I know you're lying. So who knows what else you're lying about?" Jason retorted. So much for his plan to approach the subject carefully. But his temper had trumped his good intentions. "I'm friends with these people, Tyler. I don't want you making an ass of yourself tonight."

"Well, don't worry. I'm not going to embarrass you in front of your special new friends. I'll be invisible," Tyler muttered.

Jason took a deep breath and didn't comment on the extreme unlikelihood of Tyler ever being invisible. He'd been arguing with Tyler all afternoon, but he didn't feel angry. He felt worried. "Ty, listen," he said. "What's really going on? I know you're not just here for a visit. You're in some kind of trouble, right?"

"Yeah." Tyler's voice was so quiet that Jason could barely hear him. "I'm in big trouble."

"Well, tell me what it is," Jason said. "I can help you."

"No, you can't, Jason," Tyler said. "Nobody can help."

"Whoa. That's pretty negative, dude," Jason said, surfer-style, hoping to get a smile out of Tyler. It didn't work. "How do you know I can't help if you don't tell me what's going on?"

"I just know, okay?"

Jason shrugged and focused on the road. Whatever. He wasn't going to beg.

"Unless your dad's so rich now that your allowance is a couple thou," Tyler muttered.

"You need two thousand dollars?" Jason tried to keep the shock out of his voice.

"Five, actually," Tyler admitted.

Jason let out a long, low whistle. That was a serious lump of cash.

"See, Freeman, there are things even you can't fix," Tyler said, wiping his hands nervously on the legs of his jeans.

"How'd you get in so deep?" Jason asked. "Credit card?"

Tyler snorted.

"Betting on b-ball?" Jason suggested. *Would any bookie let Tyler run up that kind of tab?* he wondered. *He'd have to be one stupid illegal businessman.*

"What does it matter?" Tyler sounded pissy now. He always sounded pissy when he was scared. Jason remembered the time Tyler had almost got bitten by a rattlesnake on a Boy Scout hiking trip. Well, actually, the time Tyler *saw* a rattlesnake on a Boy Scout hiking trip. He had been so scared that he'd cursed the thing out for two solid minutes, using words in combinations even the Scout Master hadn't heard before.

"I guess I just thought knowing who you owed the money to might help us come up with a plan," Jason answered.

"'Us,'" Tyler repeated. "There is no 'us' in this situation. There's just me."

"Hey, you showed up at my door with a problem. You brought me into it." Jason pulled through the massive iron gates leading to the Lafrenière property. "So spill it. How'd you rack up that kind of debt?" He flashed on the bottle of Ritalin in Tyler's room. "Ritalin?"

"Everyone needs some recreation once in a while," Tyler answered, without really answering. "It's nothing."

A valet in a black suit and a narrow black tie signalled Jason to a stop. Tyler jumped out of the car without waiting for Jason and headed up the long driveway. Jason took the claim check from the valet and followed Tyler, not bothering to hurry. He wasn't

eager to get to the party. He was in an even less cele-
bratory mood now than he had been when he left the
house. *Some Thanksgiving vacation,* Jason thought.
*Let's all give thanks for pissy, drug-abusing friends who
won't tell you anything.*

"There are probably five thousand bucks' worth of
those candle thingies in the trees," Tyler commented
when Jason caught up to him.

"Possibly." Jason glanced at the trees lining the
drive. Hundreds of clear glass globes had been hung
from the branches, and each one held a short fat candle and glowed with golden candlelight. More candles
gleamed from the decks and balconies that jutted out
on all the levels of the house.

"Where do they get all their cash?" Tyler asked.

"Mom's a screenwriter. Dad's a music producer,"
Jason said, wishing Tyler would get off the subject.
People in Malibu didn't walk around talking about
how much stuff cost or how anybody got the money
they had. It was tacky.

"So that chick over there who looks like the actress
in that cheerleader movie, but skinnier?" Tyler indi-
cated a direction with a slight jerk of his chin. "That's
actually her?"

Jason tried to look without looking like he was
looking. "I'd say yeah."

"Do you think she'd like to know that I have a

poster of her over my bed?" Tyler joked. "Or do you think I need a different approach?"

"I'm sure she'd find that truly flattering," Jason answered as they stepped through the double front doors and into the house. "She being beautiful and famous. And you being you."

"I'll hit on her later," Tyler decided. "Give her time to watch me from afar and become intrigued."

"Good idea."

Tyler headed over to the bar that had been set up in the entryway, complete with a hottie bartender, who was flipping bottles like she was half-juggler. "The signature drink of the evening is the pumpkin martini," she told them. "'Tinis of all sorts are available: apple, chocolate, clean, dirty. And pretty much any other kind of alcohol you want."

"Only party I've been to where there's not a line by the booze," Tyler commented.

"Well, you only have to go a few feet to find another bar," the bartender answered.

"I'll go with the pumpkin." Tyler grinned at Jason. "This is definitely the place to come if you want to forget your problems for a few hours."

Jason thought that over for all of two seconds. Tyler had a point: They could deal with all this shit post-fun. "Beer for me."

"You've got to give me more than that," the bartender told him.

"Surprise me," Jason said. She handed him a Heineken. He wasn't sure what that said about him. Maybe that he hadn't yet completely assimilated to Malibu, home of designer beer.

His eyes swept over what he thought was the living room. All the furniture had been moved out to make space for dancing, and a DJ kept everyone moving with a hip-hop/reggae mix. Clips from movies— Adam would probably be able to identify every one— were being projected on one wall. A baby floating in space. Keanu bending under a bullet. Chewbacca roaring. John Travolta disco dancing in a white suit. Mike Myers in a kilt. That freakazoid girl from *The Ring* crawling out of the well.

"So this is your life now, huh?" Tyler asked. He took a sip of his martini.

"Not quite. I still have to take out the trash," Jason answered.

"Great. Malibu party boy surrounded by excess whines about the one chore he has to do." Adam approached, his camera stuck to his face. "I think I have to use this for the trailer."

"Happy to be of service." Jason shook his head. "That thing is going to become permanently grafted to your eye if you don't put it down occasionally. You ever think of, maybe . . . I don't know, leaving it at home?"

"And face the world—and *people*—without my layer of ironic protection?" Adam protested. "Besides, you never know when a really good docudrama is going to unfold."

"Glad you guys could make it," Zach called over the music. He joined them, shaking hands all around. "Adam, my mom scored a print of the new Tarantino flick. In the screening room at midnight."

Adam lowered his camera. "You," he said slowly, "are a god."

"I have to pass on one rule from my parents," Zach told them. "We can do anything we want to the first floor and the basement—short of burning them to the ground—but the top floor is off limits."

"And you expect us to stay?" Jason joked.

"The pool and the grounds are also available," Zach told him.

"Oh, well then, I guess we can hang for an hour or so," Jason said.

"Speak for yourself," Tyler put in. "I'm never leaving."

Zach smiled. "Let me know if there's anything you want that you can't find," he said, and headed to the entryway to greet some new arrivals.

"Cool guy," Tyler commented.

"He was almost chatty," Adam added. "Those may have been the most words Lafrenière has ever said to me at one time. Maybe our birthday friend has been enjoying something more exotic than the martinis."

Jason shot a glance at Tyler. He hoped *his* friend wouldn't go looking for anything stronger than the drink he had in his hand.

"I think I must have stretched out my stomach with yesterday's gorge," Adam said. "Because I'm hungry. In my travels, I saw this phenomenal dessert station. There's actually a chef making bananas Foster."

"Do you think they have pumpkin pie?" Tyler asked. "You know it's not good to mix bananas and pumpkin." He waved his martini glass. "That's a recipe for vomit."

"Are you kidding?" Adam asked as they wove their way across the dance floor. "Clearly I haven't expressed the scope of this dessert bar. It's monster." He led the way out to the huge deck that surrounded the pool. The dessert table went on for a mile, the scent of banana liqueur and hot sugar mixing with the salty breeze coming off the ocean.

"Check it," Tyler said.

Jason watched as the chef scooped up a ladle of liquid from around some simmering bananas and torched it. He poured it back into the pan—a stream of fire hit the bananas with a whoosh of blue flame.

"Wait. I hear my name. Someone's calling me." Adam headed toward the chef.

Tyler snagged a piece of pumpkin pie, and Jason grabbed a brownie.

As he picked it up, he heard Sienna's familiar laugh. And for a second, he felt like he'd had a six-pack instead of just one beer. He turned and spotted her with Belle, reclining on matching lounge chairs the other side of the pool. Van Dyke stood next to them.

Jason wandered—in what he hoped looked like a casual way—in their direction. Tyler followed him.

"Uh-oh. We're being invaded by Michigan," Sienna said, and laughed when she spotted them.

"I'm not complaining," Belle purred.

"Remember that the insanely jealous boyfriend is probably lurking nearby," Jason warned under his breath. Tyler nodded.

"Pretty soon there are going to be more of you than there are of us," Sienna teased.

"And that would be a bad thing?" Jason asked. "You could use some good Midwestern stock in the mix. You've gotten soft out here."

"Soft? Feel this!" Sienna reached out, grabbed Jason's hand, and ran his fingers across her taut abs. Jason tried to look unimpressed.

"Gym muscles," Tyler scoffed. "Those don't count. Jason and I have real muscles, from working the land."

"Yeah, Jason, I'm sure you worked the land every weekend—with the power mower," Sienna joked.

Van Dyke and Belle laughed.

"You don't get muscles like these mowing the lawn," Jason retorted. He caught Sienna's hand, flexed, and pressed it against his bicep. He knew he shouldn't be doing it. He knew he should be keeping his hands off her. *But it's not like we're going behind Brad's back or anything,* he told himself. *We're just two friends, joking around, in front of loads of people.*

Right.

"Ooooh." Sienna gave his arm a little squeeze. "You're right! You definitely don't get muscles like that mowing the lawn. You must have had one of those mowers you ride on."

"Meow!" Belle said, grinning at Sienna.

"Just give up," Van Dyke suggested to Jason.

"Yes. I'm too smart for you." Sienna sighed, her dark eyes flashing with mischief.

Jason raised an eyebrow. "You won't seem so smart when you're dripping wet," he remarked, with a nod to the pool. He turned back to Sienna. "Watch it. Or you're going in."

"With those tiny muscles? I don't think so," Sienna shot back, laughing.

She was asking for it.

Jason lunged toward her lounge chair, and Sienna

leaped out of it with a shriek and darted away.

Let her go, Jason told himself. But he couldn't. And as he raced after her, Jason realized that Sienna was his Ritalin. And he was addicted.

"Jason, I'm going to break the kegstand record. I'm going for a full minute," Harberts called as Jason headed toward him. He flipped onto his hands, and two guys grabbed his legs. Erin Henry positioned the keg tap in Harberts's mouth and flipped it.

"One, two, three—," the crowd around him began to chant as Harberts struggled to force beer up his throat.

Sienna had disappeared into the house. Jason picked up speed, dodging the stream of beer Harberts had just started to spew, and running into the den. A group of guys from the football team were lounging on the overstuffed leather couches, watching a Super Bowl game on the plasma-screen TV. Jason caught a glimpse of Sienna running through another door and followed.

He found himself in a home gym, fully equipped. Weight machines, cardio machines, a lap pool, and Sienna. She was bouncing on a trampoline, her hair flying around her, her cheeks flushed.

Jason walked toward her. "Don't think I'm not going to carry you right back out to that pool," he warned.

"You'll have to catch me first," Sienna taunted, jumping lightly off the trampoline and slipping away through another door.

"Right," Jason muttered, picking up speed again. He ran out into the corridor, in time to see a door close. Throwing it open, he saw the library beyond and, for a split second, he thought he'd found Sienna. But when the girl turned toward him, he saw it was Lauren Gissinger. She was sitting with Dominic and two other guys, playing strip poker. Lauren was clearly braless under her thin T-shirt, and one of the guys was shirtless—except for a lacy pink-and-black bra. *Must be some rule I don't know about,* Jason thought.

"Wanna play?" Lauren asked.

"Maybe later," Jason said as he heard Sienna laugh behind him, and whirled around to see her at the other end of the corridor. He followed her into a sunroom. It had glass on three sides, plants all around, and lots of bamboo furniture. The air felt dense.

Sienna darted behind a sofa—like that was enough to stop him. Jason leaped straight over the back.

"Nowhere to run," he told Sienna, strolling lazily toward her.

Sienna backed away, laughing and reaching behind her for the balcony doors. She got the handle, twisted it, and slipped outside. Jason was out the door half a second later.

The small balcony had a wrought-iron railing all the way around it. Candles illuminated it, casting light across Sienna's face. She was close now, and Jason could hear her breath coming fast. He smiled as she backed up again—and hit the railing.

Jason grabbed the rail on either side of her, creating a wall with his body. Sienna twisted back and forth, trying to wriggle away.

"Now what were you saying about my muscles?" Jason asked as she gave him a playful push that didn't move him an inch.

"That they're very strong and manly," Sienna lied with a grin.

"That's not what I remember." Jason moved closer, preparing to drag her back to the pool. But he didn't want to take her back out to the crowd. He wanted to stay right there with her—alone.

He stared into her dark eyes, then Sienna's arms came up around his neck and her body met his. Just like in his dream, her lips parted. . . . And, suddenly, the rest of the dream came flooding back. Jason remembered Sienna's eyes—unrecognizable and full of bloodlust. He drew back sharply, confused, needing to know that she was still Sienna and not someone— or some*thing*—else.

NINE

$\mathfrak{S}$ienna looked up, startled, as Jason drew back. Her dark eyes went wide with surprise. They held no bloodlust. There were no fangs. There was just Sienna looking puzzled and then pissed off.

"Sienna, I—," Jason began, trying to explain.

But it was too late.

"Forget it," Sienna said flatly, and she turned and walked away. Just walked. The chase was over. Jason knew he'd screwed up. He'd had her. She'd wanted him to kiss her. But he'd flashed back to his dream and . . . well, that was that.

If I could just explain, he thought. Yeah. Just say, "Sienna, I wasn't trying to give you mixed signals or mess with you. I completely want you. It's just that for one minute I thought about this nightmare where you gave in to the bloodlust and attacked me." Right. Great plan.

But he had to do something. Jason pulled in a deep breath, ran his fingers through his hair, and smoothed down his shirt. Then he retraced his steps. Sienna wasn't in the library. Neither were Erin or Dominic. The two remaining guys had switched over to playing for cash.

He returned to the gym. Vivian Andersen was lying on the trampoline now, staring up at the ceiling and giggling, like there was a movie up there or something. No Sienna.

Jason skirted the glossy polished floor of the basketball court and headed into the den. His heart twisted painfully in his chest, because there was Sienna. On one of the leather couches. More specifically, on Brad's lap on one of the leather couches.

Sienna caught Jason's eye, her gaze ice. Then she took Brad's face in her hands, leaned down, and kissed him—long and deep. The kiss that should have been Jason's, *would* have been Jason's if he hadn't screwed up so spectacularly. Again.

Jason abruptly turned away. He didn't want to see what he was missing. And besides, he didn't want anyone to notice him staring.

He headed toward the pool, just to have a destination. Belle and Van Dyke passed him. ". . . to get up to the Garden," Van Dyke was saying. Jason tried to put a smile—or at least a normal, relaxed expression—on his face. To his relief, they didn't notice him. He didn't want to try to come up with words right now. He sat down in the closest deck chair and stared vacantly at the water volleyball game that had started up in his absence.

A few minutes later, Adam sat down in the chair

next to him. "Remember what I said about not knowing when a docudrama was going to unfold?" he asked.

Jason nodded.

"Well, the unfolding is happening now, I'm pretty
sure," Adam went on. "There's this slow migration
happening. People are heading upstairs—where no
one is supposed to go."

Jason shrugged. "Ever been to a party where that
doesn't happen?"

"Mia Hodges's third birthday party. Because we
were all afraid of Mrs. Hodges," Adam answered. "But
it's not just regular people going upstairs. It's only
people of the Sienna, Zach, Brad variety."

Vampires. "So they're having a little sub-party,"
Jason said.

"Could be," Adam agreed. "Could be something
else. Don't you want to know why they all suddenly
have this need to get together?"

"If they want to be alone, let them be," Jason
replied with a shrug. Right now he was just happy to
know that Sienna and Brad would be out of sight for
a while. One step closer to out of mind.

Adam frowned. "Do you remember putting on
some kind of metal hat? Maybe some electricity?" he
asked. "Because I think somebody may have switched
our brains. Aren't you the one who was übersuspicious
of our *friends*?"

"Yeah," Jason admitted. "But the way Zach handled the rogue vampire convinced me that we can trust them to deal with their own shit. I don't know about you, but I have enough of my own to deal with." Thinking of Sienna. And Brad. And Tyler.

"I just want to take a little peek. Come on." Adam got to his feet, slinging his camera strap over his shoulder. "I know where there's a back staircase."

"Adam, it's none of our business what they're—"

But Adam was gone. Jason closed his eyes for a long moment. Then he opened them and headed after his friend. He couldn't let him go up there alone.

Jason spotted Belle and Van Dyke walking up the main staircase as he followed Adam. "We're going to have to be careful or we're going to get spotted," Jason warned when he caught up to Adam at the smaller staircase off the kitchen.

"Careful is nothing like my middle name, which is Tecumseh. But, yeah," Adam answered, starting up the stairs. He slowed down as they reached the top. Jason peered over his shoulder. There was nothing to see but empty hallway. And nothing to hear but the dull thud of the music from the party.

"If we're doing this, now's a good time," Jason said. He and Adam headed down the hall. Adam paused outside a closed door, listened for a moment, then swung the door open. A bedroom. Probably a guest room. Nothing too personal in it. Empty.

Adam shut the door and they continued. Another bedroom. Also empty. They moved on to the upstairs living room, just off the main staircase. Empty.

"Something mysterious has occurred," Adam said, turning on the camera and panning across the empty sofas and chairs. "My colleague and I witnessed people coming upstairs. But having followed them, we've found nobody." Adam pointed the camera at Jason. "What are your theories?"

"I thought I told you not to come up here," someone interrupted before Jason could answer.

Jason turned to see Zach Lafrenière standing in the doorway. He didn't look happy.

TEN

Where the hell did Zach come from? Jason wondered. "Sorry. Uh, the line for the head downstairs is almost out the front door," he said quickly. "It was the rose bushes or the forbidden upstairs."

"And the rose bushes, they have thorns," Adam added, lowering his camera. "Not safe."

Zach raised one dark eyebrow, and Jason suddenly felt like a five-year-old.

"There are four bathrooms down there," Zach said, one corner of his mouth lifting in amusement. "Come on. I'll give you the tour. I think you'll especially enjoy the one off my dad's office. The toilet has a heated seat." He turned and headed for the stairs.

"I don't think I've ever heard Lafrenière make a joke before," Adam said under his breath as he and Jason followed Zach downstairs.

"Down that hallway. Third door on the left," Zach said when they reached the first floor.

"Thanks." Jason answered.

Zach turned and loped back upstairs.

"He sounded downright cheerful. And he was grinning!" Adam exclaimed. "Now I *really* want to know what's going on. I know it's his birthday, but come on. What could be happening up there to put Zach in such a great mood?"

"Vampire Twister?" Jason suggested.

"Don't be an ass," Adam said. "Seriously, what do you think they're all doing right now? They can't be having some private feeding session. They'd need humans for that."

Jason nodded thoughtfully.

"Do you think they're planning something?" Adam went on. "Something that made Lafrenière so happy that he actually smiled?"

Jason wished Adam would drop it. "Vampire bingo!" he said firmly.

"Definitely a complete ass," Adam retorted.

"Want to check out the bowling alley? Get some footage?" Jason started down the hallway. "Because, really, can you even name one truly great film that does not include a bowling scene?"

"*The Bicycle Thief*," Adam answered, falling into step beside him.

"I said truly great," Jason protested. He led the way into the basement: five bowling lanes with electronic scoring, vintage video games, two pool tables, jukebox with accompanying disco ball and strobe lights, and tiki bar. Not your regular rec room.

But even with all the toys, without the vampires—

meaning without the most popular of the popular—
there was something missing from the party. Some
kind of . . . shimmer. Or maybe it was just lack of
Sienna that was making the party feel flat to Jason.

Which meant his whole life would feel flat from
now on, he reflected, because Jason got the impression
that Sienna didn't plan on being around him much.

In the middle of his second bowling match, Jason
caught sight of Sienna just as he released the ball. So
they had returned. Jason forced his attention to the
pins and watched his ball take out all but two: a seven-
ten split. Nasty.

"Goalposts!" Harberts yelled. "That's a shot for
you, my friend." He handed Jason a shot glass of
tequila.

Nasty, but not without benefits, Jason thought. He
downed the shot. The sensation was not unlike staring
into Sienna's eyes: a long burst of fire from mouth to
gut.

Sienna looked away, wrapping her arms around
Brad, and Jason felt cold in spite of the tequila. Seeing
Sienna all over Brad sucked the pleasure out of every-
thing.

Jason didn't want to be there anymore. He worked
it out carefully in his head: one beer when they'd first
arrived, and now one shot—he was okay to drive. He

wondered where Tyler was. He hadn't seen him in hours.

"Your turn," Harberts told him.

Jason grabbed the closest bowling ball, sent it down the lane without aiming, and managed to knock down one of the pins. He decided to name it Brad. Even though Brad had done nothing to deserve being slammed to the ground by a bowling ball—except be lucky enough to have Sienna as his girlfriend.

"Take over for me," Jason called to Craig Yoder, a guy from his history class.

"You've got some catching up to do." Harberts tossed Craig the blue Cabo Wabo bottle as Jason made his way over to the stairs. He took them three at a time and followed the sound of whoops and whistles through the house and out onto the back patio. Tyler usually managed to locate—if not create—the epicenter of a party. It seemed like the place to start the search. Maybe he'd find Adam, too. He'd wandered off after the first game of bowling ended.

No Tyler on the patio. Although Jason thought his friend would have liked to be there to see Belle right that second. She was shaking her moneymaker down the top of the adobe wall that ran around the courtyard. Guys lined the wall below her, arms up. Wanting to be the one who caught her if she fell.

Dominic stood at the edge of the crowd, arms

crossed over his chest, watching Belle and her entourage, blue eyes narrow. Did any of those guys realize an armful of Belle almost certainly came with a gutful of her boyfriend's fists? Jason wondered.

He made his way deeper into the backyard and over to the pool. Who wouldn't want to be hanging in an outdoor pool in November? Especially when Maggie was floating on a lounge chair in the center, her long, golden-brown hair trailing in the water.

As Jason watched, Maggie used her fingertips to slowly paddle down to the shallow end of the pool and over to Kyle Priesmeyer, one of the divers on the swim team. She reached up, looped her hands around his neck, and pulled his head down for a kiss. The lounge chair rocked, but didn't capsize, and Kyle stretched out on top of Maggie.

Jason knew that Maggie had begun to feed on Kyle. And the guy was oblivious. To anything but the pleasure. Jason shook his head and continued his search for Tyler.

He hurried back into the house to check the mini-party kitchen, which included Adam eating a slice of white pizza and trying to explain why reincarnation was complete bull. Just the kind of conversation you could only take seriously when wasted. But still no Tyler.

"Jason, back me up here," Adam called, waving him

toward the group. "A whole buttload of people would have to be walking around soulless for reincarnation to be possible, correct? Because if there are a finite number of souls that keep coming back, and no new ones, there aren't enough souls to go around, because of population growth."

"Have you seen Tyler?" Jason asked, ignoring the question.

"But, no," a girl with bangs and an intense expression said. "All the souls available aren't inhabiting bodies all the time. The number of people on earth thousands of years ago tells you nothing about the total number of souls. There's no correlation."

"Tyler?" Jason said again.

"Haven't seen him since before we went upstairs," Adam answered. He broke away from the group and crossed over to Jason. "But you know what I *have* seen?" He lowered his voice. "A lot of our special friends circling Zach."

"You can see that every day at school," Jason pointed out.

"It's more than the usual Zach-adoration. And it's more than him being the birthday boy," Adam said, taking a bite of his pizza. "And he's still smiling. And the smiles are somehow vampire-related, because whatever is making him smile, they all know about it."

"Huh," Jason said, not wanting to encourage Adam.

"Yeah. Big huh." Adam tossed his pizza crust in the trash. "And even though I know the vampires have funded a massive percentage of our Malibu goodness, it kind of freaks me out to think of them behind closed doors, making plans. I mean, shouldn't our kind have a delegation?"

Jason shrugged. "If they're planning their annual croquet tournament, no. If they're coming up with, uh"—he glanced around to make sure no one was listening—"some kind of meal plan, yeah. But I thought we decided that they can handle themselves."

"Yeah. I know," Adam agreed. "I guess I should—"

"Adam, did you consider the animal and insect population in your theory?" called out a junior in desperate need of a growth spurt.

"Insects? So every mosquito has a soul, is that what you're telling me?" Adam asked, returning to the debate.

"I'm going to keep looking for Tyler," Jason muttered. He grabbed a soda on his way out.

He took a swig as he headed for the family room. Sometime during the party, it had become make-out central. He did a Tyler scan. Didn't see him. Jason turned away. But then, through the sliding doors leading to one of the house's many decks, he caught a flash of dark blue sweatshirt, like the one Tyler had been wearing tied around his waist.

Jason hurried across the room, careful not to step on the couple stretched out in front of the fire. Evidently in Malibu, sixty-five degrees was considered fireplace weather.

He opened the door and saw Tyler leaning against the deck's wooden railing, staring down at the ocean. "There you are," Jason said. "I've been looking for you."

Tyler whipped around. "Oh, hey."

Jason shook his head. "You haven't even been here a week and you're going native."

"What?" Tyler asked.

"You've got your hoodie zipped up to your neck like it's freezing," Jason said.

"Ocean makes it cold out here," Tyler answered, his hands jammed into the front pockets.

"What are you doing out here by yourself, anyway? I was looking for you in the party hot spots. You know, the Tyler zones."

"I wasn't out here *by myself* until a few minutes ago," Tyler said. He turned toward the ocean, then immediately turned back to face Jason. "You know what I mean? Huh? Huh? Huh, huh, huh?"

Jason laughed. "So who was she?"

"It wasn't a name kind of situation," Tyler replied.

"Well, what'd she look like?" Jason asked. *Did she have anything unusual about her?* he added silently. *Like fangs?*

"What? You're not getting any, so you need some vicarious thrills? Is that it?"

Jason decided that it didn't seem like Tyler had been fed on. He was talking fast, and his eyes were darting back and forth. After Erin had bitten him at Belle's party, Jason remembered that he had hardly been able to move. He'd felt drunk and floaty and, to be all California surfer about it, mellow. Tyler definitely wasn't mellow.

But had there really been a girl out there with him? Jason wondered darkly. Or had Tyler been hanging out with his friend Ritalin? He *was* all twitchy.

"You ready to get out of here?" Tyler asked.

"Sure." Jason had thought he might have to pry Tyler out of the party with a crowbar. His friend was a close-the-party-down kind of guy. He was glad he didn't have to persuade Tyler to leave. But it did put some more checks in the Tyler weirdness column. "Let's go tell Adam we're heading out."

Jason led the way back to the kitchen. The reincarnation talk had switched over to—with Adam in the group, what else?—movies.

"We're thinking about taking off," Jason told him.

"You're not staying for the screening? We're talking Tarantino here. Are you feverish?" Adam asked.

"Nah. Just like to leave the party at the peak," Jason told him. It didn't really make sense, but whatever. "See you at school."

"See you," Adam said.

As they got close to the front door, Jason spotted Sienna and Brad lingering in the hallway, standing close together. His heart suddenly felt as if it had tripled in weight. "See you guys later," Jason forced himself to say.

"You're leaving?" Brad asked. "Party foul. The second wind is about to hit. I can feel it."

Sienna didn't say a word. She didn't even look at Jason as he slapped hands with Brad and made his way out the door.

Tyler hurried toward the bug, his hands still shoved in his pockets. Jason followed him. He glanced back once, and saw Sienna kissing Brad again, her hands sliding up under his shirt.

I'd let her drink every drop of blood in my body if she kissed me like that to do it, Jason thought.

ELEVEN

"**O**kay, boys, spill!" Aunt Bianca ordered Jason and Tyler the next morning. "What kind of depravity went on at that party last night?"

Stellar. The last thing Jason wanted to talk about was the party. It just reminded him of his screwup with Sienna. And Tyler was no help. He just sat there gazing at his sausages as if they held the secrets of the universe. His foot, propped on the chair leg, bounced about a million miles an hour.

"That juicy, hmm?" Bianca asked. "You can't even come up with one thing you're willing to share?"

"Bowling," Jason answered. He scooped a second helping of scrambled eggs out of the frying pan and onto his plate, then sat back down at the kitchen table. "You know, it's a gateway activity. A high percentage of teens who've tried it move on to miniature golf. And once you go there, you can't get back without rehab."

"Bowling? You left *Zach's* party to go bowling?" Dani shook her head in disgust.

"The Lafrenières have a bowling alley," Jason said. "We didn't have to leave."

Tyler suddenly looked up and rolled an orange

across the table, knocking over the salt and pepper shakers. They all stared at him.

"Bowling," he explained.

Man, he was hyper. Ritalin before breakfast? Jason wondered. He glanced around the table. No one else seemed to find Tyler's behavior strange.

"It's a good thing you stayed home, Dani," Bianca said. "That's no kind of environment for you."

"You're way too young to start with the bowling," Jason's father agreed, with a smile.

"And bowling was the most scandalous part?" Aunt Bianca asked, spreading strawberry jam on a piece of toast.

"Pretty much," Jason answered. What did she think? That he was going to start talking about under-age drinking? Or give an estimate on the number of hook-ups that took place at Zach's? Or say that Tyler was probably high by the end of the night, and possibly now, too?

Bianca turned to Tyler. "Jason's being discreet. You tell us about the party. How did it compare to one of your Michigan blasts?"

"It's no different, right, Tyler?" Dani asked.

"No one ended up dead at the parties in Michigan," Mrs. Freeman pointed out, standing up abruptly and refilling her coffee cup.

"Someone *died* at a party out here?" Aunt Bianca

asked, stopping with her toast halfway to her mouth. She glanced at Dani. "You didn't tell me that!"

"It was a party on a yacht. A girl fell overboard and drowned. She'd been drinking," Jason's mother explained. "Now do you understand why I don't want Danielle at these things?"

Carrie was already dead when she hit the water, Jason thought, flashing on her body lying on the beach. Her lips blue. Eyes staring sightlessly.

"I . . . I can't believe it," Aunt Bianca murmured.

"Horrible. I can't even think about her poor parents," Mrs. Freeman said with a shudder.

"Well, last night's party was just a party," Tyler said. He used his fingers to pop a Tater Tot into his mouth, then another. He swallowed them, hardly bothering to chew, then smiled at Jason's mom. "The big difference was that the girls were wearing less clothes than they would have been in Michigan."

Mrs. Freeman actually laughed. Tyler had always been good at making her laugh. Jason's dad snorted.

Tyler grabbed the ketchup bottle, opened it, and thumped on the bottom so hard that he almost completely smothered his remaining Taters. "I even saw a bikini top floating in the hot tub," he added. Then he pointed at Bianca with a grin. "And that's all you're getting out of me."

"Did you go in the hot tub?" Dani asked casually.

Jason knew what she really wanted to ask Tyler: "Did you have anything to do with the removal of the bikini top?" Dani could never resist gossip—especially where someone she knew might be involved.

"Didn't bring a bathing suit," Tyler replied. He looked over at Jason. "Hey, man. Think you could drive me into the city when you're done?"

"Done now," Jason said, forking the last bite of eggs into his mouth. "Let's go." He got up feeling relieved. It would get him away from any more questions about the party.

"I'll meet you out there," Tyler said. "I want to grab my jacket."

"You're not going to need it," Jason told him, but Tyler was already gone.

Jason stood up and checked his pocket for his car keys. "See you guys later," he told his family as he headed out of the kitchen.

He hurried outside, unlocked the car, and slid into the driver's seat. A minute later, Tyler got in, hoodie zipped to his chin. "Any particular place you want to go?" Jason asked.

"Just Malibu central. I'm guessing I'll be able to find a post office there?" Tyler replied.

"Sure." Jason backed out of the driveway and headed for the Pacific Coast Highway, enjoying the view as usual. All that blue ocean stretching out for-ever. But he noticed that Tyler wasn't looking at the beach. He sat staring straight ahead, eyes intense, as if willing the car to go faster.

"Not like I'm trying to get rid of you, but won't it take you a few days to get home if you have to hitch? And even with those free days at school . . ." Jason let his words trail off. "I could spot you bus money. Again, not that I'm trying to get rid of you." Except that he was. Kind of. And how alternate-universe was that? Jason wanting Tyler gone? He used to wish they were brothers so he could live with the Freemans all the time.

"School's the least of my problems," Tyler said as Jason turned onto a road peppered with stores. "You can just let me out here."

"Here?" Jason glanced at the trendy restaurants and the shoe store. "You sure?"

"Yeah. Here is good." Tyler started to swing the door open before Jason had even pulled all the way over to the curb.

"You want to meet up in a while?" Jason asked. It was more than obvious that Tyler didn't want Jason anywhere around right now.

"I'll find my own way back," Tyler said as he climbed out of the car. "Later." And he slammed the door before Jason could get another question in.

"Thank you for using Jason's cab service," Jason muttered, staring after his friend. What was his deal? And what was he up to now?

Whatever. Jason couldn't do much if Tyler wasn't going to talk to him. He pulled back out onto the street and made a U-turn at the corner. He spotted Sienna coming out of L'OCCITANE en Provence. Sienna and Belle.

Without giving himself enough time to wimp out, Jason pulled into the parking space just vacated by an SUV. "Hey," he called as he got out of the car. "Impressive moves on that wall last night, Belle." He figured it was safer to say something to Belle first. Belle was always friendly.

"I made a couple hundred in tips," she joked. "Cold, hard cash. But Dom wasn't happy. He doesn't get that I just like attention. Is that so horrible?"

"I vote no," Jason said. "So what are you two up to?"

"I just bought some Olive Paste. It's the best thing in the world for sun-damaged hair," Belle told him. "Sienna's keeping me company. Not that she's actually talking or anything."

"I've talked," Sienna protested.

"Right. You said the words *venti mochaccino* about half an hour ago," Belle teased.

"Half an hour ago?" Jason repeated. "Then you must be ready for another one. I know shopping for hair products is tiring work. Not that I spend much time shopping for hair products," he added, which didn't significantly improve his not-so-brilliant comment.

Not that it mattered. All that mattered was that he got to spend some time with Sienna. Enough time so that she'd actually start speaking to him again. Possibly even want to kiss him again, in this lifetime.

"No, Belle needs to get home," Sienna said. She seemed to be talking to his left ear. "She insisted on wearing her new Jimmy Choos and she's destroyed her feet."

"I'll drop you at your car," Jason offered gallantly, thinking that even that would give him a little Sienna-time. "Where'd you park?"

"We walked," Belle answered. "Not my most intelligent decision, I admit." She shook her head at her sandals, which were nothing but some thin straps and spike heels.

"I'll drive you home, then," Jason said firmly. Score. He'd drop Belle off first, then—

"Oooh. Yes, please," Belle said, pulling Jason away from his thoughts. She slipped off the sandals and picked them up.

"Do you mind if I don't come with you?" Sienna asked Belle. "I said I'd drop in at Brad's place and help his mom pick out new drapes. I'll call and have Brad pick me up." She looked Jason in the eye for the first time. "I'd rather not put you out."

Or be anywhere near you, Jason added silently. *Got it.*

"Sure. Don't let my feet spoil the rest of the day for

you," Belle said, seeming oblivious to the conversation going on under the conversation. She turned to Jason. "Can we go? This pavement is getting hot on my poor little piggies."

What could he say? "Sure." He opened the passenger door of the bug, and Belle hopped in. Jason shut the door for her.

"Sienna, about what happened at the party . . . ," he began, taking the unexpected opportunity for an attempted explanation.

She pulled out her cell and hit a speed-dial number. "Hey, babe," she said, looking right at Jason. "Want to come get me?"

Jason gave a nod, then walked around to the driver's side of the car and slid behind the wheel. "Thanks so much. You are such the lifesaver," Belle told him. But Jason wasn't really listening.

You knew Sienna was with Brad. You've known it since the day you met her, Jason told himself. *It's better this way. Let her stay pissed at you. You shouldn't be going after her, anyway.*

"Where's that Tyler?" Belle asked. "All the girls at the party were intrigued. Some of them are planning a hunting trip to Michigan, which now seems to be Land of Cute Boys."

"He's still in town . . . someplace," Jason told her. *Doing who in the hell knows what,* he thought.

"Did he have fun at his first Malibu party? Zach's was definitely the one to go to."

"He claimed to. He disappeared for a while, which is usually a sign of some kind of fun, right?" Jason asked, grinning.

"Absolutely. I love to disappear at parties. It makes Dominic go mental, but the best amusements happen away from the crowd," Belle answered.

They drove past the police station, and Jason thought about Adam: "Child of the poor but hard-working chief of police," as Adam had described himself on the day they met. Maybe he was right. Maybe something had been going on last night with the vampires that at least a few humans should be aware of. And Belle knew Jason was in on the truth about exactly who lived in DeVere Heights.

"I noticed you and Sienna and some of the others disappeared upstairs for a while too," Jason said, trying to sound casual. "Were you having fun?"

"Yes."

Jason thought it was the first time he'd ever heard Belle give a one-word answer to a question. She didn't say anything else for the rest of the ride.

Clearly whatever the vampires had going was nothing humans were allowed to know about. But, like Jason kept telling Adam, that didn't mean it was anything bad. Right?

TWELVE

Jason noticed it as soon as he walked into the locker room for swim practice on the Monday after Thanksgiving weekend. Judging by the uncharacteristic quiet, something was wrong. The guys on the swim team were all there as usual, but they were changing in silence. No postschool, prepractice banter.

"What's up with you guys?" Jason called. "You all still in a turkey coma?"

"One of us is a thief," Harberts answered flatly.

"What?" Jason demanded, wandering over to Harberts's locker. Brad sat next to him, swim goggles pushed up on his forehead.

"The Lafrenières got robbed the night of Zach's party," Brad explained.

"They're sure somebody who was at the party did it," Van Dyke added from the next row of lockers over.

Jason relaxed a tiny bit. "So you're talking one of us who was there, not one of us on the team," he said.

"It better not be somebody from the team!" Van Dyke declared, appearing from around the corner. "That would be an even bigger betrayal."

"What was taken?" Jason asked. "A lot?"

"Just one thing. An antique that's been in the Lafrenière family for hundreds of years," Brad said. "Zach's dad freaked out hardcore this morning when he realized it was missing. He called the school and had Zach yanked from class."

"That's asinine. What's Zach supposed to do about it?" Harberts asked.

Brad shrugged.

"All I can say is that Maggie Roy is not guilty," Kyle volunteered, joining the group. "I had my hands on her all night."

"Priesmeyer just wants to advertise that he finally got a little," Van Dyke commented with a laugh.

"Hey, we're talking Maggie Roy," Kyle said.

"Been there. Done that," Harberts told him.

"You lie. We all know you're on your way to being the next forty-year-old virgin," Kyle shot back.

Ah, this was the locker room Jason knew and loved.

"What kind of antique are we talking?" Harberts asked, getting serious again.

"A gold chalice. That's a cup to you, Harberts," Brad answered. "The thief was smart, too. The chalice was locked in Mr. Lafrenière's briefcase. I guess it's usually kept in a safe-deposit box, but he'd taken it out to use over the holiday. Anyway, the thief managed to crack the lock, and he left this glass paperweight in place of the chalice. Otherwise, Mr. Lafrenière would have realized something was wrong the second he picked up the case."

An image of Tyler suddenly slammed into Jason's head. Tyler all twitchy. Hoodie zipped up to his chin. Hands jammed in the big front pocket. Because he was holding the chalice? Hiding it under the baggy sweatshirt?

A year ago, it wouldn't have crossed Jason's mind. In fact, he'd have punched anyone who considered the possibility. But since his parents' divorce, Tyler had changed. And he was desperate for cash.

But *that* desperate? Jason wasn't sure.

Then he remembered the phone call on Tyler's cell. The guy had mentioned a thirty-six-hour deadline. And Tyler had turned into an instant asshole. It had obviously been a threat. It might have been enough to make Tyler willing to do just about anything.

But the threat was nothing compared to what Tyler might be facing now. At least the guy on the phone was human.

"How can a place like the Lafrenières' not have an extremely high-tech security system?" Kyle asked.

Brad turned toward Jason, even though the question had been Kyle's. "It does. There are cameras everywhere. By now, they probably know who did it."

Jason stared back at him. Was Brad trying to tell

him something? Had Brad seen something that made him suspect Tyler, too?

Was it a warning?

"Damn! I completely forgot I have a dentist appointment," Jason exclaimed. "My mom's going to massacre me. Tell the coach, okay?"

Brad nodded. And Jason headed out of the locker room, holding himself to a fast walk. The second he was through the doors, he broke into a run. He had to talk to Tyler. Jason just hoped he'd find him in front of the TV where he'd left him that morning.

Jason raced to the parking lot and over to the bug. He vaulted into the convertible without bothering to open the door and squealed out of the lot. He stepped on the gas as soon as he hit the PCH. Seventy. Eighty. He needed to find Tyler fast.

Zach Lafrenière was a guy who took action—the other vampires counted on him for it. And Zach took care of problems—violently, if necessary. What exactly would Zach do to Tyler for stealing something irreplaceable from his family?

Jason caught sight of a figure out of the corner of his eye and slammed on the brakes. He twisted around. Yeah, it was Tyler. His friend was staring at him from the edge of the cliffs overlooking the beach on the other side of the road. "Tyler!" he shouted. "Get in the car!"

Tyler waited for a Jeep to drive past, then jogged across the two-lane highway. "Hey. Decided to walk into town," he said cheerfully.

"Get in," Jason told him again.

"I was thinking of maybe renting a board. Can't come all the way to Malibu without at least attempting to surf. Am I right?" Tyler asked.

"The Lafrenières were robbed at the party on Friday," Jason told him. He locked eyes with Tyler. "I think it might be a good time for you to be at home. A stranger in town could be at the top of their list of suspects."

Tyler nodded wordlessly and climbed into the car.

"Did you do it, Ty?" Jason came right out with the question. He pulled back onto the highway. He wanted to get Tyler out of sight until he knew exactly what the situation was. "I don't hear you answering."

"You take me to a party with you and you think I *stole* something?" Tyler shook his head sadly.

"That's not an answer." Why couldn't Tyler just give him a no? That was all Jason wanted.

"You have a Bible? I need a Bible if you're going to put me on the witness stand," Tyler snapped.

Jason glanced at his old friend. He looked as pissed off as he sounded. And Jason began to doubt himself. Maybe he'd jumped to a false—and insulting—conclusion.

"I didn't do it," Tyler told him, speaking slowly and carefully, like a kindergarten teacher giving safety instructions. "Happy?"

"Ecstatic," Jason muttered as they entered the Heights. "Sorry," he told Tyler. "I just . . ." He didn't go on. There was no explanation good enough for accusing his friend of being a thief.

"Forget it," Tyler said.

Jason pulled into his driveway—and hit the brakes fast. His stomach seized as he looked at the house. The front door hung open.

"Didn't my mom and Bianca say they had some kind of charity luncheon today?" he asked. "And Dani was going to go straight to Kristy's and stay there until after dinner."

"Yeah," Tyler said, staring at the gaping door. "And your father's at work."

Jason threw the car into park and killed the engine. He dashed to the door, Tyler right behind him.

Books, CDs, and DVDs lay all over the living room floor. The coffee table had been knocked over. The glass in his mother's curio cabinet smashed. The ottoman flipped and the bottom slit open.

Someone had come in and searched the place. And Jason knew exactly what they had been looking for.

THIRTEEN

Jason whipped around, grabbed Tyler by the shoulders, and slammed him against the wall. "Tell me again that you didn't steal an antique chalice from the Lafrenières!"

Tyler didn't look pissed off anymore. He had gone pale. "I didn't know they'd do anything like this. If I'd thought it would somehow come back to your family . . ."

But it *had* come back to Jason's family. Tyler had brought the vampires right into Jason's home. What would have happened if his parents or his aunt or Dani had been there? The thought made his body go cold, then hot with anger. "So you took it. Just admit it," Jason ordered.

Tyler twisted away from him. "I had no choice."

"Bullshit."

"You're right." Tyler strode into the living room and began picking up books and shoving them back on the bookshelf. "I had a choice. I could have let Russ kill me."

Jason followed Tyler, catching sight of the kitchen through the open door. The canisters of sugar, flour, and coffee had been dumped. The floor looked like some kind of toxic beach.

"Who's Russ?" he asked, joining Tyler in gathering up the books. He almost didn't want to know the answer.

"My dealer."

"And? Come on, do I have to yank the whole story out of you word by word?"

"I stole from him, all right? I needed some Ritalin. I got addicted to it. I didn't have the cash. Russ wouldn't front me, so I took everything he had, even drugs I didn't want. I was pissed," Tyler confessed. "Like five thousand dollars' worth of stuff."

"Christ." Jason let out a long breath. "That call I answered? That was—"

"That was Russ. He's my new best friend. Calls all the time," Tyler said. "Thanks for telling him where I was, by the way." He jammed a book onto a shelf hard enough to make the bookcase shake.

"I'm not used to my friends being chased by people who want them dead," Jason countered. He moved toward another book and heard a sharp crack. He pulled his foot back. "Great! You now owe my mother a *Celine Dion's Greatest Hits* CD." He glanced around the room. "Among other things," he added under his breath.

"Look, Russ gave me forty-eight hours to get him

cash for what I stole," Tyler said. "And I wasn't kidding about him sending somebody out here to kill me. Or at least seriously mess me up. I figured the Lafrenières have insurance up the wazoo. I thought they'd just submit a claim. No harm, no foul." Tyler lifted his arms, then let them fall to his sides. "How was I supposed to know they'd do something like this? You saw their house. They have more crap than they could use in five lives. Why would they care so much?"

"You picked the wrong thing to steal," Jason told him. "That chalice has been in their family for generations. That's why they care so much." A thought struck him like a knife in the chest. "Was it even here when they trashed the place?"

Tyler shook his head. "I sold it at a pawn shop."

"Then this isn't over. They aren't going to stop until they get it back. And, obviously"—Jason kicked the overturned ottoman—"they know you're the one who took the thing. We've got to go get it."

"With what? I wired the money to Michigan already. I have"—Tyler pulled his wallet out of his back pocket and checked the contents—"fifty-four dollars total."

"We'll figure that out later. We've got to get to the pawn shop before they sell it," Jason said. "Because somebody else might be looking to mess you up if we don't." He hesitated. "It'll only slow us down if I call

Dad now and try to tell him some version of what happened. So let's hit it," he told Tyler.

"I'm surprised you actually managed to find a pawn shop in Malibu," Jason said as Tyler pushed the buzzer next to the door.

"Rich people probably need quick cash for their dealers every once in a while," Tyler said. "It's easy to spend however much money you have on drugs. And then some."

Another buzz sounded. Tyler grabbed the door-knob and pulled the door open. Jason followed him inside. One wall held TVs, DVD players, CD players, and computers. A selection of cameras hung from the ceiling. Glass counters held an assortment of jewelry, including a variety of diamond engagement rings. It was pretty pathetic.

"Back already?" the middle-aged guy behind the counter asked Tyler. "Got some more good stuff for me?" He gave his short, graying ponytail a tug.

"We need back the gold chalice he sold you," Jason said.

"Not possible," the clerk answered. "That thing flew out of here. I only had it in the case for a couple of hours."

"Who bought it?" Jason demanded.

"This is the kind of place where people like their privacy," the man replied flatly.

"It's important," Tyler put in. "I'm kind of in a bad position."

The man shrugged. "It's also the kind of place where people are in bad positions a lot. I stay out of that."

"We only want to find the buyer so we can buy back the chalice. We'll pay more than they paid. A lot more." Jason had no idea where he or Tyler would come up with the money. A loan from Aunt Bianca, maybe? It didn't matter. For now, all he cared about was finding the chalice.

"Doesn't interest me," the clerk said. "I don't give out buyer information."

Jason pulled his fingers through his hair. "How about this? You contact the buyer for us, and tell them that we'll give them a profit if they'll sell us the chalice back."

The man pulled a rag out of his back pocket and started to polish the closest counter. "Of course, you'd get a percentage if the buyer agrees to sell," Jason added quickly.

"Give me your phone number." The man slid a business card across the counter to Jason.

Jason carefully printed his cell number on the card and slid it over. "We really appreciate this."

The guy grinned. "I'll call you if they're interested."

Jason waited. But it was clear that no call would be

made while they were standing there, so he turned and headed out.

"Thanks for doing that," Tyler told him as they walked down the sidewalk toward the car. "I shouldn't have come here. I shouldn't have brought all this into your life. Your parents have always been great to me, and—"

"Enough, already," Jason interrupted. "You completely pissed me off. You lied to me. You got my house trashed. But you're my oldest friend. Who else were you supposed to come to?"

"There was no one else," Tyler admitted.

"What do you think—," Jason began.

An SUV with tinted windows abruptly pulled up alongside them and stopped. The side door slid open, fast and soundless. Immediately, two men leaped out, and Jason saw a flash of metal in the sunlight as a piece of pipe came down on Tyler's head.

Jason launched himself at the closest assailant, but another man moved in from the left to block him. Before Jason could reach Tyler, the men had him in the van and the door was sliding shut.

A second later the guy who'd blocked Jason was behind the wheel. Jason heard the van pull away. He stared after it. No license plate.

It sped around the corner and disappeared. With Tyler inside.

FOURTEEN

Jason stared down the empty street. Adrenaline rushed through his body. Where were they taking Tyler? And what were they going to do to him when they got there?

His cell phone started to play "It's a Small World," courtesy of Dani again. Jason jerked the cell out of his pocket and hit talk. "Tyler?" he asked, knowing even as he said it that there was no possible way it was his friend.

"No, it's me. Sienna."

Sienna. The last person he'd expected. Jason hadn't thought she'd ever want to talk to him again.

"You have to get Tyler out of Malibu. Right now," she told him, her voice tight with tension.

"Too late." Jason looked down the street again, as if somehow, magically, the SUV would come speeding backward toward him and the whole abduction would happen in reverse, leaving Tyler standing next to him. "Two guys just snatched him. I was right there, but I couldn't stop it."

Sienna didn't respond. But he could hear her breathing. "I know where he is," she said finally.

"Where? Tell me."

She hesitated.

Come on, come on, come on! Jason urged silently. He didn't have time for this. *Tyler* didn't have time.

"Meet me at Zach's. At the gazebo in the side garden," Sienna instructed.

"I'm on my way." Jason started toward his car.

"And Jason? Don't park where anyone can see you," Sienna finished. She hung up before he could respond.

Jason parked a block away from Zach's. He cut down to the beach, figuring there was less chance of him being spotted if he approached the house from that way, rather than from the front. Although it occurred to him that all those decks and balconies would give anyone who happened to be looking a perfect view of him. He just had to hope no one had picked this moment to enjoy the ocean views.

He ran along the sand, his feet sinking into it with every step. Jason usually loved running on the beach, but right now he wanted some nice, hard asphalt. A surface that would let him get some traction and *speed*.

Sneakers wouldn't hurt either, he thought as he veered toward the rough wooden logs that served as stairs up the side of the cliff. A layer of sand had crept between his Tevas and his feet.

Jason pounded up the steps and and raced over to

the gazebo. Sienna was already waiting, her long, inky hair fluttering in the breeze coming off the ocean.

"Thanks for calling me," he said when he reached her. "So what gives?"

"Zach asked me to call," Sienna told him. "He thinks he owes you for saving his life," she continued. "Zach doesn't like to owe anybody."

"He doesn't owe me. He saved my life, too. But I'm sure as hell not going to turn down his help," Jason answered. "Where's Tyler?"

"Zach wanted you to get him out of town." Sienna twisted her hair into a knot to keep it from blowing in her face. "But I really don't know what you can do for him now."

"Just tell me where he is and let me worry about the rest," Jason said impatiently.

Sienna gave a reluctant nod. "He's been taken before the Council."

Questions exploded in Jason's head. "The what?"

"The DeVere Heights Vampire Council," Sienna repeated. "It's this group that makes decisions about things that involve all of . . . of us."

"Why would this council care about Tyler?" Jason demanded. "Is it, like, steal from one of you and you steal from all of you?"

"What Tyler took belongs to all of us, in a way," Sienna explained. "The Lafrenières keep the chalice because they are one of the oldest vampire families, but it doesn't truly belong to them. It's a sacred relic that has been used in our ceremonies for centuries."

Nice one, Tyler, Jason thought. *The Lafrenière house is stuffed with expensive crap. And you had to grab some precious vampire artifact!*

"So what are they going to do with him?" Jason paced the gazebo, unable to stand still. "He's already sold the thing, but we have a lead on getting it back. We just need a little time."

"I don't know," Sienna admitted apprehensively. "That's what they're deciding right now. But it doesn't look good. That's why Zach wanted you to get Tyler out of town before they found him."

"Where *is* Zach?" Jason demanded. He and Jason weren't friends. Jason didn't know if Zach was actually friends with anyone—even any of the vampires. But Zach had power and, rightly or wrongly, he felt indebted to Jason. Right now, Jason could use that.

"He's at the meeting," Sienna replied. "He's on the Council now. That's why the chalice was out of the bank vault in the first place. It was used in the ceremony to inaugurate Zach onto the Council, the night of the party. The party was given just to hide the fact that all the vampires were gathered. There was even a member of the High Council at the house that night."

So that's *why there was extra Zach-adoration at the*

party, Jason thought. "Okay, well, where does the Council meet?" he asked. His mind was racing. Maybe he could talk to the Council. Explain that he had already been to the pawnbroker. That, no matter what, he and Tyler would get the chalice back.

Or was discussion time over?

"If I tell you that . . ." Sienna let her words trail off. She pulled her thin sweater tighter around herself.

"I get it. The Council could come after you," Jason filled in for her. "Look, I won't tell them who I got the information from. Just tell me where they are."

"I don't care about me," Sienna burst out, her voice ragged with emotion. "But if you try to interfere with the Council, they could kill you. I can't let that happen, Jason. It might be too late for you to save Tyler. But it's not too late for *me* to save *you*!"

Her words were so unexpected that it took Jason a moment to process them. After all his clumsiness, he was amazed that Sienna actually cared. In the midst of the current crisis, part of him still found time to be ridiculously pleased that she did. But it didn't change anything. He reached out and touched her arm. "Sienna, he's my best friend. I can't just . . ." He shook his head. "I can't."

"In the Garden," she said simply.

Jason's eyes darted around the gardens surrounding the gazebo.

"No, up there." Sienna pointed to the roof of the Lafrenière house. Sunlight glinted off huge panels of glass.

Jason frowned. He'd been on the top floor—all over the top floor—with Adam, and yet he hadn't seen those massive skylights. And, even at night, all that glass would have been impossible to miss.

And then suddenly, he got it. He and Adam hadn't actually been on the top floor at all. There was another whole floor to the house. That's why he and Adam had seen the vampires go upstairs but hadn't seen anyone there when they went up themselves.

"Go home, Sienna," Jason said, his eyes fixed on the roof.

"What are you going to do?" she asked anxiously.

He turned to look at her and paused to run one finger down her soft, pale cheek. "Don't worry about me. Just go."

FIFTEEN

It's not like I can just go ring the doorbell and ask if I can please have my friend back, Jason thought, staring at the Lafrenière house. He pulled out his cell and called Adam. He had the strong, unpleasant feeling that he might need someone to get his back. Soon.

"Talk to me," Adam said.

"I don't have time to explain, but I need you over at Zach's," Jason told him. "I'll be . . . I should be on the roof. North side."

"Why would you—?" Adam began.

Jason hung up and surveyed the roof. Even a few more seconds could be critical to Tyler. But, since he wasn't freakin' Spider-Man, how was he going to get up there to find out what was going on? Could the ivy and honeysuckle growing up the side of the house be strong enough to hold him? Jason trotted over to investigate.

Not a great option, he decided as he gave the thick, intertwined vines an experimental tug. But the only one that seemed to be available. And, hey, Sienna had climbed up a trellis in his dream, so this had to work. "Here goes nothing," Jason muttered, and reached up to grab a handful of the vines.

He slowly scaled the wall of the house, inch by inch. Leaves tore off in his fingers, but the thin vines held. For now. He moved up one story. Then another.

He ignored the sweat forming on his palms and between his toes. He tried to keep his movements even, putting steady pressure on the vines without jerking.

Snap!

The hunk of ivy and honeysuckle in Jason's right hand broke free. His body slipped, his feet sliding off the wall. His full weight now hung on the vines in his left hand. And he could feel them beginning to give. . . .

One of the smaller balconies was just a little way above him and a few feet to the left. Jason swung out just as the vines tore. With one hand, he grabbed the balcony railing. The metal bit into his palm and the muscles in his arm burned, but he slowly hauled himself up and over the railing.

Jason allowed himself to take a couple of deep breaths, then leaned over the railing to survey the damage. There were no longer any vines in reach above him. Unless . . .

He braced one hand against the wall and got himself balanced on top of the thin wrought-iron railing of the balcony. Then he twisted his body—and jumped. He managed to grab some of the vines high up above him in each hand. His feet scrambled against the stone wall, then found purchase. He scaled the rest of the wall as quickly as possible, trying to keep his weight on each section of vine for as short a time as possible.

And at last his fingers hit roof. Sweet, sweet roof. Jason pulled himself up onto it. One of the huge glass panes was about five feet away. He crawled over, and what he saw took his breath away.

Sienna had called the meeting place the Garden. Jason had been expecting some sort of conservatory: lots of potted plants under glass. What he actually found was astounding.

Almost thirty feet below Jason, inside the house, smooth, green grass lawns stretched across the entire top floor of the Lafrenière mansion. Trees stretched up toward the windows, their top branches nearly brushing the glass. Birds of paradise, hibiscus, and other exotic-looking flowers Jason didn't know the names of blossomed everywhere. And a waterfall at the far end of the Garden splashed into a stream that meandered through the man-made glen. It looked like some kind of Eden. Extreme.

Through a cluster of trees, Jason spotted flashes of color. People, he thought. Well, vampires. The trees blocked most of his view. He'd have to move to a different window. Cautiously, attempting soundlessness,

Jason crept across the roof toward the next of the enormous skylights.

A mosaic of black-and-white stone dominated this side of the Garden. A huge glass table stood on top of it. And, standing around the table was a collection of Beautiful People. Capital B, capital P. *Make that a V,* Jason told himself. They were all vampires. But they looked like movie stars playing big-business execs. Power suits on the men. Dresses and skyscraper heels on most of the women, in colors that rivaled the flowers. Five-hundred-dollar haircuts all around. Manicures, of course. The undead knew how to take care of themselves.

Zach was the exception. Not that he wasn't a B.V. Jason had heard Dani rave about his intense dark brown eyes and his black hair and his perfect body. But Zach hadn't gone with a suit. Although Jason was pretty sure—thanks to Dani's fashion obsession—that his jeans were Armani.

As if they'd been given a signal, all the vampires sat down. And Jason felt a rush of adrenaline.

Tyler sat in one of the chairs. No, "sat" was the wrong word. He was slumped in one of the chairs, his head hanging so that his chin rested against his chest. Motionless.

For a horrible moment, Jason wondered if he was too late. Was Tyler already dead?

SIXTEEN

Jason stared at his friend. From so far away, he couldn't see if Tyler's chest was rising and falling. But after a moment, he saw Tyler's hand twitch. Tyler was alive—apparently unconscious, but alive.

I never should have brought him to Zach's party, Jason thought. *I shouldn't have let him get within a hundred yards of any of the vampires.*

But Jason knew that that was not what he should be obsessing about now. He needed a plan to get Tyler away from the vampires. And he realized that first he'd have to find out what the vampires were planning. Jason leaned closer to the glass in an effort to overhear their discussion below. He could hear nothing, but he felt something hard pressing into his chest.

Jason twisted around and slid sideways to see what it was, and found that he was lying on a latch. The massive skylight could be opened.

Could he risk it? The ceiling of the Garden stretched high—high enough to allow for full-size trees. Jason decided he could probably ease the window open without attracting the vampires' attention. He flipped the latch and gradually inched the window up. Thankfully, the skylight glided open smoothly and soundlessly. The scent of eucalyptus, bay, and grass filled the air.

Jason scanned the vampires at the table below him. Not one of them glanced up. He could see a guy in a charcoal suit talking. But he still couldn't hear what he was saying. Shit. He'd have to get closer.

Jason chose the thickest branch on the closest eucalyptus tree, which stood about thirty feet from the Council table. Without giving himself time to think, he slithered forward on his stomach and leaned down until he could reach the branch, then he grabbed hold and swung himself into the air. *Another branch, another branch. I need another branch,* Jason thought, feeling around frantically with his feet. Luckily, he was now screened by the sharp-smelling eucalyptus leaves, but he could only cling to his branch for so long. . . .

One of his toes hit something hard. Okay. Jason carefully got both feet positioned on the branch below, then inched toward the trunk. Now he could hear the man's voice, but not his actual words. He had to get closer still.

His heart pounded as he began to climb— agonizingly slowly—down the tree. He chose each step and handhold carefully, attempting complete silence.

Jason finally paused on a branch about fifteen feet above the ground. At first all he could hear was his pulse thumping in his ears. But the sound faded as his heart returned to its normal rhythm, and he found he could make out what the man was saying. He wriggled around until he could see the speaker through the leaves and branches. All eyes were on him as he spoke. No one glanced in Jason's direction.

". . . pawnbroker sold it," the man continued. "The boy doesn't have anything to tell us. He's useless."

So let him go, Jason urged silently.

"So let's dump him before he regains consciousness," Zach said, echoing Jason's thought. "He doesn't know anything. He can't connect us to anything that's happened to him."

Jason suspected Zach was more interested in making the score even between himself and Jason than in Tyler's well-being. Good enough for now. *Glad he hates to owe anyone,* Jason thought.

"That's only part of the issue," a woman with a blond bun responded. "He stole from all of us."

"So turn him over to the cops along with the security tape. Stealing from the Lafrenières will be treated seriously by our loyal men in blue," Zach said with a grin, sticking one foot up on the glass table.

The blonde stared at his top-of-the-line hiking boot in disgust, but she didn't comment.

"How many tickets did we buy to the Policemen's Ball, Dad?" he asked the man sitting across the table from him. Jason noted that Zach's father had the same black hair as Zach, but his eyes were lighter, a silvery gray.

"A more than adequate number," Mr. Lafrenière answered. He stared pointedly at Zach's foot on the table. Zach didn't move it. "I'm sure they would be happy to make things very unpleasant for the young man," he added, indicating Tyler with a nod of his head.

Unpleasant was . . . unpleasant, of course, but at this point, Jason could easily imagine much worse. He prayed that Zach and his father would convince the rest of the Council not to hurt Tyler.

"'Unpleasant' isn't good enough," the blonde insisted. "There are people out there who know the history of the chalice. If it falls into the wrong hands, our whole community is threatened. He's endangered us all!" Murmurs of agreement came from what Jason estimated to be at least half of the Council.

"So we get it back," Zach said with a shrug. "That's the solution. We get it back, and no one sees it."

Right. No harm, no foul. Jason looked hopefully at the other vampires around the table, to see if they seemed to agree.

"Our newest member of the Council certainly is chatty," put in a woman wearing a diamond ring that could choke a horse, frowning at Zach.

Zach ignored her. "We have the resources to find the buyer." Zach raised one dark eyebrow. "Or am I wrong?" His tone made it clear he was sure that wasn't a possibility.

Everyone else at the table was older than Zach. But he had their full attention. It occurred to Jason that Zach might actually have the cojones to pull this off.

"You're right," the speaker Suit answered. "And, of course, we'll do whatever we have to do to get the chalice back. But that's a separate question. We're talking about what to do with the boy."

"Kill him," a man with collar-length red hair said calmly. Jason bit his lip.

"I agree." The blond woman gave a decisive nod. "We can't tolerate such a lack of respect."

"But it's not as if he knows who we are," a woman with bloodred lipstick told the group. Relief flooded through Jason. "It's not as though he decided to steal from us on purpose."

"Does that matter?" the speaker asked.

"Not to me," the redhead answered. "I don't care about motive. I care about action."

"You care about vengeance," Zach said.

Way to go, Zach! Jason murmured soundlessly.

"That's enough," Mr. Lafrenière barked at Zach. "Being asked to join the Council is an honor. An honor that can be revoked!" He sighed. "We all appreciate the way you dealt with the last . . . situation, Zach," he added more calmly. There were several nods around the table. "But you were too impulsive. Too wild. You still have a lot to learn."

Zach dropped his foot back to the ground. "I killed that vampire because he stopped following our rules and started hurting innocent people," Zach said. "We don't murder. Or has that changed?" He looked over at his father. So did everyone else.

The silence that filled the Garden felt as if it had physical weight. Jason found himself holding his breath.

At last, Zach's father responded. "We never feed to the point of death," he said flatly.

"I understand the need to kill a vampire—or a human—who is a threat to us," an older man with a mane of silvery hair said quietly. "But I honestly don't see the danger in letting the boy live. I think we're sliding into the realms of revenge here."

"I agree. I'm not at all comfortable killing him simply because he stole from one of us," the woman in dark lipstick answered.

"All of us," another murmured.

"Murdering a thief is worse than what that vampire did, because we'd be killing calmly and rationally," put in the silver-haired man. "Not in the grip of the bloodlust."

"I don't see the point of more discussion," the speaker interrupted loudly. "It's time for the vote."

Mr. Lafrenière nodded gravely and leaned forward. "I second that."

A vote on whether Tyler lived or died. Jason shook his head in an effort to dispel the horror that was threatening to cloud his brain. He scanned the enormous room, looking for all possible exits. If they voted to kill Tyler, he would have to move fast.

He listened to the voices as each member of the Council handed down a verdict. Six to six. A tie. Now what?

"Shouldn't the decision to kill be unanimous?" someone asked.

"A fine point," Jason whispered.

"We've never required a unanimous vote before," the blonde said.

"Have you ever voted to slaughter a human before?" Zach asked lazily.

Jason saw her stiffen at the word "slaughter." Good.

"Our visitor from the High Council will be here any minute and will cast the deciding vote," Mr. Lafrenière said firmly, before any of the others could respond.

"Of course," the speaker agreed without hesitation, and there was an almost universal murmur of assent from the others around the table.

Okay, now time for a bathroom break, Jason thought. *Or everybody downstairs for coffee and doughnuts. Whatever. Just leave long enough for me to get Tyler out of here.*

Nobody moved.

If the High Council member voted the wrong way, what could he do? The closest exit—the only exit Jason could see, other than the windows—was back by the waterfall. He wouldn't be able to get Tyler over there without a fight—and he couldn't possibly fight all of them. Would they kill Tyler as soon as the deciding vote was cast? Jason wondered. Or was there some kind of ceremony that might buy him some time?

Jason saw one half of the large double doors by the waterfall swing open. The branches prevented him from seeing who had entered, but all the vampires fell silent. Now there was only the sound of rushing water and the faint rustle of leaves.

Mr. Lafrenière moved out of Jason's line of sight. A moment later, he returned with a woman. Jason could see the top of her head—dark hair in a ponytail—but that was it. Zach's father stood blocking her.

A woman, Jason thought, surprised, *but who?* Cautiously, he parted the closest branches, trying to get a better look. Was she someone he knew? The mother of someone he went to school with? Or was she from France? Maybe all the High Council members came from the homeland.

He still couldn't see her face, and he was afraid that if he pressed on the branches any harder, one of them would snap. And then Tyler wouldn't be the only one in need of a rescue mission.

"Madame High Councillor, please take my chair," Mr. Lafrenière said. "We've found ourselves at a stalemate. We need you to cast the final vote."

"Of course," the High Councillor answered, her voice low and gravelly. And somehow familiar.

She sat down, and at last, Jason could see her face. He almost fell out of the eucalyptus tree in shock.

He was looking at his aunt Bianca.

SEVENTEEN

So Bianca was a vampire.

Jason stared at her, for some reason remembering the toy bulldozer she'd given him for his fifth birthday and how she'd sat in the backyard with him for hours, using it to make a road. He remembered her visiting him in the hospital when he was eleven and had his tonsils out. She'd taught him how to play poker that day. He remembered her taking him to the best concert of his life in Madison Square Garden when he was fifteen.

And then he remembered her coming out of the pool house on Thanksgiving, leaving Joe the pool guy in there practically walking into walls and giggling. *She bit him,* Jason realized grimly. *Right there in our pool house.*

Jason's mind reeled with shock and confusion. How could Aunt Bianca—the person of whom he had so many good memories—be a vampire? How could *his mother's sister* be a vampire?

His mother's sister. A trickle of cold sweat ran down Jason's back. Aunt Bianca and his mother had so much in common . . . could that mean his mother was a vampire too? Sienna had told him vampirism was hereditary.

But . . . his *mother*? That would mean he and Dani would have to be at least half—

Jason realized his aunt had begun to speak. He shoved all his questions aside and tried to focus.

"This isn't something I want to do," she was saying, her voice cool and crisp and oh so businesslike. "But our safety has been compromised by the theft of the chalice. We can't allow that to happen. We have to show anyone who may be watching that we will do whatever is necessary to protect ourselves."

Bianca stared calmly at Tyler. "I vote that the boy should die."

And at that moment, Jason mentally disowned his aunt. She knew Tyler. She'd known him since he was a little kid. She'd had breakfast with him that morning. And now she was calmly commanding his death.

Jason frowned, his mind focused and racing now, determined to find a way to rescue Tyler. But there were thirteen vampires down there—terrible odds.

"I'll dispose of him. Not here, of course," Bianca was saying briskly. "Zach, help me get him down to my car. I think he's about to regain consciousness, and the less he sees of this place—and any of you—the better."

Jason saw a glimmer of hope. His aunt and Zach—

he felt more confident about taking on just the two of them. And maybe Zach would still be feeling indebted.

Jason's cell phone rang. His body jerked, and for the second time he almost fell off his branch. He yanked the cell out of his pocket and managed to turn it off two notes into "It's a Small World."

He scanned the faces of the vampires. A few of them were glancing around the table as if they'd heard the sound. But no one looked up. Jason checked the number of the incoming call. Adam. He texted a quick message: "Wait. Quiet."

Bianca and Zach were half carrying, half dragging Tyler toward the door by the waterfall now. Jason needed to get out of the Garden and formulate a plan, fast.

"The rest of you leave a few at a time," Bianca ordered over her shoulder as Jason started back up the tree.

The leaves trembled as he moved from branch to branch. He could only pray that his luck held. And it seemed to. No one shouted out as he grabbed the edge of the skylight and scrambled back onto the roof. Gently, he slid the glass pane closed.

Now he just had to get himself to the ground— easy, except that a chunk of his vine ladder was now missing. Jason stretched out on his belly and surveyed the side of the house. To his horror he saw that more than a chunk had gone—the honeysuckle and ivy had crumpled to the ground from the spot where they tore. There was no getting down that way.

Luckily, Jason had another idea. He inched down the section of vines that remained, then grabbed the railing of the balcony he'd used before. Now came the tricky part. There was another balcony below this one, but it was off to the right.

Jason swung out and back, building up momentum. One. Two. Three. He released the railing, letting himself fly backward through the air. He landed on the floor of the lower balcony, hard enough to knock the breath out of him for a moment.

"Are you insane?" Adam called up to him when Jason got back on his feet.

Jason signaled frantically for him to shut up, then climbed over the balcony rail and used the railing to lower himself as far as he could. He checked the bushes below him. *They should help. A little,* he thought. Then he let go.

"I don't need an answer," Adam said as he rushed over and helped Jason out of the thick, prickly brush. "I can already see you are certifiable."

"I feel like I am," Jason told him. "I just found out my aunt Bianca is a vampire. And not just any vampire. She's on something they call the 'High Council.'"

"Why do I think that's not the group in charge of Vampire Twister?" Adam asked.

"She was meeting with the DeVere Heights Vampire Council to decide what to do with Tyler. Short version: At Zach's party, he stole a priceless artifact the vampires use in their ceremonies. And the Council just voted to kill him for it. Aunt Bianca's going to do it. She's going to take him . . . wherever, and just off him."

"Wait. Your aunt is a vampire?" Adam repeated. Jason wasn't sure whether he'd actually taken in anything else. "What does that mean about your mom? And, not to get too personal, you? The whole thing is supposed to be inherited, right?"

"I thought of that." Reflexively, Jason ran his tongue over his teeth. Pretty blunt. "I'm not. I can't be. I'd have to know, wouldn't I?"

"You haven't been drinking any blood lately, have you?"

"No," Jason answered quickly. "Well, if I cut my finger or something, I lick it. Is that weird?" Suddenly, the taste flooded his mouth: salty, metallic, warm. He felt his gag reflex react. Surely that was a good sign.

"Everybody does that," Adam told him. "Do you think your mom knows about your aunt?"

"I'm not sure," Jason admitted. "It shocked the hell out of me. And there's no way Dani would know if I don't. If my mom does know what Bianca is, she's keeping it a big secret. I guess it's possible, but I seriously doubt—"

Jason stopped. He could feel the outline of a plan forming. "I'm not supposed to know about Aunt Bianca," he muttered.

"Yeah. That's kind of the definition of a secret," Adam said. "Did you hit that soft spot on your head when you fell?"

"But, listen, we can use the secret thing. Bianca isn't going to want to say or do anything in front of me that would make me realize she isn't just my regular, *human* aunt," Jason explained. He pulled his keys out of his pocket and handed them to Adam. "So, go get my car and bring it right up to the front door of the house, okay? I parked down the block."

"I saw. I'm gone." Adam sprinted away.

Jason positioned himself at the side of the house, in sight of Bianca's rented red Mustang convertible and the front door. Then waited. He mentally rehearsed what he was going to say, hoping that he'd be able to sound convincing. It's not like he was much of an actor. His last performance had been when he played a potato in the third-grade play.

He ran his fingers through his hair, pulling out a leaf, and smoothed down his shirt. He needed to look normal when he talked to his aunt. Otherwise, he'd blow the plan. "You're not going to blow it," he told himself firmly. "Tyler's life depends on that!"

Where were Bianca and Zach? How long could it take them to get Tyler downstairs? Jason wondered. They hadn't decided to kill Zach in the house, had they? No, that didn't make sense. The mess, for one thing. They wouldn't want to get blood all over the Lafrenière showplace. Unless they killed him in a bloodless way. Would they just drain him? Would they figure why not use the blood for—

The front door swung open, snapping Jason out of his thoughts. Bianca and Zach emerged, supporting Tyler between them. His eyes were open now, and he was walking. He'd clearly fall if they let him go, but he was at least able to move his legs.

"Zach! Tyler! Hey!" Jason called, strolling toward them all. His voice came out a little too loud. A little nervous sounding, maybe. But passable. "Aunt Bianca! What are you doing here?" Jason decided he would be the one asking the questions. Let her play defense.

Her eyes widened, but she answered smoothly enough. "I was dropping off a book for Zach's father," she said quickly. "Something I knew Stefan would want him to have."

So you're a vampire and *a stellar liar,* Jason thought. *Way to go, Aunt Bianca!*

His aunt smiled. "And, as you can see, I found our Tyler having a bit too much fun with Zach."

"Tyler, man, you couldn't wait for me?" Jason asked.

"What?" Tyler mumbled.

"You know I'm always up for a good time." He tapped his friend's chest, wanting Tyler to know that he was there.

"Let's get him into my car, Zach," Bianca said. "He's getting heavy." She and Zach took a step toward the red Mustang.

Jason stepped in front of them, blocking their way. "You'll be sorry if you put him in your car," Jason warned. "I know Tyler. I know his pre-puke face. And this is it. He'll ruin your upholstery. I'll drive him home."

"In what?" Bianca asked. "I don't see your car."

Zach didn't speak, but his eyes moved back and forth between Jason and Bianca like he was watching a tennis match.

"Adam's on his way over with it. I asked him to drive. I wanted to take a run on the beach," Jason explained, the trickle of sweat beginning to run down his back again. He could feel it starting to glue his shirt to his skin. "He'll be here in a sec."

"I'm not sure Tyler can stand up another sec," Bianca said, taking a step forward and forcing Tyler—and Zach—with her. Jason had to back up a little.

"Don't worry about my car. It's a rental," she added cheerfully.

Tyler's knees buckled. Zach and Bianca had to tighten their grip on him to keep him on his feet. Jason took advantage of the situation. "I got him," he said, grabbing Tyler's arm.

Bianca rushed over to the Mustang and opened the passenger door. "You can trust me to take Tyler home and tuck him into bed," she said sweetly. "Let's get him sitting down."

Phenomenal liar, Jason thought. *Pure ice.*

"That would humiliate him," Jason said. "He, uh, he has a crush on you." He turned to Zach, desperately playing for time. "You can see why he'd have a crush on my aunt, right?"

Zach ran his eyes from Bianca's dark hair to her black spike heels. "Absolutely," he announced calmly.

"Absolutely," Jason repeated. Now sweat was popping out on his forehead. Would Bianca notice? Would it make her suspicious? *Don't think about it. Keep talking,* he ordered himself. "Absolutely," he said again. "And Tyler wouldn't want the woman he's hot for—sorry, Aunt Bianca, I mean attracted to—tucking him into bed."

"Unless she was with him," Zach added.

"Right. So you should let me take care of Tyler," Jason urged. And then he heard a wonderful, miraculous sound. He glanced over his shoulder. Yeah. It was the bug. "And Adam's here with the car now, so, *no problema*. We'll cart Tyler home."

Adam pulled up right next to Bianca's car. He jumped out and opened the passenger door. Jason hustled Tyler into the passenger seat, then slid behind the wheel. Adam jumped into the tiny backseat.

This is it, Jason thought. He knew his aunt had very few choices left. Either she had to give up the kindly aunt pretence and out herself as a vampire. Or she had to let them leave.

What was it going to be?

EIGHTEEN

"See you back at the house," Bianca said, her blue eyes ice-cold.

Jason realized with a huge rush of relief that his gamble had paid off. Bianca wasn't willing to reveal the truth about herself. At least, not yet.

He smiled at her, nodded, and put his foot on the gas.

"Where are we?" Tyler mumbled.

"We are now leaving hell," Jason told him as they sped through the massive iron gates that guarded the Lafrenière property.

"Okay," Tyler said, head lolling.

Jason pulled up next to Adam's Vespa and stopped. "Thanks. I didn't have anyone else to call."

Adam nodded. "Are you going to be okay from here?" he asked. "I'm available for more sidekick duty—as long as I don't have to start wearing yellow tights or anything."

"I'm good. And no one with the middle name 'Tecumseh' can be a sidekick," Jason replied. He needed to find a place to stash Tyler. And he knew it could put Adam in danger—more danger than he was already in—if he knew where that place was.

"Call me later and tell me how it goes, Batman," Adam joked. But his eyes were serious.

Jason nodded, then started to drive out of DeVere Heights as the twilight deepened to night. His cell rang. A number he didn't recognize. He answered it. "Yeah."

"Take Tyler straight to the airport," a low, cool voice said. It took Jason half a second to recognize it: Zach. "Sienna will meet you there with cash. Terminal 3."

"Got it." Jason glanced over at Tyler. The cool breeze seemed to be reviving him a little. "And thanks."

"We're even now, Freeman," Zach replied. "Don't expect any more favors." And then there was nothing but silence.

Jason didn't care. The favor Zach had already done him was probably going to save Tyler's life. And Jason very much hoped he'd never need another favor from Zach.

He pulled out onto the Pacific Coast Highway for what felt like the hundredth time that day. PCH had a completely different vibe at night. Eerie. The ocean stretched away down below the road, a dark, endless abyss.

Jason saw headlights appear in his reaview mirror. Someone was coming up fast behind him. But who?

The car flashed its brights, blinding him for a moment. Was it Bianca? One of the other vampires from the Council? The hit squad that had picked up Tyler in the SUV?

This was a bad place to be followed. The empty beach ran for miles on one side. And now that they were outside of Malibu, there were very few exits on the other. Jason figured he could veer off into one of the little beach towns and try to lose whoever was behind him in the warren of little streets. But he didn't know the area. He could end up turning down a dead end—and somebody could end up dead.

Jason checked the rearview again. The car moved into the left lane and drew up alongside. He could see it now: a Mustang—red, like Bianca's.

"Tyler, stay low," Jason ordered.

"What's going on?" Tyler asked, frowning at him. His eyes were clearer now.

"Later," Jason told him.

The driver honked and flashed the brights again. Were they trying to get him to pull over? And then what? Just hand Tyler over to them? Jason's fingers tightened on the wheel as he tried to decide how to play it.

He could floor it—but he wasn't sure the bug could outrun the Mustang. He could slam into the other car and maybe it would knock the driver—Bianca?—out. Those seemed like his only options.

The Mustang picked up speed until it was next to Jason. He didn't recognize the driver.

He *didn't* recognize the driver!

It *wasn't* one of the vampires from the Council. It *definitely* wasn't his aunt. It was some middle-aged guy with gray hair, wearing a leather jacket and a goofy Red Baron–type silk scarf. That plus the red Mustang convertible equaled midlife crisis. Jason let out a sigh of relief.

"One of your taillights is out," the Red Baron yelled. "You're going to get pulled over." Jason waved his thanks, and the Baron accelerated around him with a cheerful *toot-toot*.

Jason immediately checked behind him. Only blackness. Unless someone was back there driving with the headlights off, he and Tyler were safe. For now.

"Can you answer my question now?" Tyler's voice had lost the muzzy quality.

"What do you remember?" Jason asked, stalling.

"I remember us going to the pawn shop and that the guy had already sold the chalice," Tyler answered. "I remember . . . smelling flowers. And was I in Zach's house?"

"You've lost a little memory," Jason told him, relieved that he had. It would make things easier.

"When we came out of the pawn shop, two guys jumped you. Knocked you out. You took a pretty good smack to the head," he explained. "That's why you're out of it. From what they said when they were beating the hell out of you, they were from that dealer in Michigan."

Tyler touched the back of his head and winced, then he turned and studied Jason. "You look pretty good. You take a seat, have some popcorn, and watch the show?" he joked, sounding more like his old self with every word.

"Nah. I'm just not as big a wimp as you are. I know how to handle myself in a fight," Jason answered, grinning. He glanced at Tyler, then checked the rearview. Still no one there. "Right now, we need to get you out of town. Those guys seemed pretty Terminator. I think they'll be back. Any ideas on where you want to go?"

"With my fifty bucks?" Tyler asked, staring out at the dark waves crashing against the darker rocks.

"Fifty-four," Jason corrected. "But no worries. Sienna's meeting us at the airport with traveling money. You just have to pick your final destination."

"Back to Michigan, I guess," Tyler said, still looking out at the ocean. "At least I have a place to crash there." He gave a snort of laughter. "My dad probably hasn't even realized I'm gone. Or if he has, he just figures I'll be back when I get hungry."

Bleak. But Tyler couldn't stay out here even if Jason's parents would agree. "Is Michigan going to be safe? With the dealer and everything?"

"He'll have got the money I wired by the time I get home. It'll be cool." Tyler turned to face Jason. "It'll be cool," he repeated. Like if he said it enough times it would be true.

"Maybe I'll come out there and visit," Jason said. "Experience a few days without sunshine and maybe some—" He stopped, his attention caught by a pair of headlights behind him. *Get a grip,* he told himself. *A lot of people use PCH.*

"Some what?" Tyler asked.

"Uh—" Jason kept his eyes on the headlights, trying to remember what he'd been about to say. He settled for, "Some of that gray, slushy snow that gets down in your boots."

"I can pretty much guarantee it." Tyler looked over his shoulder. "You don't think those are the guys back there, do you? Wanting to go another round?"

"Crossed my mind," Jason admitted. "But it's doubtful." The car behind them hung back, keeping pace from a distance.

It *was* doubtful. But by now, Bianca would have had time to get home. And she'd have realized that Jason hadn't returned with Tyler. What was she thinking? Was she coming to find them?

"Uh, I could use some caffeine," Jason said. "Maybe some barbecue potato chips. We can't be driving all the way to the airport without provisions." He glanced at the car again. It was still back there. Taking a little detour would show whether he and Tyler were just being paranoid, or if they had something real to worry about.

"My treat," Tyler answered, his eyes also on the rearview mirror.

Jason turned off on Tuna Canyon Road. So did the car behind them.

"Maybe they're after caffeine too," Tyler suggested, but he didn't sound like he believed it.

This is what Jason had wanted to avoid. Ending up in some kind of chase in an area he didn't know. He spotted the neon sign of a mini-mart up ahead. He'd only said he wanted to do a junk-food stop so they'd have an excuse to pull off the highway. But a mini-mart meant witnesses. And that felt like a good thing right now.

He sped up and pulled into the parking lot. The car—a station wagon with wooden panels that had got the *Pimp My Ride* treatment—pulled in behind them. "Let's get inside," Jason urged.

He and Tyler scrambled out of the bug and rushed into the store. An electronic bell announced their arrival. A moment later, it rang again. Jason looked toward the door. Two strangers had come in and were heading for the beer. Another false alarm. Man, he was going to be one of the few seventeen-year-olds to experience heart failure if he didn't get his paranoia in check.

Except, Jason reminded himself, what was that T-shirt slogan? "Just because you're paranoid doesn't mean they're not out to get you."

He loaded up on Mountain Dew—he felt like he'd been awake for about three days—then grabbed the biggest bag of BBQ Ruffles available. Dani would say he was stress eating. But who cared?

Tyler paid up. The Dani thought reminded Jason to reprogram the ringtone on his phone. Then they headed back to the bug. And back to the highway.

The closer they got to L.A., the more traffic filled the road. Jason couldn't keep tabs on all the drivers. He knew they could be being followed right now and not even know it. The number of cars would give cover to anyone tailing them.

"What's that up there?" Tyler asked.

"It's the Ferris wheel on the Santa Monica Pier," Jason answered.

It was hard to believe that crowds of people were out on the pier, having fun under the colorful lights. Playing Skee-Ball. Eating junk food. Giving fake screams in the stupid haunted house. How could all that be going on when his friend had almost been murdered tonight?

His mind kept returning to the expression on his aunt's face when she gave the vote that meant Tyler's death. So calm. So rational.

"I know I'm the visitor, but shouldn't we be heading toward that exit?" Tyler asked.

Jason realized that he'd almost missed the ramp to the 405. He glanced over his shoulder, then cut over a couple of lanes, just reaching the exit in time. "Good catch," he told Tyler.

"Well, it said that way to the airport, and I thought since we were going to the airport . . ."

"It's not very far from here," Jason said. He focused on the signage and managed to get them to LAX with only one U-turn, then into the big cement parking garage for Terminal 3.

Jason and Tyler left the bug in the garage and cut across the bumper-to-bumper airport traffic to reach the terminal. Jason did a Sienna scan. There were lots of people around, but it wasn't as though she was easy to miss. She wasn't there yet.

"Let's check out the flights to Michigan." He led the way over to the bank of arrival/departure monitors.

"There's one in a little less than an hour: Midwest Express," Tyler said.

Jason did another Sienna check. This time, he saw her. He waved, and she hurried toward them without smiling. All that emotion she'd shown when she'd tried to stop him from going after Tyler was gone.

"We found a flight," Jason told her.

And, after that, everything happened very quickly. Tyler bought a ticket with the money Sienna gave him. He had to go directly to security for check-in, and they weren't allowed to go with him past the metal detectors.

"So, I guess I'll see you in Michigan sometime. Maybe," Tyler said when he was two people away from the detectors.

"Yup, I'm coming. And I'm going to whip your butt in basketball," Jason replied with a grin.

Tyler surprised him by grabbing him and hugging him hard. "Thank you. I'm going to get it together," he promised. Then he walked through the metal detector and disappeared from sight.

It was then that Jason realized Sienna was no longer standing next to him. He spun around and saw her striding toward the closest exit. "Sienna! Wait!" he called. She didn't turn around. It was like what had happened between them in the gazebo had been erased from her memory.

Jason sprinted after her and grabbed her arm. "I said wait!"

She whirled around to face him. "Tyler's on his way to the plane. You don't need me anymore," she snapped, trying to pull free. "And in, oh, maybe another two seconds you'll be wanting to get away from me, anyway, right? You obviously can't manage to feel the same way about me for more than two minutes at a time."

Jason did the only thing he could think of. He kissed her. Fast, before she had time to react. Hard, because he had been wanting to for so long.

Everything fell away except the feel of her mouth on his. Complete inferno.

A passenger in a hurry let his heavy suitcase slam into their legs, and they stumbled apart. Sienna reached down and rubbed her calf.

Slowly, the world around Jason came into focus. There were people everywhere. All he wanted to do was kiss Sienna again. But this wasn't exactly the place. "Let me walk you to your car," he offered.

"Okay." She was back to not quite looking at him as they headed outside and crossed the street to the garage. "I'm glad that Tyler's okay." She paused. "And you, too."

"It got a little hairy there for a while. It would have gone a lot differently, a lot worse, without you and Zach. Thank you."

"I'm on the second level," she answered.

He opened the door to the stairwell and let Sienna go in ahead of him. Maybe they could just camp out here on the cement steps. Never go back to the real world. He glanced at her, wishing she had a little screen running across her forehead that spelled out her thoughts.

"What?" she said.

Jason realized he'd been staring. "I was just wondering about my aunt, the High Council member," he said. Because he couldn't tell Sienna what he'd been really thinking. And, anyway, he did wonder about his aunt.

"I wanted to tell you about her. But she didn't want anyone in your family to know," Sienna said. She opened the door to the second level of the parking garage and they walked over to her Spider.

Jason hated watching her slide behind the wheel. They'd hardly had any time together. And who knew when they'd be alone again.

Sienna turned the key. The Spider gave a groan of protest. "Not again!" Sienna cried.

Excellent—the Spider came through for Jason yet again. How much did he love that car? So very much. "Guess you need a ride," he said, feeling a grin spread across his face.

Sienna got out of the car and slammed the door. "I guess I do."

Half an hour later, Jason pulled back on to PCH, the lights from the Santa Monica Pier glittering in the darkness. It no longer bothered him to see people out there having fun. Eating bad food. Playing games. Pretending to be scared by plywood monsters. Making out on the sand under the boardwalk. Having Sienna with him changed everything.

"Tyler should be boarding his plane right around now," Sienna said.

"Yeah. And by now, my aunt must know for sure that he's gone." Jason shook his head. "I have no idea what to expect when I get home."

"She'll probably act completely normal. Maybe a little worried because she expected you at home." Sienna reached out and put her hand over his for a brief moment. "She's not going to want the DeVere Heights Council or the other members of the High Council to know she let Tyler get away. So she won't tell anyone. And it's not like Zach or I will say anything. I think Tyler's pretty safe."

"Can I ask you something else?" Jason went on, without waiting for a yes. "You said being a vampire is a hereditary thing. And Aunt Bianca's a vampire, right? So that should mean my mom is . . . and Dani and me?"

Sienna laughed. "Don't sweat it. You're not a vampire, neither is Dani, or your mom and dad."

"So, how come? Bianca's adopted?"

"No. Well, not that I know of," Sienna answered. "Your aunt is more unusual than that—she's a human who chose to become a vampire."

"That's possible?" Jason asked curiously. It hadn't occurred to him that there might be more ways than one of becoming a vampire.

"The only way a human can become one of us is if they bite back, if they drink the blood of a vampire as the vampire drinks from them," Sienna explained. "Usually, it doesn't ever happen because a vampire won't allow it. It's too much of a risk. When you're a born vampire, you grow up knowing that you have to protect yourself and your kind. You know how important it is to keep your nature a secret. But it's different for a turned vampire. They have so many ties to the human world. There's a much greater chance that they will put us in danger by trusting the wrong people."

"I don't think Bianca has told my mom, and she usually tells my mom everything," Jason said. "But if *turned* vampires are sort of mistrusted, how did she get to be on the High Council? How'd she get to be a vampire at all?"

"Stefan loved her so much that he was willing to risk everything for her," Sienna said simply. "If a vampire with less power and prestige than Stefan had turned a human, the rest of the vampires would probably have banished him and your aunt. Or worse," Sienna told him. "But Stefan was descended from one of the very first families on the first High Council, formed back in the Renaissance. He was hugely respected, so Bianca was accepted. And when he died, Bianca inherited his spot on the High Council. She's more famous and powerful among vampires than anyone in DeVere Heights." Sienna laughed. "It's kind of like you're related to a rock star."

"A rock star who can decide if someone lives or dies," Jason replied grimly. "It's going to be hard to walk into the house tonight and act like I don't know any of this."

"But you have to," Sienna told him, a little of the intensity that had been in her voice in the gazebo returning. "I'm not sure you'll be safe if you don't."

"I will. It'll be okay," Jason reassured her as they drove through the massive gates leading into the Heights.

"It won't be okay until the chalice is returned," Sienna said with a sigh. A breeze caught her long hair, blowing it across Jason's cheek, bringing that mix of scents—green apple, and vanilla, and the ocean—that was pure Sienna.

"I'll do whatever I can to get it back," Jason promised. He turned onto Sienna's street, then into her driveway. He turned off the engine, and the car fell quiet.

"So, well, good night," Sienna said. But she didn't move, didn't reach for the door handle. She turned toward Jason.

He suddenly felt aware of every nerve ending. And of his pulse quickening as he looked into Sienna's eyes. He leaned toward her—until their lips met. And Jason knew that, in spite of Brad being his friend, in spite of Sienna being a vampire, he never wanted that moment to end.

And then his cell phone rang.

Sienna started to pull away, but Jason looped his hands in her hair, holding her close.

The phone continued to ring. Jason ignored it. He had been waiting for this kiss since the beginning of Thanksgiving vacation, which felt like a million years ago now.

He felt a jolt of adrenaline as Sienna's tongue brushed his. *It was definitely worth the wait,* he thought.

NINETEEN

Sienna gently eased away from him. "I have to go in," she whispered.

"Okay," Jason told her. "But we have to figure all this out." "This" meaning him, Sienna . . . and Brad. Jason's friend, Brad. Sienna's boyfriend, Brad.

"We will. I promise. Just not tonight." Sienna climbed out of the car and hurried up to her front door. He watched her until she had unlocked it. She turned and waved as she slipped inside.

Jason watched as the door closed, and imagined her heading into her bedroom. *Thinking about me?* he wondered as he started the car.

He checked his phone as he headed home. Seeing that he had a voice mail, he entered his code and listened. The pawnbroker. He had the chalice. It hadn't been what the buyer wanted, after all. Jason could have it back—but it would cost seven thousand dollars.

Seven *thousand* dollars. Might as well be seven million. *Where am I going to get that kind of money?* Jason wondered.

But a new worry shoved that thought aside when

he pulled into his driveway. He could see a light on in the kitchen. Someone was waiting up for him.

Jason parked the car. As soon as he got inside the house, he headed straight for the kitchen. *Might as well get this over with*, he told himself. As he had expected, his aunt was sitting at the table. The floor had been swept, the counters wiped down, everything was back in place.

"So there you are. Your parents were worried, what with the break-in and all. So was I," Bianca said. "I didn't tell them I had expected to see you here when I got back. That would have worried them even more." She took a sip of coffee.

"Thanks." Jason took a seat across from her.

"Where's Tyler? Passed out in the car?" Bianca asked. Her voice was relaxed, but there was a steely glint in her blue eyes. *She's dangerous*, Jason thought. *And not just because she's a vampire, but because there's something hard and cold and calculating inside her.*

"I took him to Starbucks to pump some coffee into him after we left Zach's," Jason explained, making sure to look his aunt in the eye. "But he got a call from his dad when we were there. Got ordered home. I guess he didn't exactly have parental clearance to come out here."

"Tyler went back to Michigan?" said a voice behind him.

Jason looked over his shoulder and saw Dani standing in the doorway, dressed in her monkey pajamas. "Yeah. He needed to get home," he told her. "He said to tell you good-bye."

"His father wouldn't even let him come back and get his things?" Bianca asked, and Jason could hear a note of suspicion in her voice.

"He didn't bring anything with him," Jason explained. "Like I said, he didn't really have permission to come visit in the first place."

"Is he okay?" Dani joined them at the table. "I'm worried about him."

Bianca reached out and covered Dani's hand with her own. Watching his aunt with his sister put Jason on edge. *She'd never hurt Dani—or any of us,* he told himself firmly, trying to believe it.

"Tyler's always seemed like a boy who knows how to take care of himself," Bianca told Dani. "I'm sure he'll be fine."

So she'd leave him alone? Was that what she was saying? There was no way to ask Bianca that without revealing that he knew the truth about her. *And* that *wouldn't be smart,* Jason thought as he headed upstairs for a few hours' sleep before school. *At all!*

Jason wrote out a check to cash for seven thousand dollars. His hand shook a little as he signed his name.

His parents would implode when they found out he'd withdrawn a major chunk of his college fund.

No other choice, he told himself as he got in line for the cashier. No way was he taking more money from Zach. Jason had brought Tyler into the Lafrenière house. What had happened was his responsibility.

A bell dinged. Jason checked the lighted number on the monitor in front of him, then headed over to Window 3. He half expected the cashier to refuse to cash the check—even though he was at his own bank. But she just asked to see his driver's license, then had him sweep his ATM card through the machine and enter his PIN.

Not much more than a minute later, he was walking back out into the afternoon sunshine, carrying seven thousand dollars in cash. He went directly to the pawnshop. Maybe there were people in the Heights who routinely walked around with that kind of money on them, but Jason just wanted to get rid of it.

The pawnbroker with the ponytail buzzed him inside with a wide smile. Why shouldn't he be smiling? He was about to make a two-thousand-dollar profit for jack.

"Do you have the chalice?" Jason asked.

"If you got the money, I got the chalice," the man replied evenly.

"Plus more than a twenty-five percent profit," Jason muttered.

The guy shrugged. "If it's too much, I'll keep the thing. I'm sure I can sell it again."

They stared at each other. The man knew exactly how desperate Jason was. Jason had made the mistake of revealing that on his first trip to the pawnshop. No point trying to negotiate now. Jason pulled out the wad of cash and shoved it across the glass counter to the pawnbroker.

The man counted it, fast and efficient. Then he reached under the cash register, pulled out a paper bag, and handed it to Jason. Jason peered inside. The chalice was there. It almost seemed to glow, even in the dim light of the shop. And it *pulled* at something in Jason. He wanted to take the chalice out of the bag and just hold it for a minute. But he closed the bag and hurried back out to his car. The chalice wasn't for him. The safest thing was to get rid of it as soon as possible.

Jason slid behind the wheel—and froze. A man was watching him from across the street. He tightened his grip on the chalice. Did the man know what was in the bag?

A truck rumbled down the street. It blocked the man from Jason's view for a few seconds. And when the truck had passed, the man was gone. Jason glanced up and down the street; there was nobody to be seen.

He fired up the bug, telling himself that he was being paranoid, but the desire to get the chalice back where it belonged had just got stronger. So he didn't pass Go, didn't collect two hundred dollars. He drove straight to Zach's.

Zach met him in the driveway before Jason could reach the front door. "I wasn't expecting to see you here again . . . so soon," Zach said.

"Hello to you, too." Jason thrust the paper bag into Zach's hands. "Something I think you'll be happy to see."

Zach opened the bag, and raised one eyebrow. "You keep coming through for us, Freeman."

"*Now* we're even," Jason told him.

Zach gave a reluctant smile.

"Don't expect any more favors," Jason added, and Zach's smile widened into a grin.

Jason swung himself back into his bug and headed for home. Things were back to normal.

As normal as they ever got in DeVere Heights.